bea   st,
running down the curves of the

My fingers traced up the path the droplets had taken
from his forearm back up to his collarbone and to his
cheek. They circled the mauve ribbon of his soft lips,
back and forth, until he opened his mouth to kiss my
fingertips.

I licked my lips as his arms reached around me and
held my naked body close to his.

"You must think I'm a beast," he announced.

His words glided over my mouth between his kisses.
"And why would I think that?"

"Remember when you told me to take what I
wanted?"

Heat rose in my neck and cheeks. Had I said that?
Not that I would ever take it back. "I suppose I did say
that, didn't I? How does that make *you* a beast?"

Adam moved to the futon and lowered me onto it.

"Because I want to take a little more."

BEST OF LUCK ELSEWHERE

TRISHA HADDAD

Genesis Press, Inc.

INDIGO LOVE SPECTRUM

An imprint of Genesis Press, Inc.
Publishing Company

Genesis Press, Inc.
P.O. Box 101
Columbus, MS 39703

Copyright © 2009 by Trisha Haddad

ISBN: 13 DIGIT : 978-1-58571-290-8
ISBN: 10 DIGIT : 1-58571-290-6
Manufactured in the United States of America

First Edition

Visit us at www.genesis-press.com
or call at 1-888-Indigo-1-4-0

DEDICATION

This book is dedicated to my grandmother, Helen Haddad, who told me "Love, real love, is limitless. And isn't that wonderful?"

And also to Derek, who proves each day that this is true.

CHAPTER 1

I have rarely read about a murder like the one you have orchestrated here. Brutal and disturbing. An excellent murder.

I did, however, find it hard to connect with some of your characters. Even if your main character is a murderer, he still needs a character arc or the readers may never really sympathize with him, the way you want them to.

Unfortunately, we will be unable to accept your manuscript for publication. Thank you for considering J Press.

Best of luck elsewhere,

S. Rain Orwell
Mystery Editor
J Press

You think that S. Rain Orwell decides the fate of your masterpiece of a novel. That she's the one who orchestrates either its glorious life in the hands of mystery fans everywhere or its violent demise with a tactfully worded rejection letter for a tombstone. Everyone thinks that. But even though your cover letter is indeed addressed to Ms. Orwell and your rejection letter is sent under her name, I, Eliza Tahan, am the one that you actually want to sweet-talk. So don't bother adding to your cover letter a sentence praising her judgment in manuscripts, saying you loved the recent bestseller that she handled. And don't gush over how much fun you had on your recent trip to San Diego and how you passed her office building on your way to Horton Plaza. Sure, she has the "final say" as to whether J Press will accept your manuscript, but I'm the one who decides if she'll even see it.

I read your submissions. I write your rejection letters.

I'm the assistant editor, a "submissions manager" of sorts. Your manuscript, and many more like it, land on my desk each day. I decide, based on your cover letter, synopsis, and first few pages, whether it gets sent to one of our sadistic interns who have no qualms about stuffing your SASE with a rejection letter, or if it deserves a little extra attention. If you've interested me during the above-mentioned first look, your manuscript will follow me home for a more thorough read while Liam, my roommate, plays video games on his Xbox 360.

If your manuscript makes it home with me but doesn't make my final cut, I'll write you a personalized rejection letter to let you know what I liked about it and what needs work. But if your novel is outstanding, I'll write a report for S. Rain Orwell as to why she ought to spend her valuable time with your masterpiece. I don't promise anything after I hand the manuscript and report to Ms. Orwell, but you've made it further than 95 percent of your fellow writers by this time. Good job.

Now, you may think that all this supposed power would make me haughty. Quite the contrary! I know I'm good at my job, but, like many people in the publishing industry, I would much rather be an author than an editor. I want to write, but I just haven't. Not since I finished college six years ago. So what if my college writing professor was certain that I was going to usher in the era of "The New Great American Novel," a title she gave to the multi-ethnic-woman-writing-powerful-fiction movement she was predicting was coming up in the literary world. I may be Arabic-American and African-American, but this multi-ethnic woman is not producing *any* fiction, let alone the "powerful" kind.

And with every manuscript I reject, I also weaken my own confidence in my talent.

So, please, don't shoot the messenger. Don't stab her. Don't throw her in the bay with her hands tied behind her back and rocks in her pocket. Don't plot some kind of elaborate and ghastly act of violence against her. Remember, I've read your mystery submission and know what evils your mind is capable of!

Just go easy on me with your rage.

"Are you the one who crushes people's dreams?"

I looked up from the letter I'd just finished signing with my boss's name, surprised to realize that the question was directed at me, and that it came from a handsome stranger with a smile playing across his lips.

"Excuse me?"

He waved his hand in the direction of the stacks of manuscripts on my desk. "You crush people's dreams."

"These are manuscript submissions."

"And you're lining them up to reject them, right?"

I was about to answer, *Not purposely, but that's how they'll most likely end up,* but I caught myself. He'd just been in the editor's office, where only our star authors were welcome. And I knew that even star authors were once just writers rejected by multitudes of publishing companies. So instead I replied, "Of course not. I get to read them and find the ones that are right for J Press."

He shot me a sideways glance, and then looked down at the letter on J Press letterhead. I slid the paper to the side, trying to be nonchalant.

"And the manuscript that goes with that letter?" he asked.

"Wasn't right for us."

"You're Eliza Tahan, aren't you? The assistant editor?"

"That's right. I help Ms. Orwell decide what we publish."

As though on cue, S. Rain Orwell emerged from her office. Tall and slender, with graying hair colored raven black, today she was clad in a black pencil skirt and white silk sleeveless blouse adorned with one wide gold cuff bracelet. Rain certainly looked the part of an editor of the mystery department at J Press, a woman who'd launched her fair share of literary careers. She adjusted her black-rimmed glasses and caught my eye.

It was only when the handsome stranger followed my gaze to my boss that Rain smiled, softened, and moved toward us.

"Eliza, my dear," she cooed at me in a way she would never do if there wasn't a visitor standing there, "I see you've already met Adam Mestas."

"Adam Mestas? You're one of the book section editors for *The San Diego Union-Tribune*." I fixed my eyes on the man standing in front of me.

This was the book section editor whose articles and reviews I read in the paper every Sunday? The man teasing me about crushing people's dreams vanished, and suddenly I saw how truly stunning he was.

I stood breathless, staring at the tall, young Mexican man who wrote with the grace of someone many years older. I was silenced as much by his youth as by his sensuous lips and his wide shoulders under the smart navy suit jacket. His jaw showed the faintest hint of what would be a shadow within a few hours.

When he turned to look at Rain, I caught a glimpse of a long, black ponytail. My fingers ached to touch his hair. Could it possibly be as silky as it looked from this angle, in the sunlight that streamed through the floor-to-ceiling windows?

Rain giggled, playfully resting a hand on Adam's forearm. I cringed. If anything was worse than my boss's usual tyranny, it was the mask she wore when someone important or useful happened to be around.

Adam turned back to me.

"It's nice to meet you, Ms. Tahan."

He held out a hand, and I shook it. He stared at me with midnight eyes full of expectation. Was he expecting me to apologize for my stunned silence, or to profess my lust? "You, too, Mr. Mestas. I appreciate your writing. I'd never have guessed you were so young."

"I hadn't guessed you were so young, either, when Ms. Orwell described you to me."

Rain broke in. "I called my good friend Adam this morning about getting *Vehicular Manslaughter* reviewed in the book section next month, right before it's pubbed."

"Oh yeah? That's great." For the first time I noticed Adam was holding the galley of the book. The stark white cover and black letters didn't hold the slightest hint of the bold, blood-spotted final cover design that I knew was currently with the author for approval.

"He's a tough negotiator," Rain continued, "but I think we came to a reasonable agreement, don't you, Adam?"

"I want to write an article about what happens to a manuscript submitted for publication at J Press," Adam explained. "Ms. Orwell suggested I interview you."

"Me?"

"Would you be up for it?"

My eyes darted to Rain, who nodded sternly out of Adam's line of sight.

"Of course, but I'm leaving on vacation tomorrow."

"Then are you available now?"

For a little privacy, we made our way to a small conference room on the north side of the floor.

"This is an amazing view of Balboa Park," Adam commented as we entered.

"Yeah, not half bad, is it? One of the benefits of being twenty floors up."

"Do you go there on your lunch breaks?"

What lunch breaks? I thought. "Not as often as I should."

"But you *have* been to the San Diego Museum of Art, I hope? If not, I'm taking you there right now."

"I've been," I replied with a laugh, and instantly wished I hadn't. Attempting to reopen his invitation, I followed it up with, "Of course, I can't get enough of the place."

There was silence for just a moment, as we both stared out the window. Complete, electric silence. I saw in the faint reflection his eyes darting to steal a glance at me.

Finally I spoke. "Have a seat, Mr. Mestas. Where shall we start with this? Do you have questions for me?" I brushed my wavy black hair from my face.

Once we actually got down to his questions, the interview was quite short and much less exciting than the interviewer himself. If it hadn't been for those lips, that jaw, I might have been annoyed at the interruption on a day I was so busy.

While I spoke, Adam jotted down notes in his notebook, and I took the opportunity to watch his hands, large and tan. He held the pen purposefully; there was nothing tentative about his grip.

I answered questions about my background before coming to J Press, my role as assistant editor, and the path a manuscript takes once we receive it.

And of course, just as at any meet-and-greet party when I tell someone where I work, I was asked to name my favorite book.

"*The Wayward Bus*, by John Steinbeck," I told him.

"That's a good one."

"I'm surprised you know the book. But of course you do: You're the book section editor at San Diego's biggest newspaper, after all."

"I suppose most people wouldn't know it."

"True, you don't look like an editor. But people who read the book section would know your name."

He laughed a throaty, honest laugh. "Thanks, but I meant the book. Most people know Steinbeck's *Grapes of Wrath* or *The Red Pony*. Not *The Wayward Bus*."

Mr. Mestas looked down for a moment, and I assumed he was running over his notes until I stole a glance at his chiseled jaw and saw a hint of a smile after he looked at my hand.

My left hand.

Heat rose in my cheeks. *Pretty sly move, Mr. Mestas*, I thought, pleased with myself for catching his attention. Now with the upper hand, I queried, "Did you have anything else you'd like to ask me?"

He looked up, as though caught off guard. "What? Um, no. I think that's it for now. Can I call you later? I mean, if I have any other questions?"

I reached across to his notepad and he handed me his pen. As I grabbed it, my fingers grazed his, sending heat through my hand starting at the place where my skin had connected with his. Quickly, before I could lose my nerve, I scribbled my cell phone number in his book.

"Again, I didn't know I'd be doing the interview today, so I left my camera at the office."

Thank goodness, I thought. I looked down at the jeans I'd worn today. They weren't even sexy jeans. My favorite clothes were all in the dryer at home, waiting to be packed for my quickly approaching vacation. "I'm not dressed for a picture anyhow."

He smiled and shook his head. "Ms. Tahan, you look lovely. This is no place for false modesty."

Lovely? False modesty? "What happened to being the one who crushes dreams?"

"You gonna hold that against me?"

"I might. It was pretty harsh."

"But it got your attention, didn't it?"

Adam's eyes locked with mine. They searched deep, as though trying to figure out how I'd reply to the question he wanted to ask.

"Could I come by your place before you leave on vacation tomorrow for a quick picture?"

A quick something, I thought. But I replied, "I guess so, but I'm heading out pretty early. I suppose that would be okay though. Can you be there by nine?"

"Can and will."

I wrote out my address for him, wondering if inviting a stranger to my house was really as bad an idea as my gut told me it was. But this was not your after-school-special stranger. This was the editor of the book section of *The San Diego Union-Tribune*.

9

And this editor had a killer body.

After walking Adam to the elevator, I headed back to my desk. My phone was ringing, single rings, not double rings, which meant that the call was from somewhere in the building. I gathered up the phone on the last ring.

"Ms. Orwell wants to talk to you, Eliza. Can you hold on a sec?" It was Jane, the editor's assistant.

"Sure, Jane. Thanks."

"What took you so long to answer?" snapped Rain's voice on the line after just a moment. What a salutation.

"I was walking Adam to the elevator. Sorry."

"Not to the lobby? Damn it, do I have to do everything?"

I rolled my eyes. Adam hadn't been gone thirty seconds and Rain was back to her usual self. "He insisted I not walk him all the way down. How can I help you, Ms. Orwell?"

"Right," she replied. "I want to know how the interview went. Did he get the info he needed? It's vital that he review *Vehicular Manslaughter*. Lazy, goddamn what's-her-name who's handling the PR on this title hadn't even talked to him before I brought it up. And with summer right around the corner! If I were her supervisor, I'd have kicked her out on her—"

"Good thing you talked him into reviewing it then."

"No shit. How did it go?"

"It went fine. He didn't say when it was going to be printed, though. I forgot to ask."

"Doesn't matter. So long as he's going to review that book."

When we hung up, I pulled a manuscript from the stack in front of me and studied the cover letter attached to it, tapping my fingertips on the pages. As I tried to resist the urge to call Liam, my roommate, to tell him the news, I stared at my short fingernails. They were painted mauve and made my caramel hands look quite dainty and fashionable. Of course, the paint had matched the thin mauve stripes in my silk, button-up shirt that I wore two days ago. With the crisp white T-shirt and jeans I was wearing today, though, the mauve nails seemed sort of silly. I made a mental note to pick up polish remover before heading to the airport tomorrow.

I'm a good editor and a fantastic reader, but fashion-ista, I am not. Willpower guru I am also not, I decided, breaking down and reaching for the phone.

Liam picked up and said in a buttery smooth voice, "Hello, this is Liam Jack."

"Why, Liam, how professional you sound."

"I *am* at work. But, Lizzy, please tell me you went to the farmer's market at Horton Plaza on your lunch break and are bringing me home some delicious veggies."

Oops. I fished in my pocket and pulled out the note he'd left on the kitchen counter this morning.

Lizzy:
Don't forget the farmer's market this afternoon! Please pick up some strawberries, green beans, and maybe some

*cheese if there's some kind that looks really good. I'll repay
your kind efforts by making something fabulous for dinner.*
   —Liam

   "So, guess what!" I countered, trying to change the
subject. "I'm gonna be famous!"

   "You forgot."

   "I'm sorry. It was a sweet note, though. Thanks." I
knew full well that he'd still make "something fabulous
for dinner." He usually does.

   "Yeah, yeah. Okay, how are you going to be famous?"

   "I just had an interview with the book section editor
for *The San Diego Union-Tribune*!"

   "No!"

   "Yes! About what happens when a manuscript's submitted."

   "Did you say something about me? Like I'm your
inspiration or something? If you get to be famous, I
should be famous, too, by association." We both laughed
and then Liam muttered, "Oops, I gotta go. The boss's
heading this way. You're incredible, Lizzy, you really are.
I'll see you at home."

   With a little kiss into the phone, we were disconnected.

   It was back to writing rejection letters and, as Adam
Mestas had so delicately put it, crushing people's dreams.

CHAPTER 2

Liam always locked the front door. He knew I got home within an hour of when he did, and he knew that I unfailingly had an armload of manuscripts to balance, but the door was always locked.

When we first moved into the condo and I'd noticed his door-locking habit, I had asked him to leave it unlocked at least until I got home. He'd replied with a straight face that if the door was unlocked for even five minutes, some criminal could easily walk in and steal his Xbox and we'd never know what happened to it.

"How awful," I'd replied sarcastically.

"A *criminal*, Lizzy," he had asserted. "In our *house*."

"A *smooth criminal*?" I'd asked, but seeing that he was very serious about the issue, I had dropped it then and there. The door was perpetually locked.

Now, arms full of manuscripts, as usual, I gently tapped my forehead on the door, hoping he was downstairs and would hear me. No answer. I pressed my hip against the doorbell and from inside I heard the chime of the pause button on his Xbox, followed by some shuffling, and the door was flung open. Before even speaking, Liam grabbed one of my armfuls of manuscripts and set them on the table next to the door. I followed suit, and as soon as my arms were empty, Liam gathered me up for a big hug. "Welcome home, oh famous one! Dinner will be done in ten."

"Smells good." I smiled as he released me. Liam closed and locked the door behind me. "Italian?"

"Pesto risotto."

"Yum! You're so great."

Liam's lanky figure moved back to his perch on the floor in front of the big-screen TV. He folded his pale white legs underneath him and took up the Xbox controller, declaring, "You bet I am! Check this out!" There was a chime and he was back to his game.

"*So* great," I affirmed as I started up the stairs.

"Remember, dinner in ten," he called after I'd turned the corner on the stairs. "Be there or be eating cold risotto."

I made my way up the stairs, and then slowed to look at the picture collages on the stairwell. Most of the pictures were from college and the few years after, and most had Liam and me smiling or goofing off, as though nothing existed before we'd met. I looked at the picture of us dressed up and smiling on Halloween as Mario and Luigi, the picture of us smiling and wind-whipped on the deck of the ferry to Coronado, the picture of us smiling and showing our muscles in front of the fence we had repaired in his parents' yard. These pictures still made me smile, no matter that I saw them every day going up and down the stairs.

Then there was the picture a waiter took of him proposing to me at our favorite restaurant, the one from the surprise engagement party with all of our family, and the one of us holding the keys to our new condo. These always brought on a sad smile.

There was only one picture, at the beach with a group of his friends where Liam is half-buried in the sand and smiling and I am contributing to the burying and only half-smiling, from after the breakup.

Turns out you can have a soul mate who is not meant to be your actual *mate*.

As of last summer, Liam ceased being my boyfriend, my fiancé, my "intended," and became just my room-mate. We'd gotten along great for a while there, never fighting. We'd sleep in separate rooms, date other people, and never, ever have sex.

As a matter of fact, we rarely had sex even when we were a couple, which was a large part of why we are now platonic. We kind of always were. Sure, we smooched all the time, and there were the here-and-there innuendos that never led anywhere. I want to remember a time when we were overwhelmingly passionate about each other, but always in my memories, I am trying to seduce him, and he just concedes. We were so busy during the first few years of our relationship that we saw each other only a few days a week, and we'd get our groove on maybe once a week. I'd always assumed that once we moved in together as we kept planning, he would become the insatiable sex machine that magazines always make men out to be.

When we bought the condo and nothing changed, I wondered if he had some religious hang-up that I was not being sensitive to. So I decided it would get better after we were married and completely legit.

After a few months of living together and being turned down countless times, though, I became more hurt than sexually frustrated. I stopped re-applying my makeup and brushing my hair before heading home from work so that I'd look cute for Liam, since he obviously didn't notice. I stopped trying to get him to make love to me. When he seemed happy not to be badgered for love-making, I felt even worse. Was I not pretty enough? I began to feel very ugly. Was I a bad lover? I no longer even *wanted* to make love to him, because I no longer felt sexy. I'd gone from sexually free to ice queen in 3.2 months.

I then started to wonder, with guilt at my own self-centeredness, if he had some kind of hormonal problem. I was just getting up the nerve to suggest he make a doctor's appointment, wanting to solve this *before* we tied the knot, when I came home an hour early from work one day. He usually got home from work before me, and I'd thought my gesture of leaving early myself to have the conversation might show him that I felt it was a serious enough issue to pursue.

When I opened the door and came around the corner, however, I found my fiancé completely nude in front of the computer, eyes shut tight in ecstasy. Before he could open them, I ducked back around the corner and to the front door, which I opened and slammed shut. I heard the quick clicking of his mouse, obviously closing several web page screens, before he gasped, "Hey, my sweet! You're home early! I'm just about to step in the shower. I'll be out in a sec."

"Yeah," I replied, stricken with the fact he had chosen something so impersonal for release instead of making love to me. It was like a brutal stab to my heart.

I was available. I hadn't ever turned him down. And yet he preferred to masturbate with a two-dimensional image instead?

I'd never felt worse about myself than at that moment.

When I heard the shower turn on upstairs, I plopped down at the computer desk to take advantage of my narrow time slot, and went directly to the most recent site in the history. I reached unconsciously for the few mini-chocolates left in the little bowl we kept on the desk.

What was I expecting to find? I feared that I'd be face-to-face with fifty thumbnails of sexy naked women with straight blonde hair, creamy white skin, perky little breasts, flat abs, and hips so narrow that they were almost boyish. What I saw was more boyish than I'd expected.

Boys Next Door. Hollywood Hunks. Sexy Sampsons.

"What the hell?"

If I had to compete with the pictures I'd been expecting, I could have told Liam to get the hell out of my life and find the kind of cookie-cutter chick he wanted.

But what could I possibly say about *this*? I couldn't compete with these men. With *any* man. I was out of the picture completely.

The shower turned off, but I could not peel away from the computer. Somehow, I knew it would be better for him to see me seeing this than for me to try to bring it up later. Moments later, Liam strolled casually into the office without knowing that his life was going to change in a few seconds. Both of our lives.

He had a towel around his waist and his brown hair was dark with moisture and hanging straight to his chin. Shimmering droplets of water ran from it down his smooth chest. When he saw me, he stopped in his tracks and neither of us could say a thing for what seemed like a nightmare of an eternity.

He stood dripping and gaping until he was able to finally muster a pathetic, "Oh, Lizzy, I didn't mean for you to . . . I was just . . ."

In response all I could muster was the energy to pry my hand from the mouse, pull off my engagement ring, and drop it into the small bowl of torn silver foil wrappers which had until recently been filled with rich chocolate.

After many very difficult weeks of trying to decide what to do, trying to figure out our feelings, and trying to explain to our friends and families that we were going to "postpone" the wedding for "personal" reasons, we finally knew the relationship was over.

There was nothing to work out. No problems to solve. I hated that Liam had led me on. Liam hated that he could not make a life with me and that he had been forced out of the closet that he had been somewhat comfortable living in.

We met with a realtor to put the condo up for sale, planning to pay off the loan and split the decent profit we had made in the short time we had owned the place. Then we would go our separate ways with only baggage of the emotional sort to deal with.

While the realtor looked around our home, tears welled up in my eyes, and though I was able to push them back, Liam noticed.

"Why can't we," he started cautiously, "just stay here? We get along perfectly, besides bedroom stuff."

I shook my head sadly, staring at my sandals. "We've talked about this, Liam. Over and over. I can't commit to a sexless marriage. It wouldn't be fair to either of us." I stroked the slowly disappearing lighter band of smooth skin where my engagement ring had been. My skin was almost back to normal. I was hoping that my heart was in tow, even if it was just taking a little longer.

Liam grabbed my hand. "We can be roommates. A very easygoing kind of thing. If we stop getting along, or one of us finds someone else, or whatever, we'll just sell. The worst that will happen is that the condo will appreciate in value a little more and we'll part with more money. The best that will happen is that our life will go on just as before for a while longer, but without sex. It was the only thing that ever seemed to be hard on the relationship."

I glared at him like he was crazy, but as the realtor came down the stairs, some clarity set in. She moved down the stairs slowly and we both knew that, like all of our visitors, she was looking at our happy picture collages. By the time she made the turn and came into view, I had made my decision.

"Cute pictures," the realtor commented airily. "You guys seem like you have lotsa fun."

"I don't know if we're ready to sell," I said suddenly, as though it were an answer to her compliment. From his place standing by my side, Liam's face turned in my direction. Though I continued to look straight ahead at the realtor, I could see in my peripheral vision a smile playing over Liam's lips.

And really, what was the harm? Our condo kept going up in value. Liam began to go out a little, feeling more comfortable in his new life. I had more time to focus on work, not having to worry about my home life as I had when we were a couple. In fact, I even appreciated all the work I brought home because I didn't have to worry about my "civilian" life much at all if I was wrapped up in reading manuscripts. The situation was good for both of us. The lack of certainty about the future just gave us some semblance of freedom. And of course, Liam still cooked for me, and how many people can say that about their platonic roommates?

"Thank you for making dinner. It was so good, as always! *Bravi!*"

"*Gratzi!* I figured it was as good a time as any to celebrate."

It was a nice enough sentiment if he'd been talking about my article. But something in his voice indicated that he hadn't been. It was something else he was celebrating.

Something outside of my sphere.

I played along, delaying the news. "Ah shucks. You're impressed with my newfound fame, eh?"

"Oh! Yeah." He cleared his throat, uncomfortable, but came up with a quick save. "I'll bet ol' S. Rain was quite impressed."

"Believe it or not, she was the one who arranged it."

Liam set down his wine in disbelief. "No!"

"It's probably too 'inconsequential' an interview to take up *her* valuable time," I explained with an air of superiority, mocking my boss.

"I don't know how you can stand her."

"I *can't* stand her. I mostly just do my job and stay out of her way. You know that. Oh, by the way, Adam Mestas is coming by before I leave tomorrow to take a picture of me."

"Who's that?"

"Adam, the editor from the newspaper. He said he'll be here by nine."

"Is Rain pissed that you're taking time off?"

"Surprisingly, no. I've been worried since I booked the flight that she'd come up with some big project to cut into my vacation. But I think she's wrapped up in herself right now."

Liam snickered, "What do you mean *right now*?"

"I overheard her the other day on the phone. Her office door was open and I was walking by. I don't know who she was talking to, but she was talking about signing divorce papers, and then later heading up to San Francisco for a long weekend."

"Wow. She's that much of a bitch that even her husband couldn't stand her."

I smiled at his joke, but felt a little sad for Rain. I knew firsthand how relationships didn't just end because someone was being bitchy. I'd never ask Rain why hers ended. I'd never given her a tissue and connected with her based on my own history. But I did feel a little sorry for her.

"Okay, Liam. Enough killing time. What are *you* celebrating?"

Liam was caught off guard, but set down his fork and took a breath. This would be big.

"I think the time has come to sell the condo."

I knew it. I knew it was coming sooner or later. I was about to protest, try to change his mind, but then I thought better of it. *This will be as good for me as for him. I can finally move past this relationship.* It was a hope more than a belief.

Liam was about to continue, but I replied first. "Yeah, I think that's a good idea."

He took a long, relaxed breath. "Ahhhhh. I'm relieved, honestly, Lizzy. I was sure I'd have to convince you."

"I'm not in love with you anymore, Liam. Nor am I desperate."

"I know, I know. So I'll call that realtor from last time we were going to sell. Unless you want to buy out my share of the condo."

"With all the money I make in the publishing industry?"

"I'll call the realtor."

I looked at my watch: 9:01. Adam Mestas would be here anytime now, and I waited for him in the driveway. Leaning up against my car, I said a little prayer that he would not want to come inside and sit down—the place was a disaster area. This morning I'd done more than my fair share of tossing things around as I packed and unpacked and re-packed.

Please let him be comfortable taking the picture out here!

I watched the curve in the street, expecting Adam's flashy car to come around it any second, maybe a red Corvette or a BMW convertible. Where was he? It was 9:07.

Jittery and nervous about being late for my flight, I killed time by jogging to the front door of the condo once again to make sure it was locked. It was, and as I meandered back to the car I found myself scowling at Adam's tardiness. *What's the point in being hot if you're rude? I better not miss my flight!*

I popped the trunk to my car and scanned its contents, trying to decide if anything should be taken into the condo before I left. There were a number of manuscripts and a small stack of form rejection letters that I could attach to the manuscripts that clearly didn't make the cut. That way, I wouldn't have to remember which I liked and which I didn't like. Made it easier for the interns in the department to stuff SASEs with rejection letters, too.

I decided these probably shouldn't sit in my trunk for the next two weeks, so I grabbed the first two stacks of manuscripts and took them inside. As I headed back out to pick up the rejection letters, I saw a car coming around the street corner. I wondered if it could be him; the car certainly did not compare to Rain's Porsche. Just in case, though, still worried about having to invite him inside, I dropped the form rejections back in the trunk, thinking, *They're just as safe in here as in the house. Cleo said she'd clear a space in her garage for my car. It's not as if it's going to be sitting at LAX.*

I realized that it was indeed Adam Mestas when he nearly jumped out of the '88 burgundy Mustang. "I'm sorry I'm late. I always forget to factor in traffic on Route 78."

"I hope you didn't take Interstate 5 to Route 78 from downtown. That's going way out of the way. You could have taken—"

"Interstate 15. I know. I came from my place in Oceanside, though. I am very sorry for being late. I know you have a plane to catch."

I decided to use any guilt he felt as leverage for my argument about not going inside. "It's all right. Do you mind if we do the picture out here? The lighting is really poor in there."

"Oh!" He looked a little surprised, as though he had expected me to invite him inside. "Yeah, of course. I wasn't thinking that we'd have to go in your house or anything. I'm glad you could meet me again, even if it's just for a minute. And I came up with another question last night."

I scanned his appearance. He'd looked good in the suit yesterday, but hotter still today in corduroy pants the color of burnt umber and a white polo shirt that not only showed his tanned forearms but also hinted at an impressive bicep right where each sleeve ended.

Ask me if I'm single, I willed him. *Ask me if I'm busy some weekend later this month. Ask me out. Ask me to invite you inside right now. I'll risk letting you see the mess for the opportunity to have you pull off that polo.*

Despite my silent urging, he said instead, "It probably takes an unusual kind of mind to write a mystery novel, specifically to come up with the details of an imaginary murder. Do you ever worry about retaliation from the people you're dealing with? Maybe a disgruntled author of a rejected manuscript?"

I laughed nervously, not because I was actually frightened, but because I'd caught myself in a sultry thought and I hoped my face was masking it. I coughed to buy a moment. It was enough for a catty comeback. "It's okay: My boss's name is the one on the form rejection letters."

"Saw that yesterday. So you're safe then, I guess."

"As long as you don't make mention of that in your article, Mr. Mestas!"

"Only if you stop calling me 'Mr. Mestas.' It's Adam. Now, how about that picture? Do you want it in front of your condo? The light really plays beautifully off your face from this angle."

I looked coyly down and to the left, but then suddenly recalled his question about a disgruntled author.

"Can you get a closer shot? Like a headshot or something? Maybe me next to my car, or even in it, so you don't see where I live in the background?"

"Oh, Eliza. I didn't mean to worry you. But I understand you'd rather not advertise your personal location. Why don't you lean on the back of your car and I'll close in enough that you can't see the surroundings."

When he was done taking a few shots, I lingered, waiting for him to make a move.

When he didn't, I decided I was in too much of a hurry to just sit around waiting for him to take the initiative, and instead just offered him a firm handshake. "Well, I better get going." I got into my car, hurrying to get away from this awkward situation, embarrassed at my assumptions of his feelings. "It was nice seeing you again."

But he didn't just go, as I'd expected. Instead, he leaned on the frame of my open car door like a romantic lead in an old movie.

"Where are you going on vacation?" he asked.

Did he actually care, or was he just buying time?

"I'm going to Greece for two weeks. I'm ready for a vacation."

"I can tell. You're single-minded in your determination to get me out of here. You don't even have a little time for some friendly conversation?"

"I'm not trying to get you out of here specifically, but I *do* have a flight to catch. It isn't personal."

"Are you leaving out of San Diego?"

"LAX."

"Driving up to Los Angeles by yourself? Or are you picking up your boyfriend on the way?"

"I don't have a boyfriend. I'm meeting up with my sister, who will drive me to the airport. But I'm traveling alone. I like a good adventure."

"Adventure?" He smiled and handed me a business card. "Well, Ms. Tahan, sometimes the best adventures start on your own doorstep."

"Or in my own driveway?"

He raised his eyebrows. "Sure, with the right traveling companion."

Overhead a bird squawked as it passed us, and the slight breeze rustled the strands of Adam's ponytail. In my hand, my keys tapped lightly against each other with a metallic melody. And in the space between Adam's lips and mine sat a heavy silence that was anything but awkward.

He spoke first. "I expect the article to run in about two weeks, just in time for your return. I'll save some extra copies for you. Let's get together for coffee and I can give you the copies."

"Sure. I'll call you," I replied, trying to play it cool.

He shook my hand once more, firmly, but holding it long enough to make me certain he was on the same page I was. "Bon voyage, Eliza. See you soon."

He closed the door for me, and walked around the front of my car to his. I slid on a pair of sunglasses so I could watch him without his noticing. He slipped into the burgundy-maroon Mustang hatchback and drove off without another look my way. I read his bumper sticker as he pulled away: *I -heart- Steinbeck.*

"I love Steinbeck, too," I said aloud in the solitude of my car.

Okay, so he was evidently a smart guy with good taste in literature. His lips and teeth flashed in my mind's eye. His smile. The way his midnight eyes sparked—was it flirting?—when he said that I should call him by his first name. That long, black, silky ponytail. And of course all the other pleasing details I'd noticed while he walked back to his car and I played voyeur.

I slipped the key into the ignition, and my old Civic jumped immediately to attention, as did my CD player. The guitar strumming began and Tracy Chapman's passionate voice rose into the song.

I patted my tickets once more, slid Adam's business card into my other pocket, and backed my car out of the driveway. I turned to head for my sister Cleo's house.

CHAPTER 3

I was an English major in college, and one of the many things you cover over and over in your lit courses is that a hero-to-be must go on a journey to discover what he needs to become a hero. The circle is complete when he returns home stronger, wiser, and able to accomplish what needs to be done. Though I didn't aspire to be a hero, I suppose I was expecting my trip to Greece to be life-changing. I thought I'd return with the confidence and follow-through to move forward in my life. Accomplish my goals. Re-order the areas of my life that were so lacking.

One area was my love life. And I now had an idea of who might fill the void.

And I wanted to write a novel. Not too much to ask, right? I'd come up with an interesting idea during a creative writing class in college but had only gotten as far as a brief outline and character sketch. Then I'd dumped the notebook in a box as I moved again and again, planning to eventually exhume it and write "The New Great American Novel." Instead I'd busied myself with my flashy new job, with my intensifying relationship with Liam, and eventually with buying a condo and planning a wedding.

At this point in my life, all of my convenient distractions had fallen short, laying bare the chaos that churned underneath. And without any of the usual reasons for procrastination, I knew this had to be the right time to push forward. I was also hoping that an adventure in the exotic Mediterranean would inspire me. I'd brought a notebook full of fresh, blank pages, fully expecting to return with it filled.

My adventure failed to dramatically change me, however. The Grecian landscape was more beautiful than I'd imagined. The architecture was thoroughly breathtaking. And I'd even had my share of new experiences. But I was the same ol' me when I returned home.

My sister Cleo picked me up at the airport, and as she drove me back to her place, she was full of questions. I was grateful for the ride, but all I wanted to do was get home and get some sleep. I dreaded the hour and a half it would take me to drive home. As I stared out the window, I tried to focus on Cleo's honest interest in my adventure.

"What was your favorite place?"

"Santorini, definitely. It was beautiful."

"That's the one with all those blue-domed churches, right?"

"Yeah. Right now is the off-season, so only locals were around, no tourists."

"Except you."

"But I felt like a local."

"What town did you stay in?"

"Fira. Some of those Santorini photos you see in calendars are shot there. It's desolate in an awe-inspiring way. I stayed in a tiny pension. Very few hotels or restaurants were open, and I saw just a handful of people the entire time. I hiked around for hours, absorbing the scenery: the narrow, super-steep staircases, the stormy ocean, the deep jade hills, and the red cliffs. I lost myself in all the beauty, Cleo."

"I'll bet you could hardly believe you were there."

"Yeah. And the views were so awesome, I could hardly breathe. Tears came to my eyes. Literally. Tears."

"That sounds unreal."

"It was."

"And what did you think of Athens? I'll bet that was amazing, too, with all that history!"

"It was okay."

"Just okay?"

"Kinda blah, if you want to know the truth. And I never felt quite safe."

Cleo jerked her head around to look at me. Through her lightly tinted sunglasses I could see her large, perfectly lined eyes burning into me.

"What do you mean? Were you in danger?"

I patted her leg, trying to reassure her. "No, no. I just didn't feel as comfortable as I did on the islands. And even if I weren't safe then, I'm home safe now. No use worrying."

"I know, I know. Oh, hey, did you keep a travelogue?"

"Travelogue?"

"Yeah. Like a journal about your trip that maybe other people can read. Like when I went to Washington, DC."

"You couldn't write much about that."

"I know, not about the security screenings and meetings. But remember I wrote about all the touristy stuff? You read it, and some friends read it. Come on, Liz. You remember."

I thought of my empty notebook. "I remember. I didn't really do that. I mean, I did write a whole bunch of postcards." I thought of the cards to Adam Mestas that I'd written, addressed, and then promptly tucked away in my suitcase. I'd think it was a good idea to send *just one* postcard, but as soon as I'd finish writing it, I'd decide it was too soon for this and that I'd seem desperate. Until I saw another postcard that I wanted to send him.

In the end, I hadn't sent Adam even one postcard, and now I was relieved at my restraint. In fact, I decided I might just keep them as a travelogue. He wouldn't care if he never knew about them.

"I'll keep my eye on the mailbox then."

"Uh, yeah."

"Where did you send them from?"

"Fira, probably. Maybe one from Paros, too. I can't quite remember."

"I just love getting postcards! Mom actually just sent me one from Botswana. The picture was so beautiful. It's like getting a little souvenir, huh?"

"I didn't get a postcard."

"I got mine last week. Maybe you got one while you were away. Or she just sent me one because *I* showed interest."

I rolled my eyes. *Yes, yes, you're the perfect daughter.* "What did she say?"

"Oh, just *dumela*, and that she missed us and stuff. The usual."

"*Dumela?*"

Cleo pushed her sunglasses to the top of her head. "God, Liz. *Dumela*. She's only been using that word, geez, since she got there. It means hello."

"Okay, okay. I know that. I just hadn't heard it spoken, I guess. Don't be so damn judgmental, Cleo."

Cleo rolled her eyes now, dramatically, as if mocking me, then pulled her sunglasses back over her eyes and continued as if our little spat had not happened. Thus is the life of sisters. "So I'm getting a postcard from you from Fira and, where was it? Paros? Where else? You said you wrote a lot of them."

"Yeah, but I also wrote them to other people."

"Oh yeah, of course. Did you send some to Mom? She'll love it if you did."

"I sent some to Mom."

"Who else?"

"Just some other people, Cleo. Come on."

"Oh." She shook her head. "You sent some to Liam, didn't you?"

"Only one."

"You didn't want me to know you sent some to *him*, too."

"Just one! And I can send postcards to Liam if I *want* to," I snapped. "He's my roommate."

Cleo was silent for a moment, looking at freeway exit signs. We were getting close, and she began moving her red Corvette toward the right lane in a dance with the other cars that seemed to be choreographed to the classical music on her CD player. When she had merged and was satisfied with our safety, she replied with her usual cool, "Sorry, Eliza. I know you forgave him, and I know that should be good enough for me."

"And I'm sorry for snapping at you. I'm just so damn tired."

"So much for sleeping the entire way on the plane, eh?"

I broke into a little smile. "No kidding. What was I thinking?"

"Take a power nap at my place before heading back."

"That's probably a good idea. Would that be rude?"

"Maybe, but I'm your sister. What is rudeness between sisters? When we were little, you used to put stickers on my face while I slept."

"You used to try to break the locks on my diaries."

"Yeah, so? What is a little rudeness between sisters? Besides, I have a lot of work to do and wouldn't be much company if you were awake anyway."

"You're busy? I could have called a cab, Cleo! You should have said something!"

Cleo shook her head, exiting and turning onto the main road to her house. "You never know about those guys. They can be crazy drivers."

"We're in Orange County. Not New York!" I laughed, but Cleo remained serious.

"Bad drivers are just as dangerous in Orange County as they are anywhere else."

We both fell silent. The vision passed through my mind, as it did too often, of my sister as a fifteen-year-old in the hospital, waking up broken and swollen and asking where Dad was.

I tried to keep the memories, the pain, at bay. Every time they cropped up again, it was too soon. Too often.

"You're right, of course, Cleo. What are you busy with at work?"

Cleo came out of her own memories and replied with little interest, "Stuff for the government. Homeland Security has me on a full-time contract right now."

I thought about the questions I'd gotten in Greece. About the answers I had given, not even knowing that Cleo was here at home with clarity on the war and clarity about her job in waging it. "It's great that you can help."

"Yeah, I guess."

"Guess?"

"Well, it's just a job they want me to do. Translating some security tapes, usual stuff like that. I'm not doing much. The fact that there's a war makes it sound like what I'm doing is so much more important . . . more . . ."

"Heroic?"

"Yeah. But it's just a job. I signed the contract before Operation Iraqi Freedom."

"Is that the official name?"

"Yeah. What were they calling it in Greece?"

"Illegal."

We pulled up to her house and I didn't feel at all rude about crashing in her guest bedroom for a few hours.

When I woke up, Cleo took a break from work and made us a couple of grilled cheese sandwiches. As we talked over our lunch and cans of Diet Pepsi, all tension from the drive home disappeared. That was just how we were. Just how most sisters are, I guess.

"Have I thanked you already for dropping me off and picking me up?"

"Yes, you have. So stop it already, Liz. It was *so* not a problem."

"Yeah, but with work and the war, I'm sure the Department of Homeland Security is really leaning on you right now. I'm surprised they haven't asked you to relocate to Washington, DC!"

"They did several years ago, when I first started doing a little work for them. But everything I do can be done over the computer. They send me recordings in Arabic, and I return transcripts in English. I'm all linked in to Washington, though I don't know how they did it. I said I didn't want to leave Southern California, and all of a sudden some IT guys were sent over to set me up an office in the house, complete with super-secret connections and stuff. I don't know all the logistics because I'm not a techie. And other than a meeting here and there with other local people working with them, I'm free to leave 'the office' whenever I want. I was happy to see you off at the airport, and be the first to welcome you home."

"Well, thank you."

"Now that you've had a little nap, are you glad to be back?"

"Eh, sorta. I'm not looking forward to getting back to the grind. But I admit I'm a little excited to see my interview in print here pretty soon."

"I almost forgot! Seems like *forever* ago you were telling me about that."

"It was only a couple of weeks ago. In the car, on the way to LAX, as a matter of fact."

"I still think you should have said bad stuff about your bitch of a boss in that interview."

"I told you already, she wouldn't be my boss for long if I had."

"Because her superiors would know what an awful person she was."

"No," I corrected her, taking the last sip of my Diet Pepsi. "Because I'd be fired quicker than a manuscript with poor spelling is rejected."

"Editor-speak." Cleo smirked. "I hope you said enough to earn you some points with your boss's boss. They should know how hard you work while Rain Orwell takes all the credit."

"Can we please not talk about Rain?" I moaned. "I blocked her from my mind during my trip, and this conversation is just reminding me that I have to go face her again in less than twenty-four hours."

"Okay, okay. Let's talk about someone else you'll be seeing soon."

I knew who she was thinking of, but asked anyway, coyly, "Oh? Who?"

"The interviewer. The newspaper editor."

"Adam Mestas." I couldn't help smiling. Yeah. I had something worthwhile to look forward to back at home.

"Of course. I've probably thought even more about him than you have these past couple of weeks, which is good because you don't want to be too eager."

I didn't admit to her that I'd thought plenty about him. Instead I just laughed.

Cleo took my soda can and tossed it into the recycle bin. "Is he Arabic?"

"Um, no—"

"African-American?"

"He's Mexican."

"Hey, don't look at me like you think I'm judging you, Liz. I'm just trying to get a mental picture. Geez. Now, you said he had long hair, right?"

"Yeah."

"And romance-novel-worthy dark eyes, and a Cheshire Cat smile . . ."

"I think you're embellishing a little."

"How tall is he?"

"Tall. A lot taller than me. Six feet, and maybe a few inches."

"How many inches, if you had to guess?"

"*Excuse me?*"

"What? Six-foot-what? That's all! Any other measurements are between you and him." She laughed at her own joke, opened the fridge and, not finding anything much to share for dessert, closed it again.

"I don't know. Six-foot-four, if I had to guess."

"And is he skinny or built?"

"Cleo, I don't know. He was dressed for work."

"You said he looked more casual when he came over to your place."

My mind flashed instantly to his tan biceps stretching the short sleeves of his classy polo shirt. "Yeah, how could I forget?"

"And I *distinctly* remember you saying that had a 'solid' body and a very nice *tizi*."

"You're right. I did say that." I paused, trying to decide for sure if I wanted to pull out the big guns. I hadn't said anything on the drive to LAX because I wasn't sure what my plan was. But I did now. "Oh, did I tell you? He asked me out."

Cleo gasped with joy and grabbed my hands. "*No!*" she exclaimed. "How could you have left that out, woman?"

"He gave me his card. You know, his number and everything. Invited me for coffee. I'll probably call him when I get back home."

"*Probably?* You *will* call that man. And you'll go out and have a blast and then you'll marry him and I'll be your maid of honor, and I'll say in my speech that one of the first things you said about him was that he had a very nice butt."

"I'll definitely have coffee with him. The rest, all of that wedding stuff, will have to be put on the back burner, I'm afraid."

"What? Why? Not because of Liam, I hope."

"Don't start on Liam now."

"I'm not! I'm just saying that you've let some other guys go because of him before."

"Yeah, when he and I were a couple."

"*And* since then. You're too self-conscious. You need to forget about all that past stuff with Liam and be careful not to let a new prospect get away because of a lost one."

It was easy for the cool sister to tell the average one not to be self-conscious. Cleo's dark skin glowed like our mother's, and she'd also inherited the trim figure of our paternal grandmother. There was no way in the world that a man could refuse her advances the way Liam had refused mine. She could not possibly know how that would affect a girl. I wanted desperately to change the subject.

"You're just jumping the gun, that's all. I *will* call Adam this week, and I *will* go to coffee with him if he still wants to, and I *will* call you afterwards with all the details. Will that do for now?"

"I guess it'll have to."

"Yes, it will. Because the caffeine from the Diet Pepsi is kicking in and I'm going to drive home now before I get sleepy again."

Cleo wanted nothing more than for me to have a safe drive home, so she was quick to help me load my luggage into my car. And she sent me on my way with two ice cold Diet Pepsis in my cupholders, just in case.

I was dead tired by the time I got home. As soon as I'd lugged my suitcases into the living room and flopped down on the couch, I pulled out the unsent postcards to Adam Mestas.

I'd bought the first one in the stack while waiting for my flight at LAX. A photo collage of Hollywood on the front. What an impulse buy! I'd filled it out on the plane, and the words on the back were like a voice from the past, excited with the adventure that was just beginning, both my trip and the prospect of our relationship:

Dear Mr. Mestas:
Thank you again for being flexible with the interview time. It was fun to do it, and nice to get to know you.
I'll see you in a couple weeks.
Eliza Tahan

I blushed as I read the last sentence, remembering the words appearing on the card and knowing I'd never send it.

As embarrassing as it was, and maybe narcissistic, too, I really wanted to read what I'd written on the other unsent postcards.

Dear Adam Mestas:
I had a stopover in London, and it was my first time here. I didn't have much time but I was able to spend a few hours in the British Museum. I mainly wanted to see the

Reading Room, which you can see in the picture on this post-card. I thought you'd appreciate it, being a book person like me. I hope it isn't weird to be sending this.

I hadn't even signed my name before I'd changed my mind. I thought of my trip to the British Museum, and everything I hadn't written on this card. Though I went to see the Reading Room, I ended up liking the Egyptian artifacts the best, since they made me think of my dad. Of course, if he were alive and there with me, he wouldn't have liked them as much and probably would have had some comment on the European effect on the Middle East, and how all these artifacts were stolen goods. But I'd still thought of him, and that felt nice.

And I could not help remembering that, though I'd had time to write postcards to a near stranger, I had not started my novel. I hadn't even cracked the notebook full of fresh, blank pages.

I couldn't have been missing Adam. We'd only just met. I wondered with a sickness in the pit of my stomach if writing to him was just an excuse for not feeling inspired enough to write anything "real." Was so much missing in my life that I had to grasp at a professional acquaintance?

The picture on the front of the next card made my heart stop all over again: white-washed buildings, blue domes, steep staircases. I felt the powerful wind over my body, as though I were climbing those steps all over again. My throat tightened as it had each time I had walked up to a church on the island.

Hi Adam—

I'm in Fira, and I took a long walk this afternoon. It's breathtaking, and even though it was knock-down windy, the views of the quiet streets and the wind-whipped ocean were worth battling the weather. The sun is out now and the wind has died down, so the ferries should be coming back to Santorini tomorrow.

Not looking forward to coming home. I can at least look forward to that coffee with you.

Until then,
Eliza

There was no question about this postcard—it would never reach Adam. None of them would, for that matter.

I looked around the living room. Geez, was I already ready for another vacation? I felt almost sick to be back. Back to my messy room, back to my hellish boss, back to the knowledge that my trip to Greece hadn't changed my life.

I sighed and began dragging myself upstairs, away from the most adventurous two weeks of my life and towards the mundane life I knew would eventually smother me.

After my shower I lay on my bed for a half hour, towel around my head and robe around my clean body. *What was I thinking, buying those cards and writing them to Adam? Waste of time. Waste of money.*

At least I had the sense not to send them. Otherwise he'd have evidence of my interest.

I sat up purposefully, the towel falling off my head. Shiny, wet obsidian hair fell around my shoulders.

"And what's so bad about that?" I asked aloud. "So what if he knows I'm interested? Am I so afraid of being rejected that I'm going to practically reject him?"

It was still best not to have sent the postcards, that much was true. But as far as my potential with Adam Mestas, I decided then and there that tomorrow I'd call him and set up that date. Even if I felt self-conscious, he'd never know it.

Inspired, I decided that tomorrow I'd print out the available positions in other departments from J Press's intranet site and apply to the interesting ones.

And I'd start my novel. Become an author as well as an editor.

And I'd start pricing studio apartments downtown and show some enthusiasm about selling the condo.

And tomorrow I'd begin filling the void.

And tomorrow I'd start rebuilding the self that had been torn down.

CHAPTER 4

I was running late for work the next morning, and having Rain yell at me was not how I wanted to start rebuilding my life. While gathering my things, I noticed the answering machine light blinking, and vaguely recalled waking to the faint sound of the phone ringing late last night and deciding in my jet-lagged daze that there was no way I was dragging myself downstairs to pick up the phone.

I listened to the messages while I hastily made my breakfast. Nothing was of much interest until Liam's voice came on.

"Lizzy—it's Liam! I'm sure you're home safe and sound and sleeping off the jet lag. You probably won't have even noticed that I'm not there, but in case you did, I just wanted to let you know that I met a friend the other day and I've been staying over at his place for a while. I'll be back tomorrow. Oh, and can I *please* borrow your car tomorrow night? Mine isn't there, as you will have noticed, but it isn't with me, either. I tried to start it up the other day and all of a sudden it didn't work. The mechanic thinks it's an electrical thing. He's probably taking me for a ride, but it's still better than trying to do it myself. We're going out tomorrow night and James uses public transportation to get around, but how lame for a date. So can I use your car? I hope you had a great time and I—"

His message had been too long. Both for the answering machine and for me. The beep cut him off just in time. I balanced my granola bar on a can of V-8 juice for my breakfast-while-commuting and headed out to work.

Every inch of my desk was piled high with manuscripts that I was going to have to catch up on, and on top one of the piles was a note that read:

> *More for you on my desk.*
> *Sue*

I moaned. What was a vacation when it just meant that you'd make up the time you had off in working overtime for the next few weeks? And since I was salaried, overtime meant "my own time."

I was there early, and so when I entered the interns' office in search of my additional workload, I wasn't surprised to find it completely empty. I came in here at least once a day to drop off rejected manuscripts with the interns. Usually it was bustling with college kids working hard and trying to network in the company, so it was eerie to be in there when it was so empty. I walked slowly along one side of the room. There was a long desk attached to the wall, and every few feet there was a sign on the desk with a name. Stacked in each section were manuscripts waiting for something—to be sent to me or another assistant editor, or to be sent back to authors. And tacked to each wall, like unauthorized divides, were personal items belonging to each intern. One intern had photos of his family, presumably on the East Coast if the foliage in the background were evidence. Another intern had pictures of her friends, and your run-of-the-mill Kittens Calendar. At Sue's section of the desk, I noticed that her wall was covered in inspirational quotes.

I found the stack of manuscripts meant for me. I was shocked to see, however, that they already had reports for Rain attached. Had Sue given her own reports on these submissions? I looked at the top one. The poorly written, too-short report ended:

> *Recommendation: Publish this book!*
> *PR Suggestions: Oprah would love this book about a strong woman.*
> *Report by: Sue Talley, covering for Eliza Tahan*

And Rain had evidently seen the reports too. In red pen she'd scrawled right on the report:

> *Who is Sue Talley and why is she covering for Eliza? This report is almost as awful as the manuscript. I'm sending back the rest of these reports and won't look at them again until Eliza sends them to me herself.*

"Dammit," I muttered. I had a little empathy for Sue, who'd just gotten a taste of the side of Rain's personality that we were all used to. And maybe I had a little pride that Rain had implied something positive about me. But mostly I was upset that Sue had taken it upon herself to "cover" for me. Who did she think she was? I leaned over to pick up the mountain of manuscripts, ready to get them back to my desk.

Just then, Sue appeared beside me. "You're back!" she exclaimed, surprised and rubbing her wrist nervously.

"Yeah, and I saw your note about the additional man-uscripts in here—"

Sue's eyes fell upon the stack in my arms. "Oh, before you go, let me take off those reports. Ms. Orwell didn't like my writing the reports for you—"

"Who said you were supposed to do that?"

"No one. I was just helping."

"You shouldn't have. I was only gone for a couple of weeks."

"But things were piling up."

"I expected that. I have a system. I'd set time aside to do this stuff when I got back." It was a lie.

Sue was quiet, rubbing her wrist. I couldn't tell if it was a nervous habit or something patterned to calm her anxiety. But then she dropped her hands to her side and in an instant shoved them deep into her pockets.

"Gosh, Eliza, I'm sorry. I was just trying to help. And maybe get my name around. But believe me, I regret the whole thing. I've regretted it ever since Rain returned those reports."

"Okay, don't worry about it. I appreciate that you wanted to help out. And I understand what you mean about getting your name around. I used to be an intern, too, you know. I know how it feels being in a sea of other people wanting a job here after college. It's just that I could get in trouble if Rain thought I was passing my job off to someone else."

"You're not going to get in trouble."

Sue replied with more certainty on the subject that I had. An optimism due to her lack of experience with Rain, to be sure.

"Anyway, let me take off those reports so you can give them a fresh look. Pretend I never did them." She snatched the report with the red scrawl from the top manuscript. "Did you read what she wrote?"

"Yeah. But don't let it get to you, Sue. Rain can be really hard on people."

"When I saw her note I wished that this was a regular job so I could just quit. But if I quit my internship, I won't get any college credit for it. I felt, I dunno, embarrassed and trapped, but also worried that she might recognize me and yell at me in front of everyone. And yet," she said thoughtfully, "I guess Jane gets the brunt of Ms. Orwell's temper and she could leave any time, but she never does. So maybe I wouldn't just up and quit either."

Lowering my voice so it wouldn't carry, I confided, "I'm sure Jane doesn't want to be an assistant forever, and one day some position will open up here that she wants. If Rain gives the hiring manager a thumbs-up, she'll be set. I think Jane understands that, and that's why she's sticking it out. So, when it gets tough here, Sue, just know that it will help your career to be in the good graces of such a respected editor."

"Thanks," she said with a smile, ending the conversation on a positive note. "Hey, you're awful chipper today. I hope you're not so happy to be back because your vacation was a flop or something like that!"

"No, no, no. A hundred times no," I replied with a laugh. "I had an amazing vacation. I think I'm just feeling a little better about, you know, everything. I've just had some time to think about what I want and about moving forward in life. I guess I feel kinda inspired right now." I drifted out of the interns' office, which was slowly coming to life with activity.

When I reached my desk, I decided to start with voicemail before hunkering down with my stacks of manuscripts. And was I glad I did. The first message happened to be from none other than Mr. Adam Mestas.

"Hello, Eliza." His rich voice slid through the phone. "I know you're on vacation, but I wanted to leave you a message to remind you to call when you get back so I can give you those copies of the article. They're going to print today for the Sunday edition, and I've put in for the additional copies. Just give me a call when you get a chance."

He left his number and I dialed it straight off, while I still had my nerve and while I was busy enough with the work I had waiting for me to sound reasonably professional when I spoke to him. Otherwise I might be too shy with the knowledge of the unsent postcards, of the thoughts of him dancing through my mind for the past two weeks.

In true phone-tag form, I got his voicemail. "You've reached the desk of Adam Mestas, editor for *The San Diego Union-Tribune* book section. I'm either away from my desk or on another line. Please leave a message with your contact information and I'll be in touch soon."

I cleared my throat during the beep, and then said, "Hello, Adam. This is Eliza Tahan at J Press returning your call. I'm back from Greece and I'd love to get together to get the copies of your article. Thank you for setting that up. Feel free to stop by the office today, or even the condo this evening. Otherwise, just give me a call back and we can set up a different time. You have my cell phone number."

Although I spent the next half-hour sorting all the papers on my desk, my attention was mostly on the phone in case Adam were to come by. My mind was also utterly preoccupied with the thought that he might come by the house tonight. I admit it was more than a little forward of me, but he'd had no problem coming by before for the photo, so it wasn't way out of left field for him to come by to drop off some copies of the article. I found myself hoping he'd come by tonight, hoping that he still had that simmering interest that seemed to spark the last time we'd met.

I decided then that it was definitely time for a coffee break. I put notes on all my stacks of manuscripts, demanding that they not be touched, and headed down to the first-floor Starbucks.

As usual, many of my colleagues were sitting at the small tables gossiping. I wondered how long they would be down here. And how long before Rain came down on one of her raids. In reality, she would come down for tea once in a while and, upon seeing her peons sitting around, she'd fly into a rage followed by a meeting later that day with threats to fire people who sat around on company time.

"Tall mocha frapp," I ordered, "and Toby, *please* don't tell me the calorie count on that!"

Behind the counter, Toby smiled his goofy nineteen-year-old smile.

"You don't need to worry about that kinda stuff anyway, Eliza." Smooth little guy. Most people interacted with the baristas just to order their drinks and move on. I imagined that it was a bummer working in a coffee shop attached to an office high rise. It would be so much more inspiring to work in a coffee shop in Hillcrest or La Jolla or somewhere, where wanna-be hippies would come in and hang out all day and chat with you and know everyone in the place. But an office building?

I was quite fond of Toby and his adorably awkward flirtation attempts. He always made me feel good about myself. In fact, he'd asked me out after he found out Liam and I were off. Doubtless he'd heard it from one of the shameless office gossips in the café. I'd told my young admirer a gentle but firm "no."

As I was leaving, a small, cool hand caught my wrist. "Eliza!" cried Carrie, the assistant editor for children's books. "How was Greece?"

I took a sip of my mocha frappuccino. "It was great. Beautiful. I spent most of my time on the islands. Santorini was my favorite."

"And you saw those houses with the blue roofs. I love those." She nodded enthusiastically, auburn waves bobbing in her face.

"Those churches, yeah. They were gorgeous."

"I'm glad you had fun. You deserve it, what with Rain always at your throat. And your engagement being called off and all."

Bitch! Trying to ruin my happy mood! "You and the other gals from children's should clear out of here before Rain goes on one of her tirades. I know she's not your boss, but she can cause havoc anywhere in the company."

"Or anywhere in the world, right?"

One of her companions spoke up from their table. "I think we're safe for now. Rain isn't in the office yet this morning."

"Not in?" Rain was *always* in.

"Nope. I went over to talk to her about this book that's a mystery for kids, to see what she thought of the mystery aspect of it, and her assistant said she's been out for a few days."

Mystery indeed.

Carrie chimed in. "But wasn't she going on vacation, too?"

"She was going to San Francisco, but she's supposed to be back." I thought of the note to Sue on the stacks of manuscripts.

"She hasn't been back, though."

I shrugged it off. "Maybe she got hit by a trolley in San Francisco and is never coming back."

Carrie didn't laugh at my attempted joke. Her eyes focused right past me. *Don't be Rain. Don't be Rain. Don't be Rain,* I chanted inwardly as I turned.

"Ms. Li," I said with a small smile to the HR manager. "How are you?"

The look on her face was strange, and she looked at me while speaking to everyone in the café. "Okay, back upstairs all of you. Go straight to the HR conference room. We're having an urgent meeting."

"Dang it," I heard Carrie mutter from behind me. "Now we're in for it. Pink slips to go with our coffees."

Could this really be the last straw? It was HR this time, and not some maniac supervisor. *Oh well,* I told myself. *I wanted a change anyway, and a change is a change.*

I spent the elevator ride to the fifteenth floor mentally calculating how long it would take me to finish my novel, send it to publishers, and start getting royalty checks. No severance package would cover the time that would take. I knew better than anyone that writing a book was the easy part and getting it published was the difficult one. So instead, I started thinking about the jobs I could do with my knowledge and background.

The elevator opened to a crowd of people, all trying to squeeze into the HR conference room. We could technically all fit, with standing room only. As we shuffled slowly in, I leaned over to Carrie and asked, "Is this our entire company?"

Carrie shook her head, the fear of being fired easing from her face. "No, looks like just books. I don't see anyone from finance or marketing or anything. But all the books interns and assistants are here, too, so it isn't an editorial issue. All I know is that they can't fire everyone in books. So, I guess we can assume this is about something else. Thank goodness."

"Yeah," I replied hesitantly, as the door closed behind me. "Thank goodness."

"Are we all here?" Ms. Li asked.

I wondered how long it would be until the claustrophobia kicked in. "Thank you all for coming." She looked upset, but not angry; uncomfortable, but not uncertain of what she was doing. "I'm sorry for the short notice. I sent an email around this morning, vague as it was, about this meeting, but I know some of you wait to open your email until later in the morning."

Someone next to me who had been herded up from Starbucks muttered, "I thought it was optional and deleted the message."

The person next to him on the other side said, "Whatever she sent is probably buried somewhere in the fifty status query emails from authors I've got sitting in there."

Ms. Li continued, "As you all know, I am Ellen Li and, as the HR manager, I am afraid I have the task of giving you all some very bad news."

My stomach dropped. Were our jobs being outsourced? Was the company being sold to a New York house? I didn't want to move to New York. A wave of whispers spread through the room.

"Quiet, please. I'm sorry to inform you that S. Rain Orwell, the editor for our mystery books department, has passed away." Ms. Li was not expecting the collective sigh of relief that followed, but she had to have realized that this relief was for the continued safety of our jobs, not the loss of an editor. Within a few seconds though, the collective shock set in. She chose this point to move forward.

"Ms. Orwell was in a car accident. On the night of the accident, she was heading to a meeting with an author. This just shows what a dedicated editor she was, what a vital part of our organization. On the way to the meeting, on Interstate 5 near Carlsbad, it seems she had a dispute with someone and it resulted in her car going over into the lagoon."

The noise from crowd began to grow. Questions. Fears.

Ms. Li held up her hand. "Please. We don't know much yet. The police have only told us that it was a hit and run, and that they don't have any suspects yet. They know it was a truck that hit her and that it was able to drive away from the scene. The authorities have not been able to locate it. They expect it was alcohol-related or maybe even road rage, but they are not ruling out that it was something more serious."

Now we were all quiet, as though Rain were moving among us in the crowded room, peering at whoever might have hated her enough to kill her.

"We will be having counselors in to talk to those who may need them. If you'd like to make an appointment, just email my assistant." She cleared her throat. "The police will be in throughout the investigation to look around and to talk to some of you. Many of you knew Rain well, and may have some information about any malicious intent aimed at her. I will personally be calling those who they'd like to talk with so that you can set up appointments with them. Are there any questions?"

No one moved until Jane's thin, pale arm rose above the heads in the crowd. Ms. Li nodded. Jane's usually weak voice now sounded empowered. She asked, "Who will be taking Rain's place?" I could only see the top back of her head, but I noticed that her blonde ringlets were still; she was unmoved and unmoving.

"We'll accept résumés for the next couple of weeks. I'm hoping that by the end of the month we'll have completed interviews and brought in a new mystery editor. Anyone interested, of course, is encouraged to apply."

"But didn't Rain leave some kind of game plan? Didn't she have someone in mind to follow her?"

"Rain didn't know this was going to happen. So I'm not sure what you mean."

"No, of course not. It's just that . . . Well, she wasn't that far from retirement. She *must* have spoken to you about suggestions for when she retired."

The room was getting uncomfortable. People realized they were hearing a private conversation. A private argument.

"No, I'm afraid she didn't. But I wouldn't worry about it. We'll have someone to fill the position very soon."

Jane clammed up, and the discomfort in the room began to dissipate. But Jane then mumbled something, and Ms. Li leaned forward, putting her hand to her ear. "What was that?"

"Oh, I was just said that a month is a long time. What am I going to tell all the authors that call me looking for the mystery editor?"

"Eliza Tahan, the current assistant mystery editor, will naturally be handling Rain's basic duties for the time being." Ms. Li directed her attention toward me, and everyone in the room seemed to follow suit. "Eliza, please stay after the meeting to chat about this."

Everyone turned back to Ms. Li. Except for Jane. Her body twisted toward the back of the room. Her wide, hazel eyes darkened and her small features peered past the shoulders around her. When I caught her eye, it was obvious that she was not pleased with the answer, and a chill swept through me.

CHAPTER 5

I worked the rest of the day amid a buzz of chatter. Most of my colleagues could not concentrate on their work after the news about Rain. But I had long ago learned to block out drama from my professional life. I'd learned the skill in high school after my dad died and I still had to finish SATs and finals and graduate. I had honed the skill when my engagement to Liam had been broken off. I still had to find and secure a handful of promising manuscripts for next year's list deadline.

Now I had to do it before taking on Rain's work. I knew that I'd have to think about Rain at some point, but my workday was not that point.

It turned out that the point would be on my way home. Not that I didn't try to head it off. I turned on the radio, but three stations were playing the same Top-40 song, one was playing a commercial for Sea World, one was reporting on traffic, and my beloved KPBS was pleading for donations in their latest membership drive. Thoughts of Rain overrode them all.

I'll never see S. Rain Orwell again. Ever. She won't be watching me in the office, waiting for me to screw up. I'll never again run into her at Balboa Park's Museum of Art on a Free Tuesday during our lunch break.

These things, I decided, were not too bad. That was the truth that I could never admit in the office, when she was there and definitely not now that she wasn't. Rain had been a bitch to me, and treated almost everyone as inferiors. She made people feel bad about their work, about their lives, and about themselves. With no Rain, J Press's mystery department might be a much more positive place to spend the workday.

I glanced out the passenger-side window at one of the military planes heading into Miramar Air Station. I turned my head back at the sudden flash of red taillights and had to slam on my brakes to avoid hitting the truck in front of me.

My heart rate quickened. My adrenaline rushed. *I'd almost had an accident.*

Is this how Rain felt when she saw the truck coming toward her? Did she know she was facing the end?

Despite my better judgment, I let myself imagine Rain getting into that silver Porsche of hers for the last time. Ms. Li had said she'd been on her way to meet with an author. It was a good guess that the meeting was probably with J Press's star author, J. D. The country could not get enough of J. D.'s free-spirited motorcyclist "Jace Jordan," who traveled from town to town solving mysteries and saving the day. Men loved the exposition on Jace's motorcycle and the sexy women he encountered. Women loved that though Jace could have any of those sexy women as easily as James Bond, he never gave in to temptation. At the end of each book he was on the phone to his long-time girlfriend, who was waiting on the other coast. The motivation for Jace Jordan's travels was to get across the country to his woman, but each town—each book—held another mystery to solve that slowed down the road trip.

I knew that J. D. had mentioned in a call to Rain last week that he wanted to end the series and send Jace Jordan home to an ultimate mystery that put the girlfriend's life in danger. Rain was collected and professional on the phone, but as soon as she'd hung up, she'd had a fit.

When she had turned her hysteria on me, she threatened, "If I can't stop him, Eliza, you'd better find out next best-seller in those stacks of manuscripts. And you'd better do it real soon."

Rain just couldn't let "Jace" get home to his girl and end the series. She would have come up with an argument to convince J.D. to extend the road trip for a few more books. I couldn't think of what the argument would be. It seemed reasonable to me to let J.D. move on to something else. If J Press handled his request with grace, he'd continue with us for his next book. But Rain was a star of an editor, and she'd have had a plan to convince him to write more "Jace" books and continue to publish with J Press for any future books as well.

The meeting to which she was heading had to have been with J.D.

Had she been nervous about the meeting, not paying attention to the vehicles around her as she drove north on

Interstate 5? Or was she confident in her negotiation skills, so confident that she hadn't concerned herself much with the truck closing in on her car until it was too late?

What was her reaction when she realized that the truck was getting close? Maybe she pulled over into the right-most lane; she did drive a Porsche, after all. Not a car to be reckless with.

I imagined a sudden screech of tires, the jolt of impact as the truck turned deliberately into the Porsche, ramming her driver's side and sending her plowing over the edge of the raised freeway and into the lagoon.

It would have felt like long minutes, though it had only been a matter of seconds.

The crunch of the truck against her car. The pain shooting over every inch of her body. The crushing sound of the divider that didn't stop her car from going over the side of the freeway and down the embankment. The whirl of her stomach as she turned upside down, right side up, upside down. A splash, and the feeling of cold salt water stinging her open wounds.

Rain must have felt the pain.

And then felt nothing at all.

Great, and now I'm sobbing. Sobbing for very few of the reasons I ought to be sobbing, but sobbing nonetheless. I wasn't going to pretend, like so many of my colleagues, that she would be missed. That it was "our loss." I cried now for the tragic end to a life. It was a mean life, but not evil, and not deserving of such a tragic fate.

I cried in fear for the people I loved. For my mom, for Cleo. Why hadn't the mythical forces of the universe protected Rain? Why hadn't they protected my dad?

And when would they fail me, or again fail someone I loved?

Liam wasn't home yet, but I decided to stay in for the night, not just because my crying had drained from me any energy to go out, but also because I remembered Liam wanted to use the car. I was in a "cherish your loved ones" mood right now, and I might as well cherish him by handing over the keys if he ever did come home.

I unloaded the manuscripts from the trunk in two trips and dropped them on the floor next to the sofa. With a dramatic, draining day behind me, I felt justified at having a little floor-picnic for dinner. Main course: mint and chocolate chip ice cream. Side dish: white zinfandel. I sat on the floor with my back against the couch and a manuscript in my lap and dug the sturdy spoon into the pint of ice cream.

At that moment I heard a rustling at the door. In a split second, my lethargy was drowned in adrenaline. My pulse quickened.

It's Liam, I told myself, hoping I wasn't lying. *I haven't seen him in two weeks, and here he is. That's good, right? So why is my stomach twisting? He'll want to update me on the plans to sell the condo. And I can talk about the thing with Rain. That might make me feel better.*

But no key entered the lock. No roommate entered the house.

There was a tap on the door, hesitant at first, and then more confident.

"Who the heck . . .?" I muttered as I slipped quickly past the window, hoping not to be seen in the narrow gap between the curtain panels. On tiptoe, I looked out the peephole.

The figure on the other side of the door was facing away from the door, but it was definitely not Liam's sleek figure. I wanted to see who it was, but to turn on the light would confirm that someone was home. The tall, masculine figure shifted uneasily, and I noticed he carried something bulky under his arm.

I thought then about Rain, about the fact that she might have been murdered.

My stomach dropped and I groaned audibly. Through the peephole, I saw the man turn, face invisible in the dark entryway. He leaned toward the peephole. I backed away, though I had tested the thing before we bought the condo and there was no way this psycho could see in at me. But he knew I was here. The idea that I might be murdered because I'd groaned at the idea of murder was an irony that did not escape me.

But then I heard footsteps. Had he left? I looked through the peephole again, but the man outside was still there. I watched another figure approach the door, sure my only defense against *two* murderers on my doorstep was flight. Then a familiar voice pierced my fright.

"Hey buddy, what do you need?" Liam's voice came muffled through the door. "Selling the paper? We already get it."

I moved my fingers to the deadbolt, planning to unlock the door in a hurry if he needed to escape inside with me.

The other man's voice was unexpectedly gentle. And familiar. "I'm looking for Ms. Tahan. I've only been here once, but I was sure this was the house."

Liam moved around the man, patted him on the shoulder. "The light's on inside, so she should be here. Let me get her."

Liam inserted his key into the lock, and I heard Adam's voice drop. "You have a key? I didn't realize Eliza had a boyfriend."

"Eliza's boyfriend? Not quite, buddy—"

Liam didn't have a chance to finish his reply before I threw open the door. "Hi, Adam. I wasn't expecting you."

Liam looked from Adam to me and back, and then moved inside, giving me the slightest hug on the way in. I stepped aside to invite Adam to follow Liam in.

"With everything going on today, I'd kinda forgotten that I said you could swing by."

Adam's brow was lightly furrowed as he watched Liam with some concern. "Sounds like you had a tough first day back."

Liam dropped his bag on the couch and looked up. "Sorry to interrupt you guys, but Lizzy, did you get my message about me borrowing your car?"

"Yeah. How did you get here?"

"Shelly from the desktop supplies department at work gave me a ride. She lives over in Escondido. I think she has a crush on me, though. Not looking forward to conversation about *that*."

I turned to Adam in explanation. "Liam works at a place that sells office supplies to big companies."

"I'm in the paper department. It isn't the most glamorous job." Liam rolled his eyes, and then turned to me.

"So can I use your car tonight then?"

"Why not?" I replied and tossed him my keys. As chilled as Liam was in the situation, it was clear Adam was not comfortable.

"Oh, I'm sorry. Adam, this is Liam Jack, a friend of mine who will evidently be stealing my car tonight. Liam, this is Adam Mestas, the editor who interviewed me."

"Good to meet you, man," Adam nodded, and the muscles in his neck released.

"You too," Liam replied, and absently began moving toward the door. "Lizzy, I'm outta here. Thanks for letting me borrow your car."

"No problem. See ya."

Liam was out the door when he turned and noted, "By the way, the front door wasn't locked. Adam Mestas could have been a murderer for all you knew!"

With a laugh, he disappeared into the dark night and I shut the door behind him.

My stomach turned and my eyes blurred, as I willed myself to be cool, keeping my back to Adam.

"You okay, Eliza? Do you want me to go? I just came to drop off these newspapers."

If I don't turn now, he'll leave for sure. If I do turn and he sees me getting all emotional, he only might or might not leave.

I turned and forced a smile. "Sorry about this. I'm kind of on edge today. I couldn't see who you were with the porch light off and sorta thought you were a murderer."

Adam set down the newspapers immediately and touched a warm hand to my elbow, leading me to the couch. "Eliza, I didn't mean to scare you. You said in your message that I could come over."

"I forgot."

"But you thought I was a murderer?"

"I know. It was something of a dramatic conclusion."

"So tell me why you jumped to it." We settled on the couch.

"Something awful has happened."

"You didn't love Greece?"

"I did." I turned toward him, tucking my legs underneath me to get comfortable.

"Then what's the bad news?"

"By the way, Liam is just a friend."

"I understand."

"Really."

"I believe you, Eliza, okay? Just tell me what's bothering you."

"The thing is, I went to work today and . . . and Rain is gone—"

"I thought this was supposed to be bad news to you." Adam laughed. "Her, ahem, reputation hasn't escaped me. Sweet as honey to us when she wants a book reviewed, but we can all hear her ordering you guys around as soon as we walk out of the office."

"Yeah, but she's really gone. She's *dead*. There was a terrible car crash. They think it might have been caused on purpose. She might have been *murdered*."

"Oh, Eliza. I'm sorry. I thought you were trying to lighten the mood and . . . holy crap." He leaned into me, hesitating, unsure of his place in comforting me. I suppose he figured he'd let me talk it out and that might give him an idea of his place.

Wrapping an arm around my shoulder he insisted, "Tell me everything."

It turned out that listening was exactly what I needed from him. By the time I'd run out of things to say about the accident, about my mixed emotions, he was holding both my hands in his and staring into my eyes seriously.

"It sounds like some random accident," he said when I finished, "not a targeted murder. I don't think you have anything to worry about. Accidents happen much more often than murders, you know."

"Really?" I sniffled. "Accidents happen more than murders?"

"I'm guessing."

"Did you just make that up?"

"No."

"Yes, you did."

"Well, okay. I did. But it sounds accurate, doesn't it?"

I swatted him, cheering up a little. "I hope your fact-checking at work is better than in conversation."

He laughed, warmly, and I could see his soft tongue behind those white teeth. I instantly drew my eyes away, hoping he hadn't seen me looking at his mouth. He had, and he placed one of his massive hands against my cheek, urging my gaze back to his face. I felt the slightest hint of roughness on his fingers, and I wondered if it were evidence of his years of note-taking. Or did this suave professional have a few backcountry manly man hobbies in his personal life?

"Are you feeling a little better, Eliza?" Adam asked, his voice melting over me.

"Yes. Thank you for listening. I didn't mean to go on and on."

"I'm glad to help you."

He moved the slightest bit, so slight in fact that if I had not been studying his face I might not have even noticed. *Is he about to kiss me?*

My adrenaline rushed. My mouth tingled at the sight of his lips coming closer.

I swallowed, my lips parting ever-so-slightly. Adam's lips, also parted, were close enough for me to feel their heat. I waited. It had to be his move.

And he made his move. In a split second the space between our mouths was gone and his lips were against mine. A kiss like his lips whispering secrets against mine. He briefly pulled back and stared into my eyes as though he were searching for my reaction to his whispered kisses.

He found my answer in my lips instead, as I pressed them to his urgently.

Adam's body reacted to my invited passion. He pulled me closer, fingertips grazing the sides of my breasts.

My mind raced. *This is what I want. This is all I want. Let this pleasure go on forever until death and never stop.*

Death. My train of thought had failed me, had led me in the wrong direction. I instantly realized it as soon as the thought had crossed my mind. And I felt again my eyes burning from the tears. The anxiety in the pit of my stomach at the possible murder of my boss bubbled up. I pulled away.

Adam's hand dropped to his lap. He didn't speak, but only stared at me, his midnight eyes fixing on mine, and then on my lips and back to my eyes again. I was the one who had pulled away first, and so it was me who had to speak first. Explain how our passion had failed so suddenly. He waited for me.

"What a day," I announced awkwardly. "The thing with Rain's really just sapped me."

"Are you asking me to leave?"

I placed a hand on his. "You don't have to go just yet."

His eyes traveled to my hand, and then back up the length of my arm to the place where the jade of my undone top button hit the caramel of my clavicle.

"What would you have me do here, Eliza? What would you like me to do for you?"

The choice raked inside me. Another day I'd have asked him to take me. There, on the couch. And then on the staircase. And then upstairs on my bed. But the emotions churning inside of me—the fear and guilt and anxiety—would not have let me enjoy it, enjoy *him*, as much as I would on another day.

I turned my head away from him, and he didn't need a verbal reply.

Adam stood and went to the door. "Here're the newspapers. I'll leave them on this table."

"Th—thanks. I'll show you out."

I made my way to the door and opened it for him.

Once outside, he turned back to me. "Maybe it's an inappropriate time right now for a date. If so, please tell me. But if not, what do you say to meeting sometime next week for lunch?"

"That would be nice."

"All right. Great. I'll talk to you then."

As he walked away, the place on my cheek where his hand had touched me burned sweetly.

CHAPTER 6

By the following week, I could barely muster the motivation to drag myself out of bed in the morning. I had worked twelve-hour days the previous week, and chased them with a weekend dedicated solely to getting caught up on reading manuscript submissions. As of Monday I was *still* not caught up, albeit closer than I'd been on Friday. Early mornings and late nights were blending into one another, and I felt understandably sick to my stomach at the thought of walking into the office on Monday morning.

But HR had told me Friday that I could start on Rain's messy office today, since the police had gathered everything they needed. I decided that if I wanted to be promoted to Rain's position permanently, I'd need to really be a shining star while the post was a temporary one. I had to march into work this morning, walk right into Rain's office, sit in her chair, turn on her computer, and make them all my own.

On Friday Adam Mestas had called me again and we'd made plans for lunch on Monday. Now, on a groggy Monday morning, the promise of seeing Adam again in a social setting carried my limp body into the shower. The water pulsed onto my skin, awakening it, sharpening my senses.

It's a date, he'd told me. My first date in months. And not because I was lowering my standards, but because a man met them.

Once out of the shower and toweled off, I slipped into my favorite pair of black slacks: plenty of darts in the back to clear my *tizi*, and a flat front with side zipper to minimize my little belly, just as the tags had promised. Like most pants on my five feet, four inch frame, they were a little too long with flat shoes, but hung just right with my black ankle boots. I buttoned up a silk, long-sleeved shirt in deep jade to match the lacey underwear I'd chosen. Even if it was just a lunch date and he'd never see them, wearing them made me feel sexy, and that was just as important.

Liam was already in my car in the front yard, and I heard him honk the horn. I leaned into the mirror and brushed on mascara, left eye then the right, saying to my reflection, "Girl, you just let him wait for you."

I added a stroke of plum lipstick and stepped back. I looked more together than I felt, but my confidence was improving. "Adam Mestas, you are one lucky man."

Liam had tired of honking the horn like a five-year-old, and I took my time getting to the car, out the front door with a stack of manuscripts in one arm and my small black purse slung over the other.

I opened the driver's side door. "Pop the trunk, will ya, Liam?"

"Your wish is my command," Liam replied and, with the push of a button, the trunk popped open.

"Then I *wish* you'd find your way to the passenger side. You're borrowing my car—again—but while I'm in it, I am still the commander of this vessel."

Liam made his way to the passenger side as I dumped the stack of manuscripts in the trunk. Once in the driver's seat, I turned to him and raised an eyebrow. "Liam, I *know* you hate seatbelts, but this is *my* car and it is a rule for my car."

"What should it matter to you if I wear this thing? Please. If we get pulled over I swear I'll pay the ticket."

"Come *on*," I urged. "No one cares about your shirt getting wrinkled. We've been over this so many times . . ."

"Maybe not in your job, Lizzy. But I need to impress both my employer and my clients who are looking to buy thousands of dollars worth of paper for their companies. Not *everyone* communicates solely by email and telephone."

"Will you impress your employer and clients if you get to work late? Because I can tell you that I'm not going anywhere until—"

"Fine!" Liam submitted with obvious frustration playing across his fine features. "I can't wait to get my own damn car back so that I don't need to bow to your every little whim." His seatbelt clicked.

"Thank you. And believe me, I *also* can't wait until you get your shiny SUV back so we don't have to have this argument again for a while." I began backing up.

Liam sighed and looked out the passenger side window, pouting.

We were out of the driveway and now moving forward. "Okay, so you'll drop me off at work, and then I'll take the commuter bus back home, right? Because I don't know yet whether I'll get back in time for you to go on your date."

"Sounds like a plan."

"I actually have a date today, too, you know."

Liam cocked his head in surprise. "What was all that talk about taking the bus home? A cover for where you'll really be spending the night?"

"Yeah, yeah, tease me all you want."

"I'll stop, but just tell me who this lovely gentleman is. Is it the guy who came over the other night. With the long hair?"

"It is, indeed. He's an editor from *The San Diego Union-Tribune*'s book section. The one that interviewed me."

"That's right. A fellow literary person, at that. By the way, has that interview been published yet or what?"

"Yeah. Adam brought over copies and I left one with your mail," I replied. "Didn't you read it?"

"No. I guess I forgot."

"Thanks for your support, Liam."

Liam wasn't deterred or defensive. "Do you . . . *love* him?"

I turned my head when we stopped in traffic. Liam's dark blond hair was slicked back, most of the blond-frosted tips at the back of his head, as it usually was in the morning for work. By his date tonight it would have fallen forward and he'd look as cool and trendy as ever.

"He's just very interesting and we're meeting for lunch."

"Lunch?" Liam asked skeptically. "That's not really a date, you know."

"It *is* a date. He said 'It's a date,' and he at least is an honest person."

Liam was quiet. I felt guilty for insinuating that *he* wasn't truthful during our relationship. Of course, he hadn't been truthful, so why the guilt?

The rest of the car ride was pretty uncomfortable. Liam didn't seem angry, but then again, I couldn't see his face as he was turned entirely toward the window. At one point I seriously considered just dropping him off at his office and telling him to rent a car if his date was so damn important. But just being within eyesight of my office building, where I knew I would find something resembling order, calmed my passionate side.

When I pulled up in front of my building, I got out. My apology was limited to "Have a good date tonight." His acceptance of my apology was limited as well: "You, too." And that was it.

By 10 a.m. I had completely forgotten the awkward morning drive. I was now dealing with a job that no longer held the order I was used to having at work. I was overwhelmed with the mess on Rain's desk, overwhelmed with the emails in her inbox, overwhelmed with the number of voicemails, and frustrated with Jane's constant requests to "put someone through" to me. I kept telling her that if they weren't from the office, to put them through to voicemail. I needed to figure out what the hell was going on here before I could answer any questions from authors, PR people, agents, *anyone*.

She'd argue with me for every phone call.

"But this is Monaka Williams. Rain said she'd have a contract to her by last week and it isn't even back from finance yet. What should I tell her? That you're going to track it down and push it through? She's one of our most promising new authors, Eliza. You know that. We *can't* afford to look bad in front of her."

I'd reply, "I know. That's *why* I can't talk to her right now. Just tell her what you told me, that it is with finance and we'll get it out as soon as possible."

She'd sigh but do as I requested.

In all honesty, I was already fed up with Jane when I excused myself for a coffee break and headed to Starbucks downstairs. For once, I understood why Rain always seemed so mean to her. But this was really surprising, since Jane had always been so sincere and kind to me in the past. She had *never* said a sharp thing to me before, but this morning she just could not be decent to me. In fact, she was being borderline unprofessional.

As usual, Starbucks was crowded with my colleagues, but no one was in good spirits yet. Out of the corner of my eye I noticed a mass migration back to work as I was handed my drink. Turning, I saw Ms. Li standing before me.

"I need to talk to you," she said quietly, moving over to one of the small tables. I followed her and she began, "As you know, the police have been gathering evidence about Ms. Orwell's death."

"Yeah. Did they find something that will help them catch the guy who hit her?"

"They say that in her pocket they found a death threat. It makes them think that the accident was first-degree murder."

"If she had a death threat, why wouldn't she have brought it to the police? Why would she keep it in her pocket?"

"Someone in her neighborhood told the police he'd been taking his dog for its evening walk when Ms. Orwell came out of the house and went to her car in the driveway. She asked him if someone came around and put ads on everyone's cars. He said she was mad, complained that it was the kind of thing that should happen in Wal-Mart parking lots, not in a neighborhood like theirs."

"Sounds like something she'd say."

"He said when she pulled the piece of paper off the windshield, she looked scared. He told her he hadn't gotten anything on his car, and then he said she looked at her watch, stuffed the paper into her pocket, and told him thanks and goodbye."

"That was it?"

"Not quite. The death threat had been written," Ms. Li touched my hand, "on the back of a rejection letter from J Press."

I felt a chill rush through my body. Ever since we'd heard about Rain's death, people in the office had been speculating whether it was a planned murder. But no one had said anything about a rejection letter.

"Was it a personalized letter? It would have had a name on it. Or if they tore off the name there are still not a lot of people that Rain personalized letters to. We could narrow it down. I keep copies of all my reports to Rain— we could use those as a starting point."

"It was a form letter, I'm afraid. I don't know why the murderer would have assumed she was the one who rejected them. The police don't know if it came from an author or from someone inside the company. You know, someone who would have access to the letters."

"The form letter has her name on it. Any author would have assumed it had come from her."

"Rain sent form letters?" Ms. Li asked, arching an eyebrow.

"No. We send form letters to those authors whose manuscripts I've read and decided to reject. Rain insisted that her name be on all outgoing correspondence. She said it gave the impression that there was someone 'competent' here. She said no one would argue about a rejection from her. I'm actually the one who reads and rejects most manuscripts. The interns scan the cover letters and first pages for grammar and spelling errors and if the submission's fine, they pass them on to me."

Ms. Li grabbed my right hand firmly. "I'll let the police know that little detail. For now, anyway, I actually came to tell you that the police would like to talk to you."

"Me?"

"Yes. They want to talk to people who might know something. They probably chose you because you worked so closely with Ms. Orwell. They're going to be talking to Jane, too. And they've already talked to me, of course. I'm sure it will be very informal." She handed me a card and said, "Can you give them a call this morning? I think they'd like to see you sometime this week. Please feel free to go down there on company time."

"I'll call," I replied, taking the card.

When I smiled at Jane as I entered the office, she just looked annoyed. I wondered if she was angry or nervous about having to talk to the police. Because I was uncomfortable with being associated with Rain's murder in any way, I decided to cut Jane some slack.

In Rain's office—my temporary office—I looked distractedly through Rain's desk calendar, trying to figure out what I should be doing outside my own reading duties, trying to procrastinate on calling the police. On her calendar, Rain had scrawled:

> *Follow-up call to J. D.*
> *Proof corrections due back for S.I.N.*
> *Ms reports due from ET*

I called through my open door to Jane, who was sitting at her desk right outside the office. She didn't answer, and I got up to check if she was even there. She was.

"Did you hear me call?" I asked.

"On the phone?"

"You were on the phone?

"No, I was asking if you called on the phone." She rolled her eyes and I could scarcely believe this rudeness.

"No," I answered curtly. "Through the doorway."

"You should have just called me. Just press six, five—"

"But you're *right here.*"

"So then it was easy for you to walk out here and talk to me."

"But Rain always—"

Jane slammed the pen she was holding down on her desk. "You're not Rain. Now what do you want?"

Heat rushed to my cheeks. I was struck dumb for a moment, and it was all I could do to cast a glance around the room to see if anyone was watching this spectacle. In my mind our conversation had been very loud, but evidently it was not as no gaze was cast on us. All eyes were down on their work. I set a hand onto Jane's desk and leaned a little closer to her, speaking softly, trying to keep my cool. I was supposedly her boss now, and as much as I wanted to, I couldn't start my reply with *Now listen here, bitch!* Instead I said, "What's the problem, Jane? We were always okay before, you and I."

She picked up her pen again and turned slightly away from me, as though she didn't even want me that close to her.

"What?" I insisted. "What in the world do you have against me?" Even as I said it, my stomach turned to think that she might have a problem with my race. My gaze hardened, as if daring her to go there. She wouldn't get away with it, not from me and not from J Press.

She looked up from the paper she had been writing on. "Why are you trying to start an argument with me, Eliza?"

"*I'm* trying to start—?"

"All I want to know is why you were calling me from across the office."

I stood up straight again. Enough diplomacy. I had to work. "Has J. D. had been told about Rain yet?"

"I told him."

"Okay, good. That's all I wanted to know. It didn't have to be a big production."

"You're welcome. I figured he needed to be told right away. He *is* our star author, after all, and *no one* else took the initiative."

"Rain had a note for a follow-up call on her calendar and I just wanted to make sure—"

"I've taken care of it." Jane was entirely focused on her paper now, and I realized that the conversation was done.

"Good. Glad you're doing your job." She was about to mutter something else, but I turned and walked back into the office, wanting to have the last word.

As I crossed the follow-up call off Rain's calendar, the *esprit d'escalier* hit. All the things I should have said. She had no right to treat me that way.

I couldn't sit still. Popping up from the chair, I paced back and forth, following the wide window.

I should have told her that her behavior was inappropriate.

I should have told her that I used to feel sorry for her because of how Rain abused her, but that I now understood why Rain had to act that way.

I should have told her that she's lucky I'm not Rain, or else she'd never work another day at J Press.

I should have forced her to tell me what her problem was.

I should have told her that I knew the police wanted to talk to her. I knew that would make her understandably nervous. I should have told her that was why I was putting up with her behavior. That my tolerance was not going to last much longer.

I moved to the door and glanced at the back of Jane's head. Her curls stopped moving for a split second, so I knew that she knew I was there. I didn't speak, but simply shut the door.

Back at my desk, with a barrier between myself and my bitchy assistant, I tried to focus on the tasks on Rain's calendar. Obviously, I was not expecting manuscript reports from E.T. as that was myself and I already knew that I had come across no new manuscripts that I wanted to pursue further. All that was left was to follow up on the author's proof corrections for a sequel called *Safety in Numbers*.

Like all but the most successful authors, this one had a full-time job and thus it was her answering machine that picked up when I called her house. "Hi, Amy. This is Eliza Tahan at J Press, calling to follow up on your proof corrections. We haven't received them yet and so I'm just checking to see if you have any questions. The book looks great, and I'll be looking forward to getting your corrections so it can be ready for the scheduled time."

Then the only call I had left to make was to the police. I pulled out the card that Ms. Li had given me. After a half minute of fret and a twisted stomach, I glanced up at the clock. Less than two hours to my date. Being worried about calling the police would not make me a fun date, I decided. So, for the sake of romance, I was going to stop procrastinating. I took a deep breath and dialed the police station.

"Wilson," was the husky answer to my call.

"Um, this is Eliza."

"This is Detective Wilson. Who is this?"

"Eliza Tahan. I'm at J Press. Our human resources manager said that you wanted to talk to me about Rain Orwell."

"Sara Orwell, you mean?"

"*Sara* Orwell?"

"Yes. The editor that was killed."

"In a car accident, yes."

"She was killed in her car. And you are Eliza Tahan." I heard him shuffle through some papers. "Ah yes, the assistant editor. Can you come down to the station to talk with me this week about Ms. Sara Orwell?"

Sara? Of course she was too much of a wannabe hippie to go by a biblical name. Her "S" initial had always been top secret, but I kind of assumed it was a normal name that she was hiding. "Rain" was much more exciting and glamorous.

"This week?" Adam's handsome face popped into my mind's eye and I replied too quickly, "Not today. I mean, I can't do it right *now*. Can I come in some other afternoon this week?"

"Not a problem. Let's say three o'clock on Thursday. Would that work?"

"Yeah, that would be fine. I can reach you via trolley, right?"

"Yes. We're on the Blue Line. I'll see you in a couple of days."

After we hung up, I felt much more at ease. What a kind, hearty voice. This wasn't going to be a gruff interrogation under hot lights. Not a "Where were you on the night of the murder?" To which I'd answer, "I was in Greece, officer, I swear!" This was going to a friendly conversation about my job, Rain's job, and who I knew that would like Rain dead. Two weeks ago we'd have *all* liked her dead. Everyone in this office *and* most of the people who sent her a manuscript for consideration. But really, none of us would have had actually gone through with it. *I ought to tell him that,* I thought confidently. *It might be helpful for them to know that no one liked Rain, but that we are decent enough not to have killed her.*

I smirked and looked up. The door was open slightly and Jane was standing there with a stony look on her face. "Why are you laughing?" she demanded quietly.

"I was just—nothing, Jane. Did you need something?"

"No," she replied, turning to leave. "I just thought I heard you say my name."

At ten minutes to noon, I looked up from a contract that I'd been trying to decipher. I had just enough time to run a brush through my hair and add a little lipstick before making my way downstairs and out of the building into the sunlight. I entered the mocha granite of the Wells Fargo Building, nodded at the security guards, and then took running steps to make it into one of the elevators before the doors closed. "Three please," I said with a smile to the other person in the elevator, who was blocking the buttons.

She pressed the button and replied, "Going to the deli?" I nodded and she continued, "They're the best. I've gained five pounds since I started working in this building."

I exited at the third floor and the lady in the elevator said, "Bon appetite," as the doors closed. I made my way down the hall and to the last room on the left. One of the best delis, in my opinion, in all of downtown. Not that I was specifically excited for the food this time.

I scanned the long line at the counter as well as the indoor eating area, seeing no sign of Adam. When I looked through the windows to the large balcony, I spotted him right away.

He'd seen me first and was already out of his chair and on his way inside.

"Eliza!" He greeted me with a wide smile, hand extended. We met in a handshake. "So great to see you again. You still have that Greek glow to you."

I blushed. My caramel skin felt instantly *bronze.* "Thank you. It's good to see you, too."

He put a hand on my back lightly and looked at the menu above the counter. "Let's go ahead and order and we'll get started on our meeting."

My heartbeat quickened at his touch, but my stomach dropped at the change of vocabulary from "date" to "meeting." What had I been thinking? But I nodded, and when we reached the counter, I ordered an egg salad sandwich, not worrying about the calories because *obviously* this wasn't a date anyway.

When we sat down, Adam became instantly shy. He stared at his hands for a moment before admitting, to my dismay, "I almost canceled our meeting, you know."

"Well, that's a good start," I muttered sarcastically. "You're just flattering me now."

He held out his hands with a surprised look. "Hey now, I just meant that when you told me about what happened to your boss and then I immediately . . . um . . . made a move, that really seemed to turn you off. Which I guess I can understand. I felt like a bit of a creep when I left your place the other day. Like I had been dishonoring the dead."

I looked down at my sandwich and leaned over the table to explain in a low voice, "I *am* sorry about that, Adam. About closing up, you know. It wasn't about honoring or not honoring Rain. It was just about how I was feeling right then."

"I don't know if that's better or worse. 'It's not you, it's me.' Come on, Eliza."

"I'm out with you now, aren't I? So if you're a creep, so am I."

Adam smiled, loosening up. "You're right. Let's get this *date* rolling then. Have you read my article yet?"

"*My* article, you mean?"

"*My* article *about* you." He laughed easily now.

"Not yet. I checked the picture, not that I was being vain, but I wanted to make sure I didn't look horrible or something. And then I set the article aside to read when I could focus on it. I need to catch up on some reading for work, and sometimes it's hard to split my attention between personal business and work."

I could see that he was disappointed. I tried to draw him in. "Do you have that problem, too? Mixing work and personal life?"

"Not really," he said with a shrug. "I mean, I do mix them—obviously, since you and I are here— but I don't find it to be a problem for me."

"You're lucky then. But how did you think the article turned out?"

"Great. I'm sure you'll have an increase in submissions addressed specifically to you, now that people think they have an 'in.' Plus, your picture came out really nice, so you may have some calls come in that are *not* business-related at all."

"You're flattering me, Mr. Mestas."

"You know, you never did tell me about your trip."

What to tell? It was not the life-changing journey that a solo overseas backpacking adventure is made out to be, but it was also the best time I'd had in a long time. So I just said, "Great. It was great."

There was a smirk and then, "Oh, please, Eliza. We are both word people, and all you can say about your two-week 'adventure' in Greece is that it was *great*?"

I looked at him sideways and then took a sip of my water. What to say? "When I got off the ferry on Santorini island, it was windy and cold and I had forgotten my jacket. I hadn't slept in two days since I went straight from the long plane ride to Athens to the bus to Piraeus to the ferry to Santorini. I accepted a ride from the first hotel person who offered me one, since there is a twisty, steep cliff road that goes up to the towns. He told me that he had rooms for twenty-two euro and that I could look at them and then decide if I wanted to stay. That's how I ended up in Fira. I didn't stay at that hotel, since the guy who took me up there was a little slimy and I didn't feel comfortable there."

"Slimy?" Adam broke in, confirming my suspicion that he had, indeed, been paying attention.

I chose my words as though I was picking them right out of a thesaurus, taking my time. "Yes. I think *slimy* is the best word. When we got to the hotel he increased the price to thirty-five euro, which made me mad on principle. But when I tried to leave, he blocked the door and said I took advantage of the ride and that now I had to stay there. Who wants to spend the night in a hotel where a slimy guy has the master room key, right? So I squeezed past him and made it out the door, deciding for sure that I was *not* going to go back.

"I wandered the streets trying to find an open hotel, but everything was closed since it was off-season. I guess 'wandered the streets' sounds a little dark for what it was really like, but the sun was setting and I was afraid I'd be stuck staying at the slimy guy's hotel. Finally I stopped at a little market where someone suggested I try the Pension Delphini, which was open. That ended up being the place where I spent my entire time on Santorini. I mean, you know, where I slept."

Adam frowned. "It almost sounds as if you didn't have a good time."

"I know. I wanted to tell that story first, but I actually *did* have a *great* trip, a beautiful and memorable trip, one of my best vacations. I guess the thing is that it wasn't really what I was expecting. Moments like that just kinda kicked into my mind how everyone had been right about how I should have reservations and a traveling companion for a vacation. I hated that they were right." *Why am I telling him all this?* I wondered. *Does he make me feel that comfortable, or maybe that listened-to, that I can tell him the darker side of the story that I've not mentioned to anyone else who's asked?*

"When you were heading out for the airport, you called it an 'adventure,' not a 'vacation.' And sometimes the more risks you take, the more fun you end up having. Did you really end up having fun, when it came down to it?"

"Other than those first few hours on Santorini, I sure did." I thought about how I must have gotten good vibes from Adam right off the bat to be able to trust him with my weaknesses. Plus, I was a little flattered that he remembered my use of the word 'adventure' from our conversation weeks ago. I decided to bare a little more of my soul. "To be honest, Adam, you're right in the fact that I was expecting this trip to be more than a vacation. I'd forgotten that I told you I was going on an adventure. I didn't really admit this to anyone, but I wanted it to be this *glorious, life-changing* adventure. As if the earth or some of those places were supposed to speak to me and tell me what to do with my life. Inspire me to make needed changes."

"The earth can't do all that. And history can't be depended on to inspire your spirit."

"If not history and landscape, then what?"

Adam smiled wryly and noted, "Maybe partly yourself and partly someone who inspires passion in you."

"Someone passionate?"

"You never know. Now, tell me one of the good memories."

I took a bite of my egg salad sandwich before continuing. "Right next to the Pension Delphini was this little fruit stand with all kinds of bright, deeply colored fruit. I went there every morning I was on Santorini to grab something to eat for breakfast while I explored. Those rich, bright hues contrasted with the white walls. The sun coming through the distant cloud cover gave the sky the appearance of a blank sheet of paper. They're pictures forever pressed in my mind. A good memory.

"One morning I saw the oldest lady. She was really short and round and wrinkly, with wind-chapped skin.

She was wearing a black dress and black shawl, and a black hood covered her hair. The wind blew little wisps of hair out from under the hood, and they matched the white-washed walls. She bought an orange—just one orange—right ahead of me and then moved easily over the uneven stones and up the hill. I bought my fruit and then followed her to a bakery around the corner, then watched her as she bought bread. Then she climbed a really steep hill in this long black dress and these chunky heels, smiling at the kids running down it, nodding and chatting with whoever passed her. In one hand she held the orange, her big black purse was over her wrist, and under her other arm was a long loaf of bread."

"And she became your picture of Greece."

"Exactly. I spent time hiking in Ia, the most beautiful village in the entire world. One afternoon I lost myself exploring the relics at the Monuments of Greece museum. I rode a moped around the island of Paros, passing rolling hills and men fishing for octopi. I climbed on a sixteenth-century castle in Naousa that was almost entirely submerged in the sea. I saw the Parthenon. I shopped in the bustling Plaka in Athens. But the picture in my mind of a smiling old lady in a black dress and heels climbing a hill with an orange in one hand and loaf of bread under her arm, chatting and laughing and passing white-washed walls with bright blue domes and vibrantly painted doors . . . that is my picture of Greece."

"Breathtaking."

"I never wanted to leave," I answered.

"Fantastic," Adam said in a hushed breath.

His enthusiasm was genuine and incredibly sexy. I looked at my sandwich and wondered if he could sense my attraction to him.

Adam leaned back in his chair and folded his hands behind his head. "I've always wanted to see Greece. As a kid all of our vacations were to visit family in Baja. I suppose that now as an adult I have no excuse not to go."

I blinked, and for a moment envisioned Adam, bare-chested, his arms wrapped around me, the wind whipping through our hair after a long hike along the caldera to Ia.

I resisted the temptation to bring up any mention of us going together. Instead I asked, "What family do you have in Baja?"

"My grandparents on my dad's side. All my mom's family is here."

"In San Diego?"

"No, I mean in the States. They're all in Arizona."

"And what is your family like?" Even as the question left my mouth I regretted asking. It was awkwardly phrased and so generic, and it could only lead to questions about my family.

"My family's pretty normal. I'm close to my parents, and I've got a brother and a sister, both younger, both in college. My brother's getting a degree in animal science or something. To be a vet. He likes to remind me that soon I'll be calling him 'Dr. Mestas.' And he's engaged to be married to a really nice girl working on her CPA credentials. She's just one test away from getting certified. They're waiting until he finishes school to get married."

"Sounds like they're really responsible."

"Yeah. It may sound weird, but I really am proud of my brother."

He must be as close to his brother as I am to Cleo, I thought.

Adam continued. "My sister's a little wild, but she's only nineteen, trying out her new freedom. To hear it from my parents, you'd think her one goal in life is to torment them. I think they blow it out of proportion. She's just not sure what she wants to do yet, but she knows that she wants to hang out with her friends and shop and travel right now. She's going to be studying abroad next semester in South Africa. So, she's a good kid. She just doesn't know what she wants to do in the future."

I shrugged. "Who does?"

"Yeah, really," he laughed, but I was pretty sure that he was doing now what he wanted to do in the future. He was already on his path. And he probably assumed I was, too. "They all still live in Arizona, where I grew up. I see all of them on holidays and often during the summer. It's a good excuse to go to the river."

"Do you ski? Jet ski?" I imagined his muscular arms glistening with droplets of river water. Then I turned my eyes demurely back to my sandwich, which was almost finished now.

"Sure do. My folks have a boat and we go out and just cruise around, water ski, swim, relax in the sun. One-hundred-fifteen-degree weather is *only* good when you're on the lake with nowhere you need to be anytime soon. Once I step back on land out there, I'm ready to head back to San Diego. Warm sunshine and cool ocean breezes, summer or winter. You really gotta love this city."

"America's finest," I agreed. We toasted the city with our bottles of water, both almost empty.

"What about your family?" Adam finished the last bite of his sandwich. "Your last name is Tahan, which is Middle Eastern."

"Good job," I replied. "My dad was Syrian, and my mom is African-American. She's working in Botswana right now with the Peace Corps, if you can believe it. *My mom!* After my dad . . . well, he passed away when I was a teenager. He and my sister were in a car accident, and she healed but he was just hurt too bad." I lowered my eyes and my hands to my lap, giving myself a moment to regain my composure so that I would not cry. Adam gave me that moment without question, and when I felt controlled, I continued, "Sorry, that's still just a sad memory. Anyway, after my mom got both my sister and me grown up and out of the house, she went on this inspired rampage to do something good for the world."

"I'm sorry about your dad," Adam said.

"Me, too. I didn't really want to bring that up."

"I imagine it must be hard to have something that tragic in your past and not have it at the forefront of your thoughts."

"Some people avoid that. I try, but it doesn't always work." I thought about Cleo. She could keep the past in the past. And that just made me feel that it was my weakness that would not let me keep it there.

For a moment, we just stared down awkwardly at the empty plates on the table. I noticed my watch and broke the silence. "I should probably get back to work pretty soon."

"How does the rest of your week look?"

"Oh, I . . ." I scanned my internal calendar for appointments. "I'm pretty free after work hours. Oh, but Thursday afternoon I have to see the police."

"Are they hauling you down to the station?"

"Yeah, *for questioning*."

"Of course."

Adam picked up my tray and returned it to the counter. He held the door open for me and we made our way to the elevator.

"Despite a dark turn in the conversation, Adam, I really enjoyed our lunch."

"Me, too," he replied, and he seemed to be telling the truth. "A lunch date is kind of only a half date, you know. We should have a *real* date. Not one during business hours. One at night."

"So we'd have a total of one and a half dates? How about Saturday evening?"

"Saturday is all right. But let's make that one tentative. If I can't delegate it to someone else, I may have to go to this book reading and signing thing, to interview the author. It's sci-fi." He made a face. "Let's plan something more solid in the meantime. Say Wednesday?"

"A date on a weeknight? How scandalous!"

Adam lifted an eyebrow. "Are you a scandalous kinda gal?"

"I accept Wednesday night dates. You judge."

"Can I pick you up at your condo on Wednesday, say at seven?"

I'll need to clean and dust. Buy some good wine. Talk Liam into going out for the night. But what I said aloud was, "Sure! Sounds great!" I smiled invitingly, wondering if he would move in for a kiss. This time I wouldn't turn away.

"I'll be at your place at seven, day after tomorrow. I *know* where you live." We reached the bottom floor, exited the building, and went our separate ways, kissless. I discreetly watched him in the reflection of the windows across the street. I was overjoyed to see him turn around twice to check me out. And I thought I caught him smiling with what looked in the reflection like satisfaction.

CHAPTER 7

My streak of bad luck was officially broken. I had a follow-up date planned with a hot guy and I felt my new position was inspiring me. Maybe I was just handling the easy stuff, but I was firing through it.

I checked with the typesetter on the author's proof corrections for *Safety in Numbers,* which had been turned in after my friendly reminder.

I made my very first offer to a previously unpublished writer for his sizzling mystery, which I couldn't wait to get out on the market. I had made his day.

Mediocre manuscripts were getting short comments to be incorporated into rejection letters, and I had already decided to let the interns do that. Delegating the more mundane tasks would be the only way I'd ever get all these new responsibilities handled.

I finished penning, "Interesting characters. Not quite 'mystery' enough for us. Try some independent presses with less niche," and dialed the intern department. Whoever happened to be in that day would answer the communal phone. It was Sue Talley, and I asked her to come over to my office when she got a chance. By the time she arrived, I had decided it was good luck that she had answered the phone. This new assignment might help her confidence after those remarks Rain had made when Sue had tried to "cover" for me.

Sue was in my office before I could pat myself on the back for the idea. She came in with a worried look, and I quickly assured her that this was a good meeting, and that I was sorry I hadn't made that clear when I called.

She visibly relaxed and casually looked around the office. "I'm so glad you got this nice office. You deserve it more than Ms. Orwell, anyway."

"Thanks. Have a seat. Sorry that chair is so uncomfortable. I keep meaning to bring in my old chair to replace it, but then whoever takes my desk will end up with that one." Of course, the truth was that I was sure I'd be back at my old desk soon and I didn't want to end up in the uncomfortable chair Sue was settling herself in now.

"Oh, please, no problem. Hey, you really need to redecorate this room. Seriously, it still looks like Ms. Orwell's."

I cleared my throat awkwardly. "I actually don't officially have this office yet. I'm just occupying it while I'm taking care of her stuff and while HR is interviewing for Rain's replacement."

Sue waved her hand and laughed. "Please. You will *so* get this job. Gosh, Eliza, there's no question about it."

Do I even want it? I asked myself. But I was on fire today, which pumped up my confidence and I answered my own question. *I'm up to any challenge. I'm better than Rain any day!*

I picked up the pile of papers, ten manuscripts' first fifty pages. Sue grabbed them excitedly and said, "That was quick! That one that was on the top of the stack. I thought it was good. Did you agree with Ms. Orwell's comments or mine?" As she spoke, she shuffled through the bundled pages.

I blushed. "Oh, um, actually these are different manuscripts. These were old and easily rejected. I'm still going to get to that stack you gave me, and I really want to give them my full attention."

Sue wore her emotions on her young face, and I knew she was disappointed. "Oh, sure, okay. I totally understand. Just let me know when it's ready."

"Which is the one you were saying you found promise in? I'll be sure to take a closer look at that one."

"It was the first one on the stack. It is currently untitled, according to the cover letter. So, what do you want me to do with these?"

"Well, I usually just edit the standard rejection letter, inputting names instead of *Dear Author* and incorporating my nicer comments to give them a boost. But I am so busy with Ms. Orwell's stuff, as well as my own, that I was thinking that you could do it."

Sue looked up, interested.

"You're doing so well. And I think this would be good developmental opportunity for you. What do you think?"

Sue looked at the note on the top manuscript. "I think that sounds great! This is an honor, Eliza!"

I decided then that this could be Sue's pet project. To tell her I'd have assigned it to whoever happened to be in the office would have been quite mean at this point. Sue *was* doing well, and she *was* such a hard worker. And any extra projects to highlight on her résumé would help put her ahead of other newcomers to the publishing industry.

"Why don't you roll that chair around the desk and I'll pull up the template and we'll go over the manuscript on top. Then I'll email you the template and you can work on composing those letters. Once you're done, go ahead and drop them in my inbox with the manuscripts, and I'll sign them and send them back to the intern office for whoever is doing the mailings that day. How does that sound?"

Sue rolled her chair around, nodding ferociously and smiling. She took notes as I explained what needed to be done. And I added another point to my day's confidence level.

⋙❖⋘

By Wednesday, order was returning to my office life again. Sue had returned the letters first thing that morning. All that was left to be done was read them through and sign my name. I went through them, reading them carefully since they'd have my name on them, and signed them.

I read through the final one in the pile.

Dear Ms. Edwards:
Thank you for submitting your novel Silver Strike *to J Press. I found the characters quite interesting and the story*

well-written. However, it is not clearly mystery genre, which means that we unfortunately cannot accept it to our mystery division. I suggest, however, that you try publishers with less focus on niche. This book may be perfect for the right independent press.

This decision does not reflect poorly on your manuscript, and we do wish you the best of luck elsewhere.

Warm regards,

Eliza Tahan
Mystery Editor
J Press

Not bad at all. I signed this last one and sighed in relief at not having to write these anymore. And I was glad that Sue was so happy about taking over the job. I carried the stack to the intern office's to-mail box and gave Sue a thumbs-up in passing.

"Good job, Sue. They were outstanding."

She stood up immediately. "Were they?"

I nodded and made my way to the door. "If you are up for it, this can be your own personal task for as long as you'd like it to be. You are quite the writer!"

She blushed. "Oh, thank you. I really love writing. I just love it. Even letters. I'm grateful for this opportunity! Do you think you'll have any more for me today?"

"I don't have any yet, but if I'm as productive today as I was yesterday, I'll be giving you a call this afternoon. What time do you leave?"

Sue looked at her wall calendar. "Um, today's Wednesday. My first class is at one-thirty today. Will that give you enough time?"

"Sure. I'll get through some manuscripts this morning and get you a stack by eleven. If you don't get to them today, you can finish them tomorrow."

"I actually have something going tomorrow. An all-day thing. I was planning on taking the day off."

"That's fine—" I began, but she cut in.

"No, actually, this is important to me. If I can't finish everything, I'll postpone tomorrow's thing. My boyfriend will understand. We're together all the time. He'll survive *one* canceled date."

We laughed. *Date. Date. Date.* It rang in my mind. For once, I also had a date. Tonight! Yes, a Wednesday date!

On the walk back to my desk, I couldn't stop picturing Adam and me drinking some delicious wine on my couch, talking about something really interesting but also sort of funny, laughing now and then. I stopped myself at the part when he started kissing me, and running his fingers up my back. I'd save that thought for relishing during the long commute home.

By the time that eleven rolled around, I had another stack of manuscripts for Sue, which I left on her desk while she was on the intern phone. Her back to the door and to me, she was speaking in hushed tones. ". . .

Important . . . see you every night . . . canceled only this one time . . . has nothing to do with honoring my man . . . no, I still love you . . ." I quietly left Sue in the otherwise empty room thinking that Rain would have fired her for using the company phone. Of course, *I* used the company phone almost every day, and I'd bet Rain had, too. And Rain would never have walked over here to deliver something. She'd have called Jane into her office to get it or, if Jane were away from her desk, she'd have dropped the pile on Jane's chair with no explanation, so that Jane would have had to come into her office anyway to get instructions.

I had a manuscript in hand now that I had not left with Sue. It had potential, but it was borderline chick lit, and I wanted to get a second opinion about publishing it as a mystery, so I called up another editor. I knew she appreciated a good mystery as much as she did a nice Coach bag, and she agreed to take a look at it and advise me. Finally everything on my to-do list up to lunch was crossed off.

I decided to have lunch in, and carried back to the office a small plate of vegetarian stuffed grape leaves and a Diet Pepsi from the Arabic place down the street. The owners liked me and had tried to speak to me in Arabic ever since the one time that I paid with my credit card and they had noticed my last name. I'd tried to tell them that I didn't know much Arabic, but they either didn't understand or didn't believe me, because they still tried. So instead of arguing, I'd nod and smile and walk away with my meal and a generous helping of guilt for retaining so little of my dad's native language. What kind of daughter was I anyway?

The answer to that question popped up on my computer as I checked my personal email while picking up a stuffed grape leaf with my fingers. The only message in my personal email box was from Cleo. She reported that she had spoken with Mom, who was doing well, teaching English in a small village in Botswana. She noted that Mom would be moving soon to an office-type job. Mom wasn't happy to leave the school, but willing to go if that was where she was most needed. Cleo noted that she herself was happy about the move, because she worried about Mom in the village. Cleo then made a joke in Arabic, but I understood so little of it that I only got that it was a joke at all when she wrote in caps "HAHAHA" afterwards. What kind of daughter was I? A lesser daughter. Cleo was the star.

Every time I began comparing myself to Cleo, I was forced to remember that she had much more to prove than I did, which had pushed her to greater heights. I would not want to be the star if I had to go through the explosion that created it.

I always made an effort to keep my personal life separate from my professional one, and I knew it was a bad idea to open this Pandora's box in the middle of my workday. Nevertheless I automatically pulled from my wallet the one picture in it, and got ready to face the sadness. Yes, right in the middle of the workday.

The picture was of our family. Mom and Dad and Cleo and I, shortly before the accident. We are all sitting by the fireplace in the living room and laughing. Mom is leaning against Dad's shoulder to keep her balance and I could still hear their simultaneous laughter which sounded like music. Every year we would invite some of the older church members who might not have family to our house for Christmas dinner. That year, one of the older men from the church took this family picture for us. But of course, in his usual way, Dad cracked a joke just as the camera snapped and we were all cracking up. Once we all got hold of ourselves, the man from church asked if we wanted him to take another picture. Dad had said no. It was one of Dad's favorite pictures, and he'd kept it in his wallet.

Ever since I'd retrieved this picture from my dad's wallet, I'd tried to remember the joke he had told. I never could remember it, but it didn't really matter. I liked how happy we all looked. We were always laughing back then.

Now I looked closer at Cleo. The picture had obviously been taken before Cleo's laser surgery. Her glasses sat crookedly on her nose. Few pictures showed her with her glasses on, as she usually yanked them off before the shutter clicked. I guess she'd been laughing too hard in this one to remember to pull them off. She was hugging a Stephen King novel to her chest, *Christine,* though it could have been any of King's novels. Everyone at school was reading his stuff that year, except me. My name is probably still on the high school library's waiting list somewhere, edging toward the top with the rest of the uncool kids who did not catch onto the trend until everyone's name was on the hold list. Maybe at my reunion, they'd assign me *The Shining*, with a stamp that reminded me to return it in two weeks. The librarian would warn me that there were other uncool students waiting for it, so not to be late.

Cleo was definitely cooler than me. Certainly before the accident, at least. Maybe even after, when her friends stopped talking *to* her and began whispering *about* her. When she withdrew from her old life, she dedicated her time to studies and became known again throughout the school, this time for being the smart one.

At the moment that the picture was taken, there was no way that any of us could know that this would be the last Christmas photo of our family. Only four months later Cleo, a happy-go-lucky fifteen-year-old with a learner's permit tucked into her purse, climbed behind the wheel of my dad's Chevy Sprint and changed our world forever.

I had been in the library finishing a report so I didn't see it happen. But my imagination pieced together the scene from the accounts I had heard and my mind played the reel over and over. Dad pulling into the school parking lot and waving Cleo over to the car. Dad getting out and moving to the passenger side, dropping the keys in her hand as they passed one another. Cleo giving him a peck on the cheek, excited but not losing her cool in front of anyone who might be watching. Cleo climbing behind the wheel, Dad buckling up and making a joke before getting serious about instructing her driving. He probably praised her on the way she maneuvered out of the parking lot.

She insists still that she just forgot to put her glasses on, but I knew her better than anyone else and I was sure that she planned to put them on once they were away from the school. She never wanted her friends to see her in glasses. Not that such detail mattered much now. But I always wondered if she might have seen the truck speeding toward the passenger side if she'd had them on. She might have been able to see that it was not slowing down for the stoplight. Of course, she was just learning to drive and might not have been driving defensively. And Dad was about as defenseless as he could be when the truck barreled into his door.

Like everyone in the family, I was overcome with grief for a long time. I lived in a shadow world where I was only concerned with my own despair and with fear for the next tragedy that might hit my loved ones. Slowly, slowly, I began to focus on finals, then college, then Liam. I welcomed these distractions when they came, and the hole in my heart became just a fact and no longer a preoccupation. Cleo had no such distractions. Her injuries kept her out of school, giving her endless time to ruminate, to drown in her guilt. Finally she, too, finally found ways to continue living. By the time she was back in school, it was clear that she had about as much interest in reconnecting with her friends as they did in reconnecting with her. Though Cleo refused to speak about the accident, she clearly chose to cling to Mom and me.

Before I knew it, my entire lunch hour had passed, and I was sitting there with cold grape leaves and a picture, sobbing. It wasn't fair. Dad had been too young to die. Cleo had been too young to have to deal with that kind of guilt. We should be the family in the picture *still*.

I didn't want to be the perfect daughter if it took going through what Cleo had gone through.

I checked my email once more before getting back to work. Another message had come in from Cleo. I opened it and read the short note: *P.S. Mom said to tell you she loves you and misses you. Meant to tell you in the last message. Cleo.*

I wrote her back immediately, drying my eyes.

Cleo: Thanks for the P.S. I needed that. Eliza.

Now, back to work.

After such a sad lunch hour, I was relieved to return to fiction. I contacted a handful of authors with the happy news that we were interested in seeing their complete manuscripts. This was a pretty good job when it came to taking my mind off real issues in my life.

CHAPTER 8

By six o'clock on Wednesday I still had no idea what I'd be wearing when Adam showed up at seven. Liam hadn't been any help since he'd taken off with my car as soon as I'd come home. I gave up and rang Cleo, falling onto my bed, trying to avoid the piles of clothes.

I'd almost hung up, thinking it was about to go to voicemail, when she picked up breathlessly. "Cleo?" I asked.

"Eliza! What's up?"

"Are you with a guy?"

She laughed. "Kinda. But not the way you think. Jorge is a friend and . . . well, someone I'm kinda dating. He's working on my car right now and I had walked over to his garage to see how it was going. On my way, I had a *brilliant* idea to pick up a couple things at the little market down the street, without considering how I'd feel walking back with four grocery bags over my arm. Let me tell you—"

"Not a good idea?"

"No. I should have taken the other car and just *driven* over to Jorge's and then *driven* to the market. What was I thinking? I'm not in Europe or Oregon, for heaven's sake. This is Orange County! I shouldn't feel bad about driving everywhere. Everyone else does."

"You're preaching to the choir, sista. You don't have to convince a Southern Californian of the virtues of the automobile."

"So, that wasn't why you were calling then? To be preached to?"

"Not tonight, I have a date. A second date."

I could hear Cleo's leather couch squawk as she plopped into it. I instantaneously recalled the buttery-softness of the tan leather and knew she was at this moment about as comfortable as a person can be.

"With the newspaper book editor?"

"Yes, Adam Mestas. We went for lunch on Monday, too."

"A second date? Wow, Eliza! From the description you gave me before . . . woo."

"I can't figure out what to wear, Cleo. An immature problem, I know. But still . . ."

"And where are you going?"

"When we spoke earlier today he said he was thinking he'd take me out to dinner and then to something more active."

"Active as in . . ." She stretched the words out like a rubber band and they snapped back with, "Physical?"

I sat up and stared in the mirror. "I don't know, that's the thing. I was not sure how to ask him. I couldn't quite say, *Are you planning on seducing me, or are we going to play miniature golf?*"

"Oh, no. That would not be the thing to say."

"So how do I dress?"

"Wear something cute underneath, in case a seduction is in order. And you need to wear something nice, but probably not a dress in case you're going to batting cages or something. Do you have some slim-fit black slacks?"

"I have every kind of black slacks I can find at a good price."

"Okay, try those with some kind of hippy-romantic shirt. Do you have a tunic-style shirt, with an interesting print?"

"Hmm . . ." I sorted through the shirts in my closet, and pulled out a hippy-looking shirt in a wispy fabric with wide sleeves. "It isn't quite a tunic, but it wraps around and ties in the back. It's red with a red-orange and orange pattern. I think it will do."

"Yeah, and with all those oranges, definitely wear a bright blue necklace or sash or something. There you have it. Abracadabra. How much time do you have left?"

I glanced at the clock. "Thirty minutes. He better not be early. I'll call you tomorrow to let you know how it went. And thanks, Cleo."

"Fashion Coordinator Extraordinaire at your service," she replied and hung up.

I threw on her suggested outfit, complete with "something sexy," something lacey and red, underneath. I added strappy black heels and a chunky blue necklace that I'd made during my short-lived hobby of jewelry design shortly after Liam and I broke up and I needed something to occupy my time and hands so I didn't binge away my blues. The outfit looked great. I looked great.

The wispy shirt gave me an excuse to pull my hair up off my neck and into a high ponytail, and I was ready to go. Ready to go to dinner and ready for whatever active thing followed.

He wasn't early, and I decided I ought to be doing something interesting when he arrived, so it didn't look like I had spent all evening getting ready and waiting, even if I had. I grabbed *Positively 4th Street* by David Hajdu, a book I had read before getting into publishing, and opened it to somewhere near the middle, reading a section about Bob Dylan joining Joan Baez on tour in the early sixties. What started as an attempt to look like I had an interesting mental life ended up reminding me of the days when I'd read constantly. I'd keep a book in my purse to read in elevators and while waiting in lines. At night I'd start reading after dinner and read myself to sleep. In fact, I now realized that I hadn't read anything other than mystery submissions since I had started my publishing career. I needed to reclaim my nights as my own.

The doorbell sounded and my heart raced. I marked my page with my index finger and trotted casually to the door, throwing my ponytail over my shoulder, in case he could see me through the window.

"Hey Adam!" I said cheerfully as I threw open the door.

I instantly took in his classy outfit, confident stance, glowing face. His matte black tie sat boldly against his brick red silk shirt. A ribbon of black hair had come loose from his low ponytail and was slashing dramatically over his right eye. He pushed it out of the way and it was all I could do to keep from swooning.

"Eliza, hey," he said with a dazzling smile, as though he hadn't expected me but was happy that I happened to be here. I wondered if that were practiced, or if he just had a natural way of making a girl feel good about herself.

"Come on in," I invited, stepping aside.

He closed in on me and his musky cologne swirled around me, intoxicating me. I didn't recognize the scent, but I knew it would be forever connected to this moment. He ran a hand up my arm, my draping sleeve giving way so that his palm connected with my cool skin. "You look great, Eliza. Stunning."

I blushed and looked down. I noticed how his black slacks skimmed at the right times and then fit snuggly in just the right places. "Thank you. So do you."

He moved his hand to my cheek. "How refreshing it is to hear a woman say 'thank you' in reply to a compliment, instead of refuting it."

I raised my eyes to his. "I'm not like other women," I heard myself say breathlessly before I even thought to check my response.

Adam leaned down, and with his lips close to my ear he whispered, "I know, Eliza."

And then there was contact, glorious contact. His warm lips touched ever-so-gently the place on my neck right below my ear. I turned my face, and our eyes met.

"So, you said on the phone that we'd have dinner and something *active*," I whispered.

He misunderstood. It was my hint that our something active could be now, could be this and what came next. My hint failed.

Adam pulled away and straightened up. "Right. I'm so sorry, Eliza. I thought you . . . I guess I just read that wrong. You're right, though, I did promise you dinner."

You're kidding me! You took my hint the wrong way! But even as my mind was throwing this back I knew it was unfair to rely on hints. "I didn't exactly mean it that way," I tried, but the electric moment was over, short-circuited by awkwardness and explanation.

"Well, I have a couple ideas, but I'm not sure what you're in the mood for. Plus I'm not really from this neighborhood, so I don't know all the options. I mostly just got suggestions from my colleagues, to be honest."

His pre-planning gave away that he was as excited about this date as I had been. Excited enough not to simply wing it. "What did your sources come up with?"

"There's the Old Spaghetti Factory, just down the street from you. I know that the one that used to be downtown's good. Also the Fish House Vera Cruz and the California Mining Company on Restaurant Row are both supposed to be nice."

"Restaurant Row is only a few blocks from here, and there are lots of good places. But you know, the Spaghetti Factory is one of my all-time favorites and I haven't been there in a while. Why don't we go for what we both already know we like?" I replied, playfully resting a hand on his forearm. It was a solid forearm, I noted to myself. A strong forearm.

With that, we moved out of the condo and into his burgundy-maroon Mustang. I couldn't help noticing that this seemingly confident guy had a recently washed and waxed car. I wouldn't be surprised if he'd completed the picture with a new air freshener. I regained my confidence, knowing that we were equally yoked with anticipation.

He must have caught me checking out his car. Instead of realizing that I was noting the cleanliness of the thing, he assumed I was not impressed with the vehicle itself. "It's an old car, an '88. But it runs well. Has a lot of power. I've been thinking about getting a new one, but I just haven't decided what I want."

"Oh, I like your car. There's no hurry when you like your car."

"I do like it," he admitted, smiling. At least he knew I was not judging him by his car. "But I should get something new eventually. I don't think it's a good idea to show up for interviews in such an old car."

"The bad thing about your getting a new car," I countered, "is that you'd have to find another 'I love Steinbeck' sticker."

"You saw that, huh?"

"I noticed it the first time we met. I 'heart' Steinbeck, too."

"I know you do. You said your favorite book was *The Wayward Bus*."

He remembered my favorite book. "Where did you get that bumper sticker?"

"The Steinbeck Center in Salinas. It's a great museum."

"I've been meaning to go. I stopped by the old museum back in, I guess it was '96 or '97, on my way to San Francisco. It was just a storefront then. They were either building the new museum or building the funds for it."

"You've got to see the new museum. Maybe we can both go. You know, so I can get a new bumper sticker for when I get my new car." He flashed me a smile.

He held the door open for me and I climbed in, inhaling a deep breath of a brand-new, mocha-scented air freshener.

The waiter set my plate of spaghetti with browned butter and mizithra cheese in front of me and garlic-parmesan chicken in front of Adam. He asked if we'd like anything to drink other than water, but we both said no.

"Did you read my article about you?" Adam asked after I had taken my first bite.

I swallowed and hesitated and searched my mind to think of a good excuse as to why I hadn't read it. I couldn't come up with an answer in time.

"Oh, hey, that's all right."

"I'm really sorry. I've been so busy that I completely forgot. The copies are in my workbag right now. I've brought them to and from work these last couple days. I had so much else going on that it completely slipped my mind."

He waved the issue away with his hand and began cutting a piece of chicken. "Please, don't even worry about it. Just let me know when you do. I'm curious about what you think. It was incredibly hard to write, actually, and I've never before had a problem with interviews. But when I sat down to write, I found that my notes were disjointed. And I never take poor notes. I must have been," he flashed me a sly smile, "distracted. I picked up the phone to call you, but then I remembered you were on vacation. I ended up recreating parts of our conversation in the article. I hope that's okay."

"Oh, sure. I wasn't expecting anything in particular, so any format would have been fine. I do hope you made me sound intellectual, maybe even brilliant, but approachable."

"Oh, of course," he replied. "Those were the parts I remembered clearly."

"Oh yeah?" I teased. "Was it my *brilliance* that blindsided you?"

"Well, yeah. You were interesting," he grinned, "and beautiful."

I was both surprised and pleased. "I think that might have been the first time I *stunned* someone with my looks." Immediately after saying it I regretted it. Why did I feel I could say what I was thinking? What a turn-off my reply must have been. How desperate I must sound.

"Just because no one tells you when it happens, doesn't mean it doesn't happen."

I took a bite of my spaghetti to give myself a moment to bask in the compliment. So what if I could lose a few pounds? So what if my hips would always be big? So what if I would never carry myself with Cleo's grace? *He thinks I'm beautiful.*

I finished off my ice water before speaking, hoping it would rinse away anything stuck in my teeth. "Thank you. And I guess if we're being honest with each other, I must tell you that you were quite the topic of conversation while my sister drove me to the airport."

He raised an eyebrow. "Oh, really?"

"Yeah, same sorta things. I told her that you were interesting, surprising. Cute."

"*Cute*, huh?" A half smile.

"Good-looking." I looked down at my pasta, wondering suddenly if this was giving away too much information too soon. "I hope our conversation isn't laying out our cards too soon."

"Why not though? I don't know about you, but I've been through too many relationships that I hurried into without any discussion of what brought us there in the first place. I'm making a real effort to avoid the whole dating 'game.' I think that if you're honest about what works and what doesn't, and why you're both there, then you have a better chance of having it be an authentic relationship. Don't you?"

I thought of Liam, of our long and happy courtship, but despite how good it was, dishonesty had been the common theme of every day and every encounter. His dishonesty with me and with himself. "Yes. That's refreshing."

Our plates were taken away and we were served our little scoops of spumoni ice cream in tin dishes. "So, I noticed that you're reading *Positively 4th Street*," Adam commented.

I'd almost forgotten my plan to look more interesting than I actually was. But it wasn't a lie that I had been reading it. I just hadn't been reading it recently. "Oh, yeah. It's really interesting." I racked my brain to remember what I had already read.

He nodded. "Yeah, it's a good book. I can admit to being a Dylan fan, even if he comes off like a jerk in the book."

"I like him, too," I agreed, as pleased that we had somewhat similar tastes in music as I was that my reading material had spurred this topic of conversation. "And Joan Baez . . . she looks much better in the book than Dylan does."

Adam took the final bit of ice cream onto his spoon. "From what I remember, Hajdu interviewed Baez's sister as one of his main sources. That could contribute to the slant."

"Have you heard *Dark Chords on a Big Guitar*?" I asked, finishing my own ice cream.

"I have. Baez's voice is so soulful these days, now that she's older."

We exited the decadent velvet and wooden booth. "Is folk music your favorite genre, Adam?"

"No, I wouldn't say that. I like a variety of music."

"Put it this way: What's in your CD player right now?"

We walked through the front doors of the restaurant and breathed in the fresh night air. "I don't have a CD changer in my car, just the original radio and cassette player. But in my CD player at home I have Sean Paul, The Dave Matthews Band, Julio Iglesias, and Tracy Chapman that I remember for sure."

"Which Tracy Chapman album?"

"Her first one. The self-titled one. And what do you have in your CD player?"

"In my car I have Dylan, Odetta, and Tracy Chapman. *Crossroads.* It's one of my favorite albums of all time. I think I have The Doors in there, too."

"Are you an L.A. Woman?" He took my arm.

"San Diego Woman. More of an Orange County Woman, originally."

We moved toward the car, and he dropped his eyes, thoughtfully, then looked back up. "So you say that your favorites are Dylan, Joan Baez, Odetta, The Doors. It's interesting that so much of what you listen to is older music. A lot of that stuff was recorded before you were even born."

"I guess that's true." I shrugged. Interesting observation, but not so relevant.

"Has it always been that way? Dylan. The Doors. Were they always your favorites?"

"No, I used to listen to the usual Top-40 kinda stuff. But maybe when I heard the older music, I realized how much better it was."

I must have been veering the wrong way to the car, as Adam rested his palm on the small of my back and steered me slightly to the right. "Maybe."

"You don't think that's the case?"

"No, I mean, I have no idea. I just thought it was interesting."

"But why do *you* think I only like old music?"

"Wouldn't that question be best answered by you? Why do *you* think you only like old music?"

I almost answered the same thing as before, that it was just better music, but the question was good enough that I gave myself a moment to think. I kept my head down as we walked, pursing my lips while I thought. Adam didn't rush me, and I filed away my thought that he was more interested in what I had to say than just moving the conversation along. The air had chilled since we left the house, and I shivered in my thin shirt. Adam wrapped his arm around me as we walked through the parking lot, his warmth seeping through to my skin immediately.

At the car, as he began to open my door, I turned to him with an answer. "I think I prefer old music because it doesn't make me think of anything in particular. I don't have memories tied to old music."

He nodded, but didn't answer, as though waiting for me to go on. I hadn't planned to, but there he was with his eyes locked on mine, with his muscular forearm resting on the top of the door frame, his shirt clinging just slightly to his solid torso. Did this look get him his way with all the girls? It must. How could you refuse this man anything when he looked at you this way? He didn't even need to ask.

I began clarifying what I meant. "So much music reminds me of different things from my past. I had a happy past for a lot of it. But then so many of the good things came to sad ends. And it's hard to listen to music even from happy times without it making me sad. For example, I started listening to Celtic music and chant after my dad died because we used to listen to Top 40 music when he would drive me to school and so that music made me sad. And then an ex of mine got me into club music. And after that relationship ended, I tossed out all the mixes he'd made for me and picked up on folk music. Because I have no emotions tied to it." I ducked into the car.

"Good answer." He closed the door after me.

When he opened his driver's side door he smiled, maybe to lighten the mood. "I hope it works out well with us, because I'd hate for you to link Dylan with me and someday stop listening to him because he reminds you of me."

"Let's just see how things go then." In my mind I thought, *Don't break my heart.*

"Okay, so here's my idea of what we could do next, and if you don't want to, that's fine. Just say so. It's even a little weird to say, to be honest. It's just that there's this ice-skating rink a few exits down from here. The Iceoplex. A colleague plays hockey there, and he said it would make a good impression on you if I took you ice skating." We both laughed, and then he continued, more seriously. "Really, though, does that sound fun to you? Or are you more of a dinner-and-a-movie kinda date?"

Ice-skating! Not sexy, but fun nonetheless. "That sounds like *so* much fun. I haven't ever been to that rink.

I see it every day on my way to work, but then I always forget how close it is when I'm trying to think of something to do. Ice-skating is a *great* idea!"

"Then let's go work off this pasta, and after that, depending on the time, we can decide what to do next."

"So that must mean that this date is going well." I was only half joking.

He looked over and smiled, dazzling me. With his face so close, I could see the silver flecks in his midnight eyes. "Yeah. I'd say it's going well."

My breath caught and I thought he might kiss me. My mind flashed back to the garlic butter I'd spread on my bread. But he didn't kiss me; he pulled back with what I hoped was a look of regret. Maybe his mind had flashed back to his garlic-parmesan chicken dinner. I had a toothbrush in my purse. I hoped he had a mint or something. Not that it mattered to me what his breath smelled like right now, but I didn't want him to be so self-conscious that I might be robbed of a kiss.

I made it through ice-skating without falling, which I took as a good sign. I didn't get so warm while skating that I had to worry about reapplying deodorant, which I also took as a good sign. And we were "actively" spinning and sliding and laughing the entire time. Another good sign for things to come.

The best sign, though, was when Adam took my hand at the far side of the rink, raised it to his lips and kissed it gently, half on the knuckles and half on the fingers. His lips were smooth and soft against my caramel skin. The world froze in place for just the few moments between when his lips touched my skin and when he lifted his eyes and smiled.

And that was a good sign.

Even in the midst of our conversation on the way home, I was running through lines that I could use to invite him in without sounding trashy.

Would you like to come in for a bit?

Hey, why not come on in?

Shall we finish this conversation over a glass of merlot?

When he walked me to my door, Adam caught me before I could choose a line to cast out. He pulled me into an embrace and I felt myself being swallowed up in his arms, pressed against his chest, and I was breathless even before he laid his lips against mine.

The most glorious kiss in all of history, surely.

But then he released me and stepped down the first stair, away from the door. "This was a wonderful night, Eliza." He pushed a wisp of black hair away from his face. His shirt pulled snug against the muscles moving in his arm. It was especially sexy since he seemed to do it unconsciously, as though he had to deal with this annoyance each and every day.

I was confused by his backing away, my brain clouded by his kiss. "I—I had a wonderful time, too. Thank you."

I cleared my head and cast the line before I lost the opportunity. "Would you like to come in and have a drink? Some wine, I mean?"

"I would love to," he said, stepping back up, and giving me a quick kiss on the lips before he continued, "but that's probably not a good idea at the moment. Things are a little too . . . well . . . I have to work tomorrow, and I have to drive home afterward, so I shouldn't drink."

His words were a brush-off. But his discomfort indicated something deeper.

"Then just conversation? No wine?" I ventured, not yet defeated.

But then he pulled me close again, and looked into my eyes hungrily. "We've agreed to be honest, so it's my turn. You've led me toward something before, Eliza. Twice. Just to pull away. I know that the third time is supposed to be a charm, but something keeps causing you to lead me on a course to something more and then draw away from me. It's your turn for honesty."

"I hadn't been sure . . ."

"And are you sure now?"

I wasn't. I wanted it to just happen. *So I don't have to take responsibility?* My silence was telling.

Adam sighed, and ran a hand over the curve of my waist, settling on my hip. "Tell me goodnight, Eliza. I'll go, and, hey, we'll have plenty more chances. But if you're sure that you want me to come in . . ."

I turned my back on him instantly, and he stopped speaking. Our breath hung in the air.

There was the jingle of my keys, the scratch of the key entering the keyhole. I felt Adam's fingertips touch the small of my back. Still, he wouldn't let me out of making the decision. His respect for me was torment. Gorgeous torment.

When I stepped inside, his fingertips disconnected from my back. I set my purse on the entry table and looked back over my shoulder. I could see anticipation in the muscles of his neck, in his slight lean toward the door.

"Come on in." The words had barely left my lips when Adam gathered me into his arms in one dramatic lunge, closing the door on the way in.

Between kisses, he said, "Eliza, you're sure." It was a statement, not a question.

Two firm tugs untucked his shirt. My fingers found his tie, undoing it just enough to reach the brick red buttons underneath. One button undone, and another. With each, another several inches of smooth, tan muscle appeared. I thought he might not even know what my hands were doing, since his sole intent seemed to be focused on my lips, my neck. But when I reached the final button and pulled open his shirt, running my hands over his incredibly solid abs, he drew in a breath and drew back his shoulder blades to let the shirt fall off behind him.

I stepped back to take in the sight of him. The black tie slashed his perfect chest in two halves, two tight collarbones, two smooth pecs, two sides of a knotted six-pack. His tie looked like a road map, a direction, the very end pointing to something even more impressive.

He didn't stay there for my ogling for very long before closing in on me. My hands reached behind me to untie the wrap-around shirt. He didn't touch me, and he didn't breathe, watching me unwrap the light fabric from my body like a dance of seven veils, slowly exposing more and more of my body.

I turned then, unbuttoning the top button of my slacks, and swayed my way out of the entryway. Still facing away from him, but surely being followed since Adam's breath was falling against my bare shoulders, I unzipped loudly, so he'd know where I was going.

His fingertips brushed my waist before his hands grasped at it hungrily, turning me toward him. He reached around and undid my bra with precision, then pulled it off in one fluid movement.

His hands were running up my rib cage, pulling my torso up, until they stopped at the place where my breasts swelled. His thumbs met between them, curved around each, his long fingers wrapping around the sides of my rib cage. He dropped his head to bury it between my heaving breasts, kissing, nipping. When his lips tentatively touched my right nipple, lightning flew through my body.

I threw my head back and whimpered, "Oh, Adam . . ."

There was no going back, and who would want to?

I shimmied so that my slacks fell to the floor in an instant. Grabbing for his tie, I pulled Adam up to meet my eyes. "Do you believe me when I say I'm sure?"

Adam's eyes skimmed the length of my body. "Goddess," he moaned, "I'll believe whatever you tell me."

Goddess? And there wasn't a hint of sarcasm in his voice. Only want. Only a desperate desire.

"Then believe that up those stairs you'll find everything that your mouth, your hands, your body have been seeking."

I edged up the stairs, Adam in playful tow by his black tie. We'd only gone a few stairs when he picked me up effortlessly. I gasped, throwing my arms around his neck.

"And what have you been seeking, Eliza?" he asked as he carried me up the stairs.

My breasts pressed against his warm chest, and the muscles in his arm burned seductively into the sensitive area behind my knees.

He carried me into the room, set me gently on the edge of the bed. I pulled Adam closer by his belt until he was standing between my spread knees. In a moment his trousers fell.

"What I've been seeking?" I queried. One final tug and his silky boxers were on the floor. "I think I've found it as well."

CHAPTER 9

When I woke, Adam's body was spooning mine, and his strong arms surrounded my naked body. I wondered how I could get up and take my shower before he saw me so disheveled. But he was already awake.

"Good morning, Eliza." His voice was huskier in the morning. Last night it had been all velvet. He rose on an elbow to look down at me.

I turned my head and saw that—how was it possible?—he looked even better in the morning than he had last night. His long hair was undone, falling around us like a dark veil.

"Oh, good morning," was all I could think of to reply, the seductress of last night completely evaporated in the clean light of morning. "I'm sorry, I must look a mess."

"You look like a goddess," he muttered, leaning over and laying a dozen light kisses on my exposed neck and shoulders.

A blush spread over my neck, and I turned onto my back, pulling the sheets up to my chin. He pulled them back down and dusted my collarbone and breasts with kisses. "Gorgeous. You're just gorgeous, Eliza. What time do you have to be at work?"

My body filled with electricity as his hands ran over my waist, over the curve of my hip, and made their way to the insides of my thighs. He tempted me with, "How much time do we have?"

All the time in the world, I wanted to say. "We have time. I don't have to be in until eight."

Adam's hand stopped its sweet caressing.

"What is it?"

"Its 8:10 right now, Eliza. I'm sorry, I thought you had until nine or ten."

My stomach churned. I knew I'd hear about this from Jane, and she'd probably even call HR, just to try to keep me out of the running for the job. But oh, it had been worth it.

"It's okay, Adam. If I get ready now, I should be fine."

"Take the day off," he challenged. "I will, too. We'll stay in bed and make love all day. I promise it will be worth it."

"I don't doubt that it would be! But it's Thursday and—"

"You have that police thing today."

He had listened to me. He had remembered.

I must admit that I was a little out of it for the first part of my meeting with the police officer. I explained that I'd developed a little motion sickness while riding on the trolley, and Detective Wilson didn't seem to see the difference between motion sickness and a very late night, which was good. He asked me basic questions about myself, my position at J Press, and about my relationship with "Ms. Orwell." I answered it all honestly, with a little sugar-coating about my relationship with Rain.

Detective Wilson shuffled through some papers on his desk and pulled out one sheet with some notes on it, scribbled on it in the same way he had been scribbling notes during our conversation. "I spoke with Ms. Orwell's assistant already—"

"Jane?" I asked.

"Yes. And she said that Ms. Orwell was a difficult person to work for. That she gave everyone a hard time, but especially the two of you, since you all worked so closely together. Would you agree with that statement?"

"Oh, sure. Rain, Ms. Orwell, wasn't a *model supervisor*. I wouldn't say that we were friends or anything even close. She was really hard on Jane especially. I felt bad for her, and sometimes wished she'd just leave."

"Ms. Orwell?"

"No, Jane. I mean, I wanted her to leave just to show Rain how hard it would be to find someone who could do all that Jane did."

He frowned, and I noticed the deep lines carved into his forehead by a life of producing stern looks. "I also asked Jane what kept her in her position as Ms. Orwell's assistant so long, when she could have quit and been an administrative assistant in almost any company in San Diego."

"She wants to go further than just being an assistant. A referral from Rain could have gotten Jane a pretty good promotion at J Press, when the time was right. But you have to work long and hard and take a lot of crap to get that."

"Jane said it was because she respected Ms. Orwell's drive and talent and place in the industry. She was learning a lot from her and hoped to someday move into a higher position within the company. Are you sure," he raised an eyebrow, "that the referral isn't why *you* stayed? Do you have dreams of working with the big publishers in, where is it? New York City?"

I waved my hand, shooing away the very idea. "New York? No way! J Press may not be one of the most prestigious publishing houses in the country, but it *is* the best in a city where it's a dry seventy-five degrees outside when I'm out looking for a Christmas tree. No way I'd give up San Diego's sun and surf for even the most prestigious company."

"So you surf?"

"No, but I like the beach."

"Right. And you plan to stay in your position at J Press? Not many people are that satisfied in their jobs."

I glanced down. "I wouldn't say that. Heck, *you* wouldn't say that if you saw the trunk-load of manuscripts I bring home every night, and how I get paid for eight hours of work when I am actually working almost every waking hour." I laughed.

He laughed, too, but with the half-hearted, distracted laugh of a person with something on their mind other than the joke. "Yeah, I wouldn't like that. And how many hours do you usually work over your eight hours in the office?"

I thought about it, and didn't come up with an answer before he continued.

"Well, just take yesterday, for example. How many hours did you spend yesterday, over and above the usual?"

Adam's smooth chest flashed into my mind. And my impatient burning for each touch. "I usually work probably three or four extra hours a night. Yesterday was less. I went out."

"I see. So maybe you don't have a lot of job satisfaction, but you work hard, usually. Why would you say that is?"

"I really want to move up in the company, and hopefully I can move into a senior editor position at some point."

"That would be the position Ms. Orwell held until her death, correct?"

"Yeah. Believe me, she didn't take home any manuscripts that didn't already have a glowing report from yours truly. She got to read only the good stuff."

Detective Wilson sifted through his papers again. Pulling out another set of notes, he glanced over them. "Ms. Li says that you've actually now filled Ms. Orwell's position. Is that right?"

"Temporarily. Right now I'm just trying to find my way through her unfinished tasks and mine, and figure out what exactly she did all day." I let out an exasperated laugh to ease the tension I could almost visualize settling heavily in the room. It didn't work on the detective. It didn't work on me either, for that matter.

"So, you hope it'll become permanent?"

"What?"

"The position."

"I'm planning on applying for it. I can't say I'm completely sure that I want it, though. It's just that it's the kind of thing that I have been working towards, and I don't want to let the opportunity slip away while I sit back being unsure. I don't want to be an assistant editor forever. Rain never would have handed it over."

"You don't think she would have handed it over to anyone? Or just not to you?"

Uh-oh. That doesn't sound like he likes my answer. I was hoping for a quick handshake and sincere thanks for my time and a "good luck" in my ambitions.

"To anyone?" I answered. I meant it to be my answer, but it came out more like a question.

"Hmm," he muttered, again checking some notes. I was beginning to dread every time that he'd bow his head to his notes. "Yes, Jane said that you were hoping to succeed Rain when she left."

"I didn't wish an accident like this on her, though."

"Did Ms. Li tell you that we think this so-called accident might have been planned?"

"Yeah. She said it was because Rain had some author's rejection letter."

"Yes, that's one of the reasons."

"I think she said it was one of our form letters."

"And the only people who would have a copy of that letter would be someone in your company or an author of a rejected manuscript, correct?"

"Yes. But not everyone in the company would have it. Just people in our department. Other departments have letters with their own editor's name on them. It's really frustrating that we don't personalize those. They just say 'Dear Author.' I was on Rain to get that changed. A simple merge file in a Word document would make it so much more personalized. So it is just really sad that it turns out . . ."

"Did Ms. Orwell send out these letters?"

"No, the interns physically send them. But I decide who gets them. Her name's on them, though, because she was, you know, the face of the mystery department. I thought Ms. Li was going to tell you that."

"Hmm." Detective Wilson leaned forward, looking very serious. "We'll be sure that this information does not get out until we catch the person who did this. Come to think of it, I'll talk to Ms. Li, too, and ask her to have a meeting with the people in your department to discourage them from discussing the fact that you are the prime decider on manuscripts. If it was an author who killed Ms. Orwell, I guess you should be glad that they didn't know who really rejected them."

A vision of my little Civic being thrown over the side of the freeway flashed across my mind.

I said nothing and Wilson continued. "Do you have a list of authors you've sent rejection letters to—these form letters? Can you pull a list like that?"

"I'll have to ask the interns. They get me the manuscripts and send out the rejects. They must have some kind of database. I'll talk to them. Anything else?" My voice was shaky. I was ready to get out of there.

"Just please remember, Ms. Tahan, to be quiet about your job when you're out on the town. If the murderer is an author, and if the author is still in San Diego, we don't want him finding out that you were the one who really did the rejections. That would make you his real target."

Once I boarded the trolley back to the office, I collapsed into a seat. My arms fell onto my knees and my head fell into my arms. The murderer's *real* target?

The trolley began moving and I took a deep breath, shook my head to clear my mind, and sat up straight. *I can't come undone. Not about this. I'm on my way back to work, and I'll just get back to business. The police can worry about this. I've got to keep it together. But I need to remember to have the interns pull up one of those author lists.* As I reached into my workbag for my organizer and pen, my hand brushed over a stack of newspaper pages.

"Oh, no!" I moaned audibly, gazing into my bag as my stomach turned. The article. The interview.

I hastily pulled out a paper and opened to the page with my interview. My picture next to my car. Thankfully I'd overcome my camera-shyness enough to insist on a close-up so that my house would not be in the shot.

But what had I said? What had Adam asked me? Or, more pointedly, what had Adam remembered of our conversation and written about? Surely I wasn't so distracted by my upcoming adventure or carried away by Adam's good looks and flirting that I would have told him that *I* made most every decision. Rain would have *killed* me.

I scanned the article.

"In their late twenties, most people are finishing college, looking for that first 'real' job, trying to get their own apartment. Their peer, Eliza Tahan, however, as the assistant mystery editor at J Press, is a powerful force in the world of publishing. While most people her age are at the clubs on the weekends, drinking their nights away, Tahan sits in her condo and reads your Great American Novel."

So far, so good. I read novels. Who cares? No one can assume Rain is the only person who reads everything that comes in. Yet I can't help feeling that this praise for my hard work is not exactly glowing. Was Adam trying to show how responsible I am and how flaky everyone else is? Or was he trying to show that while everyone is enjoying their youth, I'm wasting mine away with their creative work? *Irrelevant at this point.*

"I decided to have a chat with this young star of the publishing field and find out how she broke in, what she does, and what she thinks of your writing."

He had written about exactly what he had alluded to in the intro.

How had I gotten into publishing? I'd answered that a long-standing passion for books led to an unpaid internship during my final two years of college, followed by an entry-level—but *paid*—position with J Press right out of college when I'd barely turned twenty-one. All my

friends had been on five- and six-year college plans, celebrating their twenty-first year by spending more time in
nightclubs and bars than in class. I, however, had been
staying up all hours reading manuscript submissions and
trying to impress my new boss. This was safe information.

But then he'd asked me what exactly I did, and
reading my answer left me in a rising panic. How could
I have responded in such a way? Was I trying to impress
him? Was I trying to stick it to Rain, thinking I'd never
return from my adventures abroad?

*"All manuscripts come right to me. I read the synopsis and
first few pages, and then decide if they should be read further,
or if they are not right for J Press at this time. If something
catches my interest, I ask the author to send the entire manuscript. When it comes in I read the rest of it. If it is excellent,
I write a report for S. Rain Orwell, the editor. Often she agrees
with me, and will follow up with a call and an offer."*

Adam had then asked what happens to a manuscript
that gets rejected.

*"It's important to remember that J Press gets thousands
of manuscripts each year, and only a small number can be
published. Just because a manuscript is rejected doesn't mean
it isn't good. It just means that it is not right for us."*

I remembered Adam's joke about me being the one
who crushes people's dreams.

I felt a little queasy—was it from the motion of the
trolley? Thankfully, Adam did not put his little joke in
the article, but there was no question as to whose opinion

determined the fate of each manuscript. And there was no question that it didn't matter how quiet I was about my job from now on. This article said it all.

I was in danger.

CHAPTER 10

I'd expected Sue to be in by the time I got back to the office, but the other interns said she'd taken the day off after all. I didn't remember her turning in any rejection letters as promised, but I'd also told her that she didn't have to cancel her plans for the letters. I refused to be the bitchy boss Rain had been. Or *Sara* had been. Or whatever her name had been. So, no big deal. I asked the remaining interns if they could pull the requested author stats and they said they were glad to take a break from stuffing rejection letters.

"What exactly do you need?" one asked.

"Yeah," chimed in another. "We don't have a real database."

"Believe me, I know," I empathized. "I've been gunning for one since I was an intern. But we used to have a spreadsheet or something. Do you still have something like that? Something in Excel?"

"Yeah. It has author name, manuscript title, address, notes, stuff like that. Is that all right?"

"That would be perfect. Go ahead and print that out for me. Everything in the last year, if possible."

The interns agreed, but noted that it would be a bit of a project, and asked if there was a deadline.

"There isn't a deadline *per se*, but just as soon as possible. It's really important. If you can't finish it tonight, just leave a note for the morning interns and make sure someone picks up the project."

I worked as late as I could. Jane had said she was surprised to see me when I returned from my meeting at the police station. Remembering the slices of her commentary that the detective had shared with me, I had replied sarcastically, "No, Jane, they didn't arrest me." I added, softening a little, that I had far too much to do to just go straight home.

She left at five, along with almost everyone in the department. Evidently, the interns had decided to leave the author-list project for the morning interns. They might have wanted a break from the monotony of stuffing rejections into envelopes, but apparently hadn't wanted to fill the time with a new project.

When the cleaning crew arrived at seven, I was still at Rain's desk, reading countless emails and trying to answer the questions from the information I could find in Rain's poorly designed filing system. She must have assumed she would never leave. Or maybe she assumed she'd never leave of her own free will. If she were forced to leave, her payback would be a job that no one could do because the key elements were hidden all over her office. Even in death she was torturing me.

A woman from the cleaning crew peeked her head into my office. "Hello," I sighed. "Is it already seven?"

She nodded. "You should go, miss. Go home to your family. This will be here tomorrow. You can do it then."

Kind wisdom, and painful wisdom. The main reason I was still here was not because I had too much to do. I was here because I had no family to go home to. Liam was out on his date in *my* car, as his was still at some shady shop with some mechanic that Liam had distrusted ever since he'd scoffed at Liam's uneducated diagnosis of the car's problem. Liam loved his car, a fairly new smallish SUV, but he didn't know anything about the guts. Cleo was in up Orange County, and reaching Orange County from San Diego without a car meant a complicated series of trolleys and trains and several busses.

I folded my things into my bag. The stack of newspapers peeking out made my stomach uneasy. I'd called Detective Wilson as soon as I could to tell him about the article, but he had already left. Now I had to face the evening alone, at the same time dealing with the fact that someone might be planning my murder.

"Ah, what the hell," I muttered, grabbing the phone. Adam had said he'd call me tonight, but maybe I could reach him first. Maybe he could pick me up. Maybe I wouldn't have to ride the bus home. Maybe I wouldn't have to be alone. I dialed.

His cell phone didn't even ring, going straight to voicemail. *Why is his phone off?* I wondered, already a little jealous of the idea that he might be on another date.

I decided to hang up without leaving a message, because I couldn't think of anything to say that didn't sound a little desperate. He'd said *he'd* call, after all.

So I dialed Cleo. She was sure to want to hear about my date, and it would be a reason to linger in the safety of the office a little longer. As Cleo's home phone rang, I wondered what time Liam would be home. Exactly how long did I have to stall? Cleo's answering machine picked up. "Come on, Cleo," I whined. "It's Eliza. I want to tell you about my date with Adam. It was good. Real good. He said I was beautiful. And . . . oh, I'll save the rest. I'd meet you somewhere halfway to chat, but Liam has my car. Last time I let *him* borrow it, seriously! Especially when I *need* to meet up with my sista to dish about my hot date!" I laughed. "Call me!"

As soon as I hung up, my cell phone rang. Adam's number appeared and my heart skipped a beat. Perfect timing. "Hello," I answered with a calm voice that didn't match my fluttering heart.

"Hi, Eliza," Adam's deep voice answered with what I took as a hint of pleasure. "I saw that you called."

"Yeah. How are you doing?"

"I'm good. I'm working at the moment."

"Late meeting, huh?"

"Yeah. But what can you do when you need a story? Listen, I just snuck away to call you but I need to get back. What's up?"

I pulled him away from work. I have to come up with a good reason for calling. "Oh, nothing. I'm sorry for pulling you away from your thing. I just had the night free and wanted to see if we could get a cup of coffee or something. Another, you know, 'half-date.' But you're in the middle of something. I'm sorry for interrupting."

"I wish I could. Remember I told you about that sci-fi thing I wanted to get out of for Saturday night? Well, I was able to trade with a colleague, but now I'm stuck at a reading for the latest get-rich-quick financial book. I'd say I got the short end of the deal, except that getting through this means I can see you on Saturday night. Unless you're calling to cancel?"

"Not at all. Saturday it is."

He paused. "Are you sure? Something in your voice sounds . . . different."

"Probably just the reception. I'm on my cell phone."

"You're okay, then? You're not regretting anything?"

"I have plenty of regret in my life, Adam, but not an ounce of regret about last night."

"I'm glad, because neither have I. So, there's nothing you need?"

I need you to meet me right now and take me home and protect me from anyone who might want to hurt me. "Nothing. Only to see you on Saturday."

"Good, then Saturday it is. I'll call you tomorrow night after work. I've gotta go."

"All right. Sorry again for interrupting."

"No problem. Talk to you tomorrow, Eliza."

By the time the cleaning woman was ready to clean my office, I was still sitting at my desk, wondering what I should do about my situation tonight.

"Good night," I told her, turning off my computer and tossing my workbag over my shoulder. I headed to the stairwell, planning to stop by the lunch room and recycle my two Diet Pepsi cans.

As I went down the stairs, I thought, *I don't actually feel like recycling these cans. I think I'm just doing this to waste time before going home to an empty house.*

I certainly didn't want to go home. If someone was looking for me, I was "in the book" because I had thought it a waste of money to keep my name unlisted. If Liam was home and the house was full of light, that would be one thing. Who'd break into a house like that? But an empty driveway in front of a dark house just waiting to be entered? It was the perfect place for a murderer to wait for his victim.

By the time I entered the lunchroom I had thoroughly scared myself. I dropped my cans in the recycle bin and looked around the room. The couch was inviting, and I wondered how long I could hang out here before someone found me. But I figured that the cleaning crew would be in soon after finishing up on my floor, so I made my way to the door. *I need to just go somewhere where no one expects me to be. I just need to kill some time.*

My eye caught a small stack of coupons push-pinned to the employee corkboard right next to the "I lost 30 pounds in 30 days! Ask me how!" flyer. Shamu arched across the top of the coupon, advertising $15 off admission to Sea World. I stuffed a coupon in my pocket and made my way to the elevators. My next stop was the bus stop.

And then Sea World. No one would try any funny business there. And no one would expect me to be there. I mean, I hadn't been to Sea World in at least a year, but for $15 off, and simply for the comfort of knowing I was safe, I was willing to spend a couple hours there before it closed.

Within an hour, I was sitting on the floor of the enclosed manatee exhibit, lazily leaning against the sea-foam green wall, enjoying the tranquility of the dimmed room and the listless new age music playing around me. One of the enormous sea cows turned and caught my eye before pushing off to float to the surface. Her nose flaps opened for air and she swallowed a mouthful of the iceberg lettuce that had been floating on the surface. I felt relaxed, so much so that even the creepy-looking alligator gar that shared the tank with the manatees did not bother me like they usually did.

It crossed my mind just once that it was sort of pathetic to have no one to count on, no safe spot to go to. As if by sisterly ESP, Cleo called my cell phone, the sudden ringtone startling me out of my daze. I hopped up and pulled the phone out, joy spreading over me to see Cleo's number appear.

I'd scarcely pulled open the phone and answered, "Cleo!" when other people in the manatee exhibit were turning and giving me dirty looks. I couldn't blame them. I was being, quite literally, a disturber of the peace.

I cupped my hand over the mouthpiece and muttered, "Hold on a sec." Mouthing "sorry" to the folks
trying to enjoy the exhibit, I hurried out the door and
into the night air.

"Sorry about that, Cleo."

"What was that about?"

"What? Are you insulted?"

"No. But what's up?"

"Guess where I am."

She was silent for a moment, perhaps waiting for me
to answer my own question. Finally she asked, "Was that
a set-up for the answer, or did you really want me to
guess?"

"Forget it," I sighed. "I'm at Sea World. Do you want
to get together?"

"At Sea World?"

"No, the park's closing soon. But maybe for coffee?"

Again, Cleo didn't answer right away.

"No pressure," I said sarcastically. "What's wrong
with you tonight?"

"It's just—just that you said on your message that
Liam had your car tonight. Does he or doesn't he?"

"He does. And I know it is a long way to come down
here. Maybe I can take the Coaster train up to Oceanside
and we could meet there. Anything further north and I'd
have to take the Amtrak."

"I can't, Liz. I have a work meeting tonight."

*And there's the reason for the awkward pauses. I'm inter-
rupting her work like I interrupted Adam's!* "I'm so sorry! I
didn't mean to interrupt!"

"It's okay. I'm just on my way now. I've got to go. But you're okay there, Liz? We can always talk about your date tomorrow or later this week."

"Yeah, I'm fine," I answered without even thinking to confide my worry in Cleo. Had the manatees and my evening at Sea World been that effective at taking my mind off my concerns? Or was I lying to her as I had lied to Adam, unable to get over the guilt of taking them away from work?

"Okay, good. I'll talk to you later, then. Oh, but before I go, what was that 'hold on' command when you first picked up anyway?" She laughed. It was slightly more relaxed this time.

"I was in the manatee exhibit, and when I answered the phone everyone gave me the stink-eye. I rushed out so I wouldn't bug them."

"You didn't turn off your phone in there? Geez, Liz, rude!"

"Yeah, yeah. I know. I'd just forgot to turn it off, and I was also waiting for you to call."

"Well, here's your call. And I can't keep Homeland Security waiting! So get back to your manatees, and for goodness' sake, Liz, turn off your phone when you're in there so you don't get on everyone's bad side!"

By the time the announcement came that the park would be closing soon, I was again in the manatee exhibit, back sitting on the floor against the wall. I was safe here and now calm enough to make decent choices about getting home and back to real life.

When the park closed, I was one of the last people to head to the gates. Out of the corner of my eye, I noticed someone staring at me. He was tall and lanky, in a tank top and baggy shorts and I could see the knotted muscles on his arms and his calves. His sandy hair flopped in front of his sunglasses which, paired with his clothes, made him the stereotypical picture of a California guy.

California Guy stood by the shrubs, just watching me. My first thought was, *I'm being checked out!* My ego had only half a moment to soar before another thought popped into my head. *I'm being stalked.* The small smile that had begun to play across my lips disappeared and I turned away. Now I was at the gate, with few people around. As soon as I went out to the parking lot and began my walk to the bus stop, I wouldn't have park security close at hand. My peace and relaxation were quickly fading. I had to keep my wits about me.

I turned back to California Guy. I'd heard somewhere that you should look a possible predator right in the eye to acknowledge he's there and to let him know you wouldn't be taken by surprise. He had turned and was leaning toward someone behind the shrubbery. Talking. Plotting.

But then he stepped away and out came Sue Talley, the intern. *Sue!* My mind raced. She was smiling nervously, trying to act natural. Was she his accomplice? Or was she his captive? Was she his next target? Was she bait?

Surprisingly, however, she walked right past California Guy and approached me, smiling. "Hi, Eliza."

I searched her face for some recognition that she was in trouble, and I noticed that her lip was cut. "Hi, Sue. Are you okay?"

"Oh this?" She touched her lip and a drop of blood oozed out. "I'm fine. I fell, is all. I'm kind of a klutz, but my boyfriend was there to help me. Please don't worry about those rejection letters. I'm going in early tomorrow to finish them up. I only have one Friday class—it's at eleven, but I'll get them all done, I promise." She was rambling, and had the deer-in-the-headlights look, caught on her date after she had told me she would cancel it. Not that I cared. I felt bad that she was so worried. And I felt silly for thinking her date was checking me out. Or plotting to kill me.

The main thing was that she was okay, and she wasn't a hostage. I sighed, considering how paranoid it was to have thought so in the first place. "The letters can wait until Monday if need be. I trust you to take care of them," I replied sympathetically.

Her hand shot back up to her mouth. She laughed nervously, but smiled her thanks. California Guy approached her from behind. Automatically my muscles tensed, based on my previous assessment of him, but when Sue grabbed his hand and pulled him closer, I was assured he was not a threat. "This is Donovan—"

"Donnie," he corrected her, reaching out to shake my hand. "Only my parents call me Donovan. And then only when I'm in trouble."

151

"Are you in trouble often?" I asked playfully.

"Well . . .," he began to reply, when Sue cut in.

"Donnie's my boyfriend. And Donnie, this is Eliza— she works with me."

"I know," Donnie replied. "You just told me back there."

He turned to me. "She saw you a few minutes ago and was a little intimidated to approach you, now that you're her boss. She's shy sometimes, but a nice girl. And she's talented, too."

Sue caught him by the arm. "Donnie, don't. Leave it."

Donnie smiled, his straight white teeth glowing under the theme park lights. "I mean, she's a talented writer. She's seriously gonna be rich and famous someday. Have you read her book?"

I turned to Sue. "You write? You've published a book?" She was in college, for goodness sake. Again I felt behind in my literary ventures. *I'll never finish my novel,* my mind accused. *And if I do, it won't be any good. And if it is, it won't be good enough to publish. And who cares if I'm Sue's boss, if she's already surpassed me in what really matters in my life—my writing.*

"No, no. I mean, I have written a book, but I haven't been published yet. I'm kinda shopping it around."

"It's so hard to get published," I sympathized, feeling instantly better about myself. "I used to write, too, and always thought it was as easy as having a good idea and then writing a manuscript. But receiving all these manuscripts every day at work and seeing how many we can't let through to a second step just really discouraged me. There's real talent out there. And of course, there are a lot of people who just don't have it."

"Are you saying that Sue doesn't have it?" Donnie demanded.

I looked him up and down. Who did he think he was? I was about to ask him just that when I realized that he was just standing up for his woman. Who was I to look down on that? So I waved him off, with a "No, no. I'm talking about me. I didn't even know Sue wrote. You should let me read something, Sue."

"Maybe. I'll think about it. I know you're busy. By the way, how are you doing on that stack I gave you before? You know, the ones you said you look at closer?"

We started moving through the gates. Donnie was already scanning for his car in the parking lot, muttering something about how you'd think his car would stand out amongst these "heaps." He was one of *those* guys.

"Actually, I started on them this morning. I'm still working through them. It takes a little longer, though, with the extra notes for your future reference."

"Ah," she muttered. "Sounds like you're sending them back. And if you're sending them back, you're rejecting them."

"Yeah, Sue, I'm afraid so. I can kinda see what you saw in them, but there was just a handful of things that really made them—"

"—not right for J Press?"

"We really need to get you away from those rejection letters, don't we?"

"No, it will be good for a career in publishing," she replied.

Sue didn't look amused, and I wished I had not made the joke.

"I think Donnie found his car. Do you need a ride to yours?"

I saw Donnie urging her along and figured I probably shouldn't ask for a thirty-minute ride to North County, especially after I'd just offended her. "No, it's all right. Thanks, though. I'll see you tomorrow."

"See you then, Eliza," she said in a tone that was missing its usual spark.

"Hey, don't worry about those manuscripts. We'll talk about them soon when I have a little more time. I think it will help you distinguish which manuscripts just can't be published. Don't give up." I looked at Donnie. "It was good meeting you!"

"You, too," he said and disappeared with Sue down a row in the parking lot.

I didn't want to take the bus home. Hell, no. I would splurge. I found the taxi pool, and slid into the car with the fewest dings and dents.

Once we got moving, the driver asked if I minded him putting on some music for the long drive. I replied that I didn't mind. Sitting in the back of the cab, listening to the driver's CD, I could distinguish a word every few minutes and realized this was an album in Arabic. I leaned forward. "Where are you from, sir?"

"Chula Vista. Why do you ask? I have a good knowledge of streets all over the county, though, so don't worry."

"I wasn't worried about that. I just noticed your music. It's Arabic, isn't it?" I wondered why I was even asking this. *Am I that lonely? What will I say if he tries to start a conversation in Arabic? That I only know a few words? Why am I starting this conversation?*

"Yes, it is." His voice was cautious.

"Are you originally from the Middle East?"

He scanned my face in the rearview mirror. Looking for signs of hostility? Trying to figure out whether I had any Arabic in my background?

"I'm originally from Lebanon," he replied. "A friend who is still there sends me copies of popular albums. Where are you from?"

"I'm from Southern California, but my dad was from Syria."

"Ah, yes," he replied. "He was from Damascus? Very close to Lebanon."

"He was raised in Aleppo."

"Good, good," the driver said. Sure enough, he began speaking in Arabic and I was lost except for a word here and there. When I didn't answer, he looked again in the mirror and saw my discomfort. "Your father did not teach you his language."

"I know what to say when someone cuts me off in traffic," I admitted with a laugh. But our conversation was now ending.

I noticed that we were heading over the lagoon where Rain had been killed, and I shuddered. It was as if her ghost were seeping into the taxi through the vents and warning me that I was next. And warning me that I had better finish reading the stack of manuscripts on my desk before I followed her. For my own sanity, I tried to turn my thoughts to poor Sue.

She tried hard, I thought. *She wrote up those reports and everything, but she was just way off base.* Those manuscripts had been truly horrible. I really needed to go over them with her. I had to appreciate her willingness to try.

And what was up with Donnie? He was strikingly good-looking in a surfer kind of way. But something felt wrong. I really didn't trust him, and maybe the chill I'd felt was actually a bad vibe. I grew less uneasy and more angry as I wondered if he might have been the cause of Sue's split lip. *He'd better not be.* Had I been so self-absorbed that I hadn't noticed that one of our interns was being abused? When did I become so damn blind to other people's problems? First thing tomorrow morning I would question her and somehow get an answer as to whether Donnie was abusing her.

When the cab pulled into the driveway, I noticed with some irritation that Liam was not home yet. My car was not back.

Once inside, I turned on all the downstairs lights and glanced at the answering machine. No blinking light.

"My car had *better* be back in the driveway when I leave for work tomorrow. I'm *not* listening to a sob story about wanting to spend the night with your *friend*."

It was a threat announced to the empty room, and then in a fit I began pulling off my clothes on my way upstairs to my room, throwing on all the light switches on the way up.

Within moments I was in a sloppy T-shirt and boxers and sliding between my sheets. At that moment, safe at home and comfortable in bed, my only fear was that these angry thoughts would lead to bad dreams about Liam, replaying the times he hurt me in his sweet ways. So I turned my thoughts to Adam, preparing clever things to say when he called this weekend, imagining our next date and making it out to be as sultry as I hoped it would be.

I drifted off to a very lusty sleep filled with sexy dreams.

CHAPTER 11

In the morning, I could see through the crack under my door that the hall light was still on. My stomach dropped. Liam still wasn't home and I had no way to work. Another taxi ride—especially all the way downtown—would cost a fortune, and waiting for a taxi to take me to the transit center seven miles away and then waiting for a bus would make me incredibly late for the second day in a row. I threw open the door and flew down the hall past Liam's empty bedroom. Pounding down the stairs in my T-shirt, I went directly to the answering machine. Still no blinking red light.

"He didn't even call?" I asked aloud, but even as the words left my mouth I knew it wasn't like Liam.

Of course, my cell phone! I found my workbag where I'd left it by the door, and fished out my phone. My thumb found the button with the green phone icon and pressed. As I waited for the phone to turn on and find a signal, I shook my head. "He must be coming back this morning to pick me up. He wouldn't just leave me without a ride to work. Even if he'd left me a message, he'd know I had no other way to work."

Finally! I thought as the phone picked up a signal and chimed to alert me to new messages. I dialed and waited, throwing a glance at the clock. I still had some time left before I needed to leave.

The computerized voice on my voicemail announced the time of the first message, 9:55 P.M., and the message began. The voice, however, was not Liam's, but Adam's. At some point after my conversation with Cleo, he had called. I hadn't expected him to. Wasn't he supposed to busy with work?

His message was short and casual, noting that his author reading was done early and that when I got home, he could bring over a movie and some snacks and we could spend a little time together.

"I know I wasn't going to call until tomorrow night, so if you're out or if you get home late, no worries. Just give me a call when you get a chance so we can plan Saturday."

I had enjoyed Sea World, but it was nothing compared to the fun Adam and I would have had, and I kicked myself for turning off my phone. Who cared what a few strangers thought about me when my phone disrupted them?

The voice announced another message, time: 12:13 A.M. The message began, but again it was not Liam. An older man's voice spoke clearly and gently, calling me "Ms. Tahan." He informed me that he was calling from our local hospital.

My throat caught.

"Your name is on the emergency contact card that Liam Jack had in his wallet. I'm afraid he has been in a car accident, and we ask that you come as soon as possible. He was admitted into the ER and, while you can't see him at this moment, we hope to be able to transfer him to ICU shortly. You can come at any time—we don't have strict visiting hours." There was an address and a phone number in case I had any questions.

I began to feel dizzy. A sharp breath in. Out. In.

I pressed "7" on my phone to save the message. There was another message waiting.

"This message is for Ms. Tahan. We have not heard back from you in response to our earlier message regarding Mr. Liam Jack. His condition is stable now and he is in the intensive care unit. He is still in a coma, but things are looking better. Please call us as soon as possible. If you cannot make it to the hospital, we need you to call with contact information for Mr. Jack's next of kin."

Stable? Intensive care unit? Coma? Next of kin?

I knew I should be speeding to the hospital but it would be all day to get there on foot. A taxi would be my chariot, regardless of the price. I was already excavating the Yellow Pages from our kitchen drawer, cell phone tucked between my shoulder and ear, when yet another message began.

"Liz!" Cleo's familiar voice boomed in contrast to the gentle hospital voices. "Damn it, Liz, why aren't you answering your phone?" Freeway noises ran all ways in the background of the message. "The hospital said they've been trying to get hold of you, leaving messages and stuff. Liam's been in an accident. He is in ICU right now. When they could not get hold of you, they called me. I don't know why he has *my* name on his emergency list, or how many people they had already called who are not picking up their phones. We are far from best buddies, but you know that and this is not the time for me to complain. What can I do but go to the hospital? I'm on my way as I speak. Come right away when you get this. I don't want to be making any life-or-death choices about *your* roommate. I'm sorry, Liz, I'm just a little anxious, a little panicked. I don't mean to scare you. ICU isn't bad. They're taking care of him. Just come right away. I want to be there to help *you* deal with this. Not be the only one there."

There was a beep and it was the end of the messages. I tried to discern the meaning of Cleo's message, clearing away all the extras that came up whenever Cleo was anxious.

I called a taxi and asked them to hurry.

I'd been able to hold back tears, busy praying in my mind, during the taxi ride to the hospital.

My voice cracked when I asked for Liam's room number, hoping they'd say he was fine now and on his way home.

But when I walked into his room, saw his torso wrapped up, his arm in a cast, and all the machines and intravenous lines to which he was hooked up, the tears began to well up in my eyes. His face with the broken nose and the stitches across his right cheekbone knocked the air out of my chest. The mid-morning sunlight was pouring through the window, making the hospital room so bright it hurt my eyes.

It wasn't the light that caused me to walk immediately out of the room, but the tears I was trying desperately to hold in. Standing in the hospital hallway, staring at the calming impressionist painting of cliffs and the sea, the tears finally made their way out.

It seemed like an eternity that I stood in the hall with my back to his door, before Cleo, who had been reading a book in the corner of the room, came out to meet me. Her arms were around my shoulders, and she was cooing my name. "Liz. Oh, Eliza . . ."

I turned, wiping my eyes, to face her. She pulled a tissue out of the purse pack she always had in her jacket pocket. "Eliza," she repeated. "You're here. Thank goodness. I was so worried about you. It wasn't like you not to come to Liam's rescue, and it was your car he was in and I just had these awful thoughts that maybe you were in there, too, and were thrown out, or something."

I looked aside and didn't say anything.

Her attitude changed to accusatory. "What the hell took you so long? I've been so damn worried! I've been here worrying *all* night!"

"I didn't get the messages 'til this morning," I sniffled. "You're the one who told me to turn my phone off."

Cleo narrowed her lips. "I meant while you were in that thing with Shamu."

"It was the manatee exhibit."

"Whatever. Don't feel bad. You had no way of knowing this was going to happen."

I looked up, my eyes cleared enough to see my sister. "What happened, anyway?" I asked, comforted by having her there.

"It was a car accident. Some drunk driver just plowed into him. The drunk driver's car was just bigger, I guess. It smashed into your Civic, then super-quick, the drunk driver sped away. The other car had to have some damage, and they're hoping that will help them track who it was." Her voice trailed off. She shook her head. "God, I'm just glad *you're* okay. This has had me totally freaked out. And I'm not easily freaked out, Liz. I was so worried about you. How can anyone sleep at night when someone they care about might be driving somewhere? Shit." She turned her head and seemed to fight back tears.

"A drunk driver?" I asked. I wasn't feeling secure enough myself to comfort her. I wanted to know the facts. Facts are cold and solid. Much easier to face than warm tears and shape-shifting fears.

Cleo choked back the tears that had threatened to come. I convinced myself that I had done her a favor. Who wants to be bawling in a hospital hall? It wasn't the time to break up over everything. Facts. I needed more facts.

"That's what we think he was. Me and the guy sharing Liam's room. He's nice enough, but bored and chatty. He just won't fall asleep and give me some peace."

"So, you've told me what happened to the car. What happened to Liam? And how is he, really?" I didn't want a list of the damage. I had seen that when I had walked in the room, spelled out in tubes and stitches. Cleo knew me, and I knew she would tell me what I needed to know.

"Liz, the doctor is going to tell you all the details as soon as he comes in. For now, well, Liam is okay, I guess. Under the circumstances. When he first came in, I don't think they thought he was going to make it. I sure didn't expect him to pull through. He hadn't been wearing his seatbelt. I mean, who *doesn't* wear a seatbelt!"

"Liam hates seatbelts. You know that."

"Yeah. After I got hold of myself, I remembered you complaining about how he never wears his seatbelt. There was that time we were all in the car together and you were trying to convince him to buckle up and he was saying that it would wrinkle his clothes and he might as well never press his shirts if they were going to be wrinkled by a seatbelt anyway."

"I remember that. We had that conversation a lot. Even just the other day, actually."

"He has some broken bones, and he hit his head really hard. They fixed all they could right now, and they say he's stable, whatever that means. He hasn't opened his eyes or anything." She glanced back into the room. When she turned back to me, she said with some surprise, "That chatty roommate of his is finally asleep! I guess that would have done the trick, just walking away from the conversation."

"I'll be quiet when I go in." I wanted to be by Liam's side.

Cleo rested a gentle hand on my shoulder. "Don't go in if you're not ready. It's pretty shocking, and you've only just pulled yourself together."

I managed a weak smile. "You think I'm pulled together?"

"See that doctor down there?" She pointed at a handsome black man in a stark white coat at the end of the hall.

"Don't tell me you've spent your time here cruising for men." I rolled my eyes.

"No, that's Liam's doctor. I think you should go talk to him and get the lowdown before going in to see Liam. I'll wait in the room for you."

"Thanks, but he looks like he's heading this way. Anyway, I'm ready to go back in there and see Liam now. I was just . . . shocked at first, I think."

"Are you sure?"

"Yeah, I'll be fine."

"All right, then. I'll let you be alone with him. And I'll tell his nurse you're here. When they couldn't get hold of you, they looked at his phone to get his parents' telephone number, so don't worry about giving the doctors their number. The doctor is on his way, like you said, and the nurse is due to check on him soon, too. She comes every fifteen minutes or so. I think she'll let you stay while she does her thing, as long as you don't get in her way."

After Cleo left I went to Liam's side. My first glimpse had prepared me to some degree, and though I was horrified at his injuries, and though my legs wanted to buckle at the thought of his pain, I moved forward and gently lifted his hand to my lips for a light kiss.

"Liam? Can you hear me?" I half-expected a hand-squeeze or something dramatic. But there was nothing. I looked at the monitors next to his bed. The readings were, as they say, Greek to me. I searched my brain for some magic words to say.

I'd once had a daydream that we were old and married (this was before, when that was still the plan) and that I was in a coma on my way to death's door. In my fantasy, Liam held my hand and read me poems. Not mushy ones, but profound ones. Rumi and Hafitz and the Psalms. To guide me to the afterlife.

But I couldn't think of anything poetic, and I didn't want to guide Liam to the afterlife. I wanted to pull him back to this life. I squeezed his hand.

Cleo entered the room, along with the doctor and nurse. The doctor shook my hand and introduced himself before trying to comfort me for an obligatory moment. That business aside, he got down to work. While the doctor was checking Liam this way and that, and the nurse was taking notes from the monitors, the doctor gave me an account of what had happened. What bones had been broken. Where he had been cut and hit. Their expectations for his coma.

"Who doesn't wear a seatbelt in this day and age?" He looked at me as though I could answer for Liam. I shrugged, just wanting him to continue. "He was admitted to the ER last night. Because he was not wearing his seatbelt, he hit his head on the windshield, which is why he has the broken nose and deep cuts on his face. His chest hit the steering wheel and broke some ribs. Being tossed around—of course without his seat-belt—caused a fracture in his right arm. His ankle was broken, too. We stitched him up, set his bones and, once he stabilized, brought him here to ICU to see if he is going to come out of this."

The doctor concluded, "Your friend is stable, and of course he is young and healthy. That really boosts his chances of making it. You know, we tried to call you sev-eral times when he came in."

"I was out," I answered softly. "My cell phone was off. So I didn't annoy people. I forgot to turn it back on when I went home and went to bed. It was late."

"Well, luckily your sister came in. And you're here now. Don't feel like you have to keep vigil over your friend, Ms. Tahan." He looked over at Cleo and smiled. "Cleo here seems to think something terrible will happen if she walks out of the room."

When he left, I asked myself if I should keep vigil. What could I do that the doctor and nurses weren't already doing?

I turned to Cleo, who was standing at the foot of Liam's bed. "I'm going to call work. I know the doctor said I didn't need to stay, but I think I'd rather."

"You have to go outside to use your cell phone," Cleo replied, keeping her eye on the sleeping roommate. "There's signs posted all over. I'll wait here for you."

"I'll use the room phone. It's a local call."

I dialed the HR manager.

"Ms. Li," I said into her voicemail, "this is Eliza Tahan, from the mystery department. A friend, my roommate, was in an accident last night and is in the hospital in a coma. I'm here at the hospital and I won't be coming in today, if that's okay. I'll try to come in tomorrow, but my friend is in really bad shape and I just don't know for sure yet when I'll be able to come in."

I left a phone number and hung up, and then made eye contact with Cleo, who had moved to the chair in the corner.

"You're out of your element, aren't you, Liz?" she whispered, trying not to wake up the roommate.

"I am. You sure do know me."

"I'm out of my element, too. Hospitals bring back . . . memories. Hey, if you're going to be here, do you mind if I take a nap at your place? I've been up all night, and I came right from a meeting so I haven't slept for too long. I don't trust myself driving all the way home before getting a little shut-eye. Plus, you know how accidents or the effects thereof really shake me up. I need a break."

"No problem, Cleo," I said, tossing her my keys. "My house key is the one with the blue plastic thingy on it. Drive carefully."

"Of course. Are you going to be okay? Got enough info to hold you for a little while before we can find out anything else?"

"I guess I don't have many options, do I? I appreciate your coming here."

"I didn't have many options, did I?"

"Hey, by the way, did they say anything about the other guy in the car?" I asked, thinking about Liam's date.

"What car? Yours? What other guy?"

"Liam was on a date with some guy. That's why I lent him my car."

"I don't think anyone else was in the car."

"He must have been on his way to pick up his date. How would someone be that drunk that early? The other driver, the one that hit him, I mean. You'd have to be drinking a while to get so drunk that you smash into someone! Don't you think?"

"Sounds like some bum who doesn't have a job. Some self-interested Hemingway who just sits around and drinks and no one knows how he can pay his rent or pay for the booze—"

"Hemingway?"

"Not literally Hemingway," Cleo laughed, her voice weak with sleepiness. She gave me a peck on the cheek. "I didn't mean to offend my favorite English major. I just meant, you know—"

"An author." I felt a little faint.

"I didn't mean an author in particular. I just meant someone who stays at home and drinks in the middle of the day. Didn't Hemingway do that?"

Did she know about S. Rain's death being a possible murder? By an author?

She didn't know about the mandate from the detective to start looking through lists of rejected authors. She didn't know that while my house didn't appear in my photo in the article, my car *did*.

Could it be that whoever hit Liam had meant to hit me?

While I sat next to Liam's bed, the day crawled by. As my original anxiety faded, I became restless. The worst part of sitting beside someone in a hospital is the unknown. The waiting and wondering and worrying, every moment a reminder of the fragility of life.

Whoever hit Liam meant to hit me. I should be in a coma now. Or dead.

I grasped Liam's hand again and squeezed gently. Had he taken my place? I didn't want him hurting, but I found myself focusing more on the fact that it could have been me. Not like "coulda been anyone," but "*shoulda* been me."

I decided I needed something solid to concentrate on. Pulling my insurance card out of my wallet, I called AAA to report the accident. I then called the police department to ask after my car. Not that work mattered much right now, but at least it was something to do. I arranged to have them call me about when I could pick up my car from the police impound yard, and they noted that I "shouldn't expect to drive it home."

I decided on another call.

"Detective Wilson," answered the voice on the other end.

"Sir, this is Eliza Tahan. We spoke yesterday about S. Rain's murder."

"Yes, Ms. Tahan."

"My roommate is in the hospital. He was driving my car when someone hit him."

"I'm very sorry," was the reply. Then silence.

"I think the guy was trying to hit me."

"You think it was on purpose?"

"Yes. There's this interview I did. I mean, I wanted to tell you yesterday but you had already left for the day. In it I said I did the rejections."

I heard Detective Wilson shuffling some papers. "Yes, I have that here. 'Ms. Orwell usually agrees with me, and she will follow up with contracts.'"

"So you read the article? All of it?"

"Yes. And it sounds like you thought Ms. Orwell was pretty useless, except to follow up with contracts."

"Please, it isn't important what I thought. It's important what I said. I did say that, and it was kind of conceited. A bad move. The interviewer was good-looking and I was trying to impress him. Rain had set up the interview right before I was supposed to go on vacation and I was angry with her. I thought I could include the article in a portfolio someday for a promotion or another job, and I wanted to look good."

"Did you complain about Ms. Orwell often to your friends and family? Not just to the interviewer, I mean?"

"No, not exactly. I wasn't telling it all over town. And never at work or anything. Just venting to a few people. Of course, it wouldn't matter anymore if I had told everyone because I told the interviewer. Any author who might have killed Rain because of a rejection knows now that he should have tried to kill me."

"Why did Rain set you up for the interview when you were supposed to be on vacation?"

I was exasperated. "Because she was mean in general, no matter what Jane and the rest of the office people say. She was not a nice person. She was selfish and didn't care about anyone else. The point is—"

"Hmmm." Detective Wilson shuffled some more papers. "That's a little harsher than just saying she wasn't a model supervisor."

Wait. Am I a suspect? I stuttered to change the subject. "That's not the point. As I was saying, if she were murdered—by an *author*—because of a rejected manuscript, then *I'm* the real target. Because I reject the manuscripts. And anyone who read that interview would know that now. And whoever hit my roommate meant to hit me. The guy who killed Rain is still in San Diego and wants to kill me!"

"Calm down, Ms. Tahan," Detective Wilson sighed. "We don't even know if it *was* an author. Lots of people have access to rejection letters. I understand your anxiety about all this. Lots of people in your company are concerned for themselves and their loved ones. And while I'm sorry for your roommate, we need more evidence to connect the crimes than just the fact that two people you know were in car accidents. However, if you can let me know your roommate's name and the time and place of the accident, I can look up the incident report and have a chat with the officer involved in the case."

"But—" I muttered. *Have a chat?*

"I will look into it, Ms. Tahan. In the meantime, please stay in contact. We may need to get more information from you."

Liam's roommate stirred, but I ignored him and didn't make eye contact, and once he settled himself he fell back asleep. I paced the room nervously. If the police didn't believe me, who would?

If the police don't think you're in danger, then maybe you aren't.

I wanted desperately to call Cleo. She'd calm me down. But she had been up all night, full of anxiety, and now finally had a chance to rest. Who was I to steal that relief from her?

My thoughts turned to Adam Mestas. Why *shouldn't* I call him? Didn't we have an increasingly serious relationship?

Increasingly intimate, my mind countered. *That's not the same as serious.*

But wasn't it common knowledge that men wanted to be rescuers? Wouldn't he be insulted if I needed help and I didn't think to call on him to be my hero?

My hero in what? In listening to my irrational fears? That will be a real turn-on. He'll be so glad you called.

I slumped down in the chair. Would Adam be there for me if I asked him to be? Would he sit next to me as I sat next to my ex, just because I needed company? Or did he just want to be with me when we were having lunch, dinner, sex?

"There's only one way to find out," I announced, standing up and making my way to the phone by Liam's bed. I dialed Adam's cell. It rang.

And rang. Four times and then the voicemail picked up.

I released a saddened sigh, and after the beep simply said, "It's Eliza. I'm at the hospital and just . . . having a rough day. Call me when you can." I paused. Should I dare to say it? How else would I know he'd be there for me? "I just need to talk."

As though some kind of divine answer, as soon as I hung up the phone I heard a moan from behind me. I turned in time to see Liam trying to shift in bed, unable to move much due to his broken body and the wires and tubes that tied him up. The breathing machine produced dramatic sounds and I rushed to his side, pounding the nurse call button as many times as I could while watching Liam with bated breath. I stopped pushing the call button and began to breathe when his eyes opened.

"Oh, Liam," I gasped.

He opened his mouth and looked at me quizzically, and moaned.

"You're awake, Liam!" I smiled, and then frowned because he'd seemed more peaceful when he had been out. Now he just looked like he was in pain and completely confused.

"It's okay, it's okay," I cooed, trying to comfort him but, afraid to touch him in case I touched something that hurt. "You were in a car accident. But you'll be all right. We're in the hospital."

He just stared at me, fear in his eyes.

Within seconds the nurse was in the room, followed by the doctor. I was ushered out, glad to have Liam in the hands of people who could help him. My own hands still had his blood on them, symbolically speaking, since I had rejected an author who might have put him here. I quivered and lowered myself to the floor and leaned against the wall, silent tears streaming down my face.

CHAPTER 12

Now that Liam was out of his coma, the nurses suggested I go home and get some rest, and I felt guiltily thankful. I was done with the hospital. I was done with Liam's staring, his struggles to make any sense of the situation.

I made sure to get outside the hospital before turning on my cell phone, spurred by the warning signs posted all over. I was planning just to call Cleo. Now that Liam was awake I didn't feel right about using his room phone. Once my phone was on, however, I saw I had a voice-mail. It was from Adam.

When I had called him, I'd felt lost, lonely, desperate. In the meantime, Liam had come out of his coma and I was free to go home.

True, I was annoyed that he hadn't quite been there for me when I most needed him. But judging from the log on my phone he'd called only shortly after my call—only, he'd dialed my cell phone, which had been off. And he could not have known where in the hospital to call. I was still a little irked, but my common sense reminded me I could not really blame him.

I pressed the button to dial my missed call. Adam picked up on the first ring.

"Eliza, are you okay? I hadn't heard back from you. I was worried."

"I'm at the hospital—"

"What hospital? Are you okay? What happened?"

"My roommate was in an accident. I've been here with him all day, but Liam's out of his coma now."

There was silence on the line. I pulled the phone from my ear to check the reception bars. Full reception on my end.

"Are you there, Adam?"

"Yeah," he replied haltingly. "Um, did you say it was Liam?"

"Yes, someone hit him while he was driving my car. He was in critical condition."

Adam paused, and when he began again his voice had lost its gentle sympathy. "So what you're saying then, Eliza, is—no, I'm sorry. I guess this isn't the right time. I'll let you get back to Liam."

I wasn't sure what had brought about the change. Surely he'd offer to be with me, or at least offer me a ride home. "I'm going home now. Liam's out of his coma, and I need some rest. I got here first thing this morning when I got the doctor's message, and I've been here all day."

"Liam doesn't have family?"

"They're out of state, so I'm his emergency contact," I replied. But then I started getting annoyed. I wasn't going to let him make me feel guilty for being there for a friend. What did he expect from me? I shifted the phone to my other ear and set my free hand on my hip with a sigh. "Adam, just tell me what's the matter. You sound upset, but I didn't do anything wrong here—and I'm not going to apologize for visiting my roommate in the hospital."

Instead of backing down, apologizing, explaining he was not upset, Adam fired back. "That's just it, Eliza. Your roommate. When Liam was at your house the other day you swore to me that he was just a friend and he was borrowing your car for the night. And now I find out that he's still 'borrowing' your car, that you're his emergency contact, and more importantly, you're *living* with this guy."

"I don't think that's any of your business, Adam." Inside, I did feel a twinge of guilt.

"It's my business that you lied to me. Did you tell him that I was just a friend, too?"

"No! I told him we were dating—"

"And he was cool with that? That the woman he's living with is dating around? Tell me, Eliza, was he in the bedroom next to us when we were making love?"

That was enough for me. "I'm hanging up, Adam. Since you obviously just want to argue about something that isn't an issue, and blame me for having a roommate instead of being there for me, I'm going to call my *sister* to pick me up—"

Adam sighed. "Eliza . . ."

"No. Call me in a few days and we'll see if we can have an adult conversation. Goodbye, Adam."

I shut my flip phone with a loud crack, the cell equivalent of slamming the phone down. Who did he think he was? I hadn't lied! Liam is a friend!

Had he expected me to give the long saga of Liam and me when all he was doing there was dropping off some damn newspapers?

I called Cleo and asked her as calmly as possible if she could pick me up.

Her hair was plaited neatly back in a French braid that tucked under at the nape of her neck. Had she redone it after her nap, or did she even *sleep* perfectly? A deep green suit, perfectly tailored, sat against her dark skin in a way that made her look both professional and avant-garde at the same time. She's darker than I, and she'd taken to the outdoors and sunlight, while I was most often found inside under a lamp and over a good book.

"New car?" I asked, trying to act normal when I slid into the Ford Taurus. "It isn't as glamorous as the 'Vette or as hip as the hybrid."

"The rental place was out of the cool cars."

"You have it so hard, Cleo. But why did you rent a car? You're one person and have three cars at home."

"One is a government-issued car. I can only use it for Department of Homeland Security stuff."

"That's right. So you have two cars left. Why the rental?"

A pause. *Damn it,* I thought, *I've offended her.*

I knew she made good money and could afford the extravagance of owning both a "fun car" and a "green car," and I couldn't tell if I was actually jealous of her success and passive-aggressively said stuff like this to make her feel bad about being a little on the materialistic side. Or did I say stuff like this innocently, and her defensive reaction was the bad behavior?

I tried to soften my question, without quite apologizing. "I mean, you have all those cool cars, and now you're *renting* a car."

She cleared her throat. "I, um, told you before about Jorge. He's fixing my car."

"I must have been so excited about my date that night when you told me that I really didn't pry about him as much as I should have." *My date. With that jealous bastard who is now mad at me for going to see my friend in the hospital.*

But then I thought about the date. He had asked if I was sure. He'd called me beautiful. He'd called me his goddess. My stomach ached.

Cleo, her eyes on the road, didn't notice my stone face. She replied to my words instead of my mood. "I was wondering why you didn't pry. Ask about him more, you know. But you were close to your own date, and I figured that was why. No worries. I'd been hesitant to bring up my being at his place, because the truth is that I got in a *little* fender bender the other day, but everything's fine. Then I had a meeting down here and I wasn't going to show up with a dinged-up front bumper. *Please.* Jorge is fixing it only for the cost of the materials."

I raised an eyebrow. "Only?"

Cleo smiled. "Okay, we've gone out a few times and he's great. He's studying to be a body shop mechanic right now and, anyway, he's going to work on it for me."

"So, what is that costing you?"

We pulled into my driveway. "Nothing I wouldn't have paid anyway."

Once inside the condo, I dropped onto the couch. "Help yourself to anything in the fridge or cupboard, Cleo."

Instead, Cleo caught my eye and sat down on the couch next to me. "You're pretty tired, aren't you? You shouldn't let Liam affect you like this. It's his own fault that he didn't use his seatbelt, and I don't think anyone wants to see you hurting for him."

"I know. It isn't that. I mean, I do feel bad for him. I don't want him to be going through this—"

"But it *is* his own fault—"

"Nevertheless. But, it's . . . Adam." I looked into Cleo's clear, wide eyes.

She grasped my hand, "What did he do?"

I laughed. "You act like you're going to call down the thunder, Cleo. Don't take everything so seriously. It isn't a big deal."

"But you're acting like it's a big deal. What happened?"

I stood up and began pacing around the room. "Everything was going so well! We connected, he seems so normal. No baggage, no issues. He just liked me and I liked him—"

"No one has no issues," Cleo pointed out, and I knew she was right. Any impression that he was "so normal" was just from not knowing him long enough.

"I called him from the hospital, and told him that Liam was there. He got all angry because I guess I had told him Liam was just a friend and now he thinks we're living together!"

"You *are* living together."

"As roommates! Not lovers, not *living* together. We just share a condo."

Cleo shook her head. "That damn Liam. Has he ruined another relationship for you?"

I made my way into the kitchen and pulled open the fridge. "Don't damn him, Cleo," I called into the other room. "He's in the hospital and you should try to find it in your heart to get over the past for now. He hurt me, but he's a decent person. Do you want a drink?"

"Do you have any liquor?"

"I have some vodka left, I think."

Cleo appeared in the kitchen next to me. "Do you have anything to mix with it?"

"Some OJ. Shall we make some screwdrivers?"

"Haven't had one of those since college."

I pulled the juice out of the fridge and grabbed two glasses. "Our day has certainly justified some drinking. And as far as Adam goes, I'll see if he calls me. If not, I'm letting it go."

Cleo watched me pouring the drinks. "A little more vodka in mine. Thanks, that's good. And if Adam *does* call you?"

I handed her a glass and toasted. "Then I'll listen to his side of the story. I'll let him blame it on his issues, his baggage. I'm okay if he's not as normal as I thought, but he's got to offer up his true self and stop blaming me."

Cleo stayed with me, but I knew she'd leave when Liam came home. She couldn't forgive him for breaking my heart, even after I'd forgiven him. She'd made it clear that she was staying with me to comfort *me*, not him.

And finally, Sunday morning, he could come home.

I have never been good with invalids, I admit that. My desire to make everything "all better" always clashed with my desire to plan for the possibility of things not getting better. One thing I knew for sure, though, was that if you're stuck on the couch with a cold or a full-body cast, you can't beat an hour of Oprah or a few good movies. The exact reason that Cleo agreed to stay for a little longer than planned was so that I could make a run to One Dollar Video. Cleo offered to go, but as she ran upstairs to get my video card, Liam grabbed my arm and whispered, "No, please! She got *Shine* last time!"

I decided I'd get one classic, one popular movie he had already seen and loved, and one documentary. The Charlie Chaplin flick *Modern Times* was a given for the classic, as was *Forrest Gump* for the pop film. In the documentary section I found plenty of films about "issues" that Liam would not need to deal with right now. One film stood out, *The Living Sea*, a video version of the IMAX movie. Liam had once thought he'd like to be a marine biologist, until he perused the science requirements for the major. So this would be perfect for him. Relaxing. Interesting. Healing. With music by Sting. Perfect.

Back at home, *The Living Sea* was definitely the most popular option. Liam wanted to watch it right away, and we started it as Cleo was ready to make her exit, sitting down to slide on her shoes before heading back to Orange County. I sat next to Liam, thinking about everything *but* the movie.

What am I going to do about my car?

How can I slip away and call Adam?

Then it happened. A song (composed by Sting most likely, since there were no words to be sung by him in this one) was about thirty seconds in when Liam started shaking. His eyes glazed over and he was no longer watching the movie. He blinked hard, shook his head, and started muttering hoarsely. I moved in closer to hear what he was saying, what was wrong. His voice got louder and more insistent. "Turn it off! Turn it off!"

Cleo and I made a mad attempt to find the remote, *any* remote, and it was I who finally clicked the TV off completely. I rushed back to Liam, who was sweating and shaking, while Cleo went to the entertainment center to pop out the DVD and put it in its box.

"I'll . . . I'll return this on the way home," she said uneasily.

I smoothed Liam's hair and tried to focus his attention on me. When he was calm, I could hold back no longer. "What happened, Liam? What was it?"

Liam looked uncomfortably at Cleo, who had not been able to peel herself away from the spot where she stood, movie in hand.

When he finally spoke, his voice was weak. "I'm sorry, you guys. That was just weird."

"Was it something in the movie?" I asked.

"That song . . ."

We waited for him to take a few breaths before he continued.

"I think that song was on the radio when that guy crashed into me. When he hit my car. Your car, I mean. It was like it got to that certain part in the song and I felt all those feelings, like fear, pain, all over. It must have been at that exact point in the song when he hit me or something, because I don't remember any of the beginning. Anyway, I'm really sorry."

Cleo glared at him doubtfully. "That song was on the *radio?*"

"Yeah," Liam said, not looking up.

I looked up, however. "Even I've heard it before, Cleo. And I don't own that soundtrack."

Cleo placed a hand on her hip and waved the movie. "They play *this* on those oldies stations you listen to?"

I inserted *Forrest Gump* into the DVD player, a sure hit, and escorted Cleo to the door. Walking her outside, I said, "I promise you that I *have* heard it. And Liam was in my car when he was hit, so one of those stations must have played it."

"There is no way they played this song on any of *your* stations. No offense."

Once outside, I closed the door so Liam wouldn't hear us. "Are you saying Liam is making it up? That he didn't like the movie and didn't want to hurt my feelings?"

"Maybe."

"That's crazy."

"He's lied before when he was trying not to hurt your feelings."

"This is different! You saw him—it was a *physical* reaction. He wasn't faking that."

"I'm just sure this was not on any radio station you'd have programmed into your car stereo or that he'd have switched to."

"You make it sound like he's more likely to *lie* than he is to listen to classical music. Give me a break."

"We both know—"

"Yes, that he can lie. We all know that, Cleo. He's lied in the past when he was trying to protect me. Protect someone, I mean. Not to avoid paying me back for my car or something like that."

"Sorry, I really didn't mean to bring up the past. I promise I didn't. I just think that he doesn't know what he's talking about on this." Cleo set a hand on my shoulder to calm me. But the subject to her was *music*, and she knew she was right. "He probably heard it on a CD. And you obviously don't have the CD in your car or you'd know it. Did you borrow it from anyone?"

"No, but that music did sound familiar. Maybe someone was playing it at work? Yeah, like background music." Was it at work though? I closed my eyes and tried to picture where I was when that music was in the background. "Probably at work. But Liam doesn't know anyone from my office."

Cleo looked at the DVD case in her hand, the morning sunlight reflecting off the glossy cover. "Right. So that's how you heard it. Could Liam have borrowed it from someone at your work? I mean, it otherwise doesn't explain why he'd have heard the song in your car."

"No, I don't think he borrowed it. And remember, he said he heard it during the accident. Not necessarily in my car."

"Well, he wasn't thrown from the car. So it had to be in your car."

"Maybe he heard it coming from the car that hit him."

"All the way from the other car?" Cleo rolled her eyes.

"Maybe the driver had it playing really loudly. Lots of people here have great sound systems, you know, teenagers and even people our age."

"But are those really the kind of people who play new age-y music?"

"No, I guess not," I conceded.

"Oh! He could've heard it in the ambulance."

"He was out by then, surely."

She bit her lip and looked off to the side in the way she always did when she was just about out of ideas. "You're sure he was unconscious by the time he was in the ambulance? Couldn't he have been maybe in and out of consciousness?"

"I don't think so, Cleo. But what if the driver had his windows down and he *was* listening to this."

"I'm not trying to be a music snob, Liz, but I just don't think some young guy cruising around with loud music pounding would have picked Sting."

She handed me back the movie, and headed over to her car.

"You may want to hold on to that. See if you can figure out who at the office has the CD."

I trembled, and that was enough to get my feelings across to my sister. I wasn't ready to rule out an author as the murderer. An author could have easily been drunk when he was going after me. But at the same time, if someone from my office was at fault, that was even scarier. Who should I blame? Who could I trust?

I watched Cleo pull out of the driveway in her boring rental car and wondered if she was going to see Jorge tonight. If he would be all sweaty and dirty from working on her car. If she would get lucky while I was at home with my invalid ex-boyfriend stewing over a real-life mystery.

I don't write mysteries. I don't think like this. I just decide what's a good mystery and how to market it. Of course, that's what got me into this spot in the first place.

I waved goodbye to Cleo, even though she was already at the end of the street. The jealousy I felt for her was much deeper than my usual sort. Usually it was something along the lines of, "Why does she have cooler cars and clothes than I do? How can we be sisters when she gets this great hair and I can't even tame mine?" Right now these things seemed inconsequential. Tonight, my jealously was something more to the effect of, "Her night will be fit for a bodice-ripper and mine for a horror novel."

It wasn't fair.

But what had Mom told us when we would cry about it not being fair that we lost our dad? Life's not fair? Yeah. That was sure turning out to be true.

Thanks, Mom.

CHAPTER 13

Liam's new friend, James, agreed to stay with him when I went to work on Monday. I met him briefly when he first arrived and I was pulling out a granola bar and bottled water to take on the bus for breakfast.

When I thanked him for hanging out with Liam, James had replied, "Oh, no problem. I guess I feel a little guilty about the whole thing. He *was* on his way to pick me up. Hell, if I had just insisted that he take the bus, he wouldn't have had to borrow your car and he would be okay."

You too? I thought. *Who doesn't feel guilty about this accident?*

I was glad to get out of the house and back to my usual distractions. However, after riding the morning commuter bus, I gave some thought as to how I could hit up Liam to go in halves with me on a rental car. The accident, if it were an accident, wasn't his fault but the fact was that I'd had a car and I had let him borrow it and now I had no car. And now I was paying eight dollars a day to take a commuter bus. It couldn't be that much more to rent a cheap little car.

My grumpy mood was most likely inflamed by the pinkish older man sitting next to me in the bus, who kept trying to look down my shirt while I tried to concentrate on the manuscripts on my lap. The dirtbag in a business suit was old enough to know better, and I felt violated. Instead of clearing my throat, confronting and embarrassing him, I just stuck to complaining in my mind about being forced to take the bus while I was still making car payments.

My mood followed me down the bus steps and across the street to my building. It followed me into the super crowded elevator, which made the ride even more ghastly that it would have been otherwise. The elevator stopped on every floor on the way up, but never seemed to get less crowded.

Once I exited on my floor, my eyes locked with Jane's across the room. I moved with precision, determined not to even look in the direction of the interns, determined to do my most immediate tasks before answering mundane questions. I stopped at Jane's desk to say hello and to get a list of those who needed to be called back. She spoke before I could even get out my salutation.

"You wanted this job so badly and you worked so hard to get it, and then you don't even show up?"

That stung. I sputtered a little and couldn't find a reply right away. At least not a reply that didn't involving taking out all my anger on her with fists and fury.

"I've been taking care of my roommate!" I choked out.

"But this is your *job*. You didn't even call to tell me you were going to play hooky."

"I *called* HR. That's what we *do* when we have an emergency. No need to call everyone on the floor to announce it."

"Ms. Orwell used to call HR *and* me."

I lowered my voice to something just above a growl, and leaned in. "You *hated* Ms. Orwell. I would have thought you'd be glad to see her and her rules gone."

Jane looked around the office. "Hmm," she muttered, and I followed her gaze. No heads were turned, but one could sense in the unusual silence that every ear was tuned in to our little confrontation. This could get ugly, and I motioned for her to follow me into my office.

Jane passed me and moved toward my desk. The door was still closing when I began. "Okay, what was that all about?"

She shrugged, tossed her blonde curls over her shoulder and raised her eyebrows, making me want to slap her. "Some people are saying you had a pretty strong motive to kill Ms. Orwell."

My breath caught and I needed a moment before responding. "What people?"

"Just some people around here."

"By 'some people' do you mean *you?*" I flashed back to the police department and my meeting with Detective Wilson. "When you talked to the detective, you made it sound like I was the murderer."

Jane shrugged again.

"How *dare* you, Jane? You had as much motive as I did. Everyone has as much motive. Everyone hated her!"

"She was a bitch, but I know her job inside and out. *I* deserved the opportunity to fill her shoes. *I* deserved this office. The authors liked me more than they liked her, and damn more than they like you. Believe me, they tell me!"

"There's more to this job than getting a few people to say they like you."

"Don't you get it? I was *supposed* to get Rain's job when she was gone!"

I grasped the door handle, ready to get the hell out if I needed to.

I should have a tape recorder. I should be wearing a wire. No one will believe me.

"You . . . you killed Rain?"

Jane's pale eyes narrowed, and she hoisted herself to a sitting position on my desk, right on top of the pile of manuscripts. She folded her arms.

My eyes searched the room for a weapon as I stalled. "You wanted this job. You thought you'd worked here long enough and should get this job. I always thought you were just looking for a good recommendation so you could move on. But you wanted to take Rain's position. She would never leave, though. And she made your life a living hell. So you killed her, thinking you'd get rid of your devil and you'd get the job, all in one swoop."

There was a pair of scissors on the desk that suddenly caught my eye. Jane followed my gaze and reached for the scissors first, hopping off my desk. I turned the door handle and readied myself to flee into the public space.

"Oh, yeah, good job, Sherlock Holmes!" Jane shouted, and then lowered her voice again. "Rain was leaving in a year. She confided that to me. She wanted to get out of this city and get away from that loser ex-husband of hers. Headhunters from the New York publishers have been after her for years, and she was training *me* to succeed her. I assumed she'd told someone else, that someone else knew about it. But she hadn't, obviously. And HR wouldn't believe me when I tried to explain it to them."

My hand tightened on the doorknob. Jane pointed the scissors at me from across the office.

"I hated Rain, but would have coped with the situation for another year to get *this* job. This job that *you* barely do and bitch about when you actually do it. It's a good job, Eliza. But then Rain had to go and die, and HR, in their infinite wisdom, had to promote by rank. Which meant you moved up and the person with the capabilities to do the job has to be your *personal assistant*."

I turned the door knob slowly.

Jane took a step toward, leading with the scissor point. "So, who has the motive here? Rain lives and in another year I get a job I've been working towards for a long time. Rain dies and you get a job you know nothing about, but that will pay you more and give you more power. *Who has the motive?*"

With that, she inched forward, keeping me at an arm's length at all times. We circled one another for a few steps, and I saw Jane's eyes about to spill tears. When she'd reached the door, and I had moved back into the office, she grabbed the door handle and waved the tip of the scissors in my direction threateningly. "I *know* it was you. I know you killed Ms. Orwell. I'm not a violent person, but if you so much as lay a finger on me, I'll fight back with all I have, I swear!" She waved the scissors awkwardly. "I have friends watching to keep me safe."

With that she pushed the door wide open and rushed out. Through the open door, I saw her drop the scissors on her desk. She turned back to me with the slightest hint of doubt before heading toward the restrooms, her head down as though she were waiting to cry until out of sight.

I breathed deeply, closing the door again.

Okay, fine, I told myself. *Jane didn't do it.*

Though my first call was far from business-related, it was my highest priority. At best it might calm me and turn my day around. At the least I'd know where I stood in one part of my life.

"Adam?" I queried, though I knew it was his voice that answered after the first ring.

"Hi, Eliza."

"How did you know it was me?"

"I recognized your voice."

"Oh. How are you?"

"I'm okay. Busy at work, but what's new, right?"

"Yeah."

"I'm glad you called me. I was going to call you tonight after work, but hadn't figured out what to say. And I didn't know if you'd ever want to hear from me."

My eyes welled up with tears and I wondered if he could hear it in my voice. "I didn't want to leave it how we did. Today has been . . . the last few days have been . . ."

"Wait, Eliza. I'm really close to your building. Can I stop by for just a few minutes? I don't want to do this over the phone."

"Do what? You can't really break up with me if we're not officially a couple."

Adam laughed, his warm breath traveling through to my soul. "That's not what I meant. I can hear in your voice that a lot is going on. I don't think a phone call is enough for me to be there for you. And I wasn't there for you the other day, and that isn't the person I want to be."

My throat caught. "Come over. I'll meet you in the lobby."

In no time, the receptionist called to announce Adam's arrival. I met him downstairs in the lobby, where he gathered me in a tight hug. Then he leaned down and whispered in my ear, "Where can we talk?"

Once we were back upstairs and in my office, door closed, Adam moved to the window and looked out pensively over San Diego bay. "This is an amazing view. The conference room where we met for the interview didn't have this view."

"It's on the north side of the building. Only the west side overlooks the bay."

"It seems like a long time ago," Adam noted, still looking out the window, "that we had that interview. When we first met, I thought you were cute, but I didn't know our relationship would go as far as it's gone."

Adam turned suddenly, and I leaned against the desk. "Eliza, we have to talk about the other day."

"Yeah, that's why I called. I mean, after spending all day at the hospital, my nerves were on end and I have a feeling I reacted differently than I would have on a normal day."

"Me, too," he replied gently. "The thing is, you called me in the morning and left a message to say you were in the hospital. I was worried all day, thinking you might be in trouble, and you hadn't called back so I couldn't help. I tried calling the major hospitals, Kaiser on Zion, Scripps, Sharp, the ones I could think of, but no one had your name as someone who had been admitted."

"I should have been clearer on the phone. It must have been terrible not to know the facts."

"You were upset, too, and I know you didn't mean to worry me. So when you called and I found out after all that anxiety that you were with this guy who you'd said was just a friend, and he's actually someone you live with . . ."

"We share the condo, but he is just a friend."

Adam moved to where I stood and put his hands on my shoulders, but he was looking down at our feet, as though he didn't want to see a lie in my eyes. "Remember at dinner I told you that I'm making an effort to avoid the whole 'game' of dating? That I wanted an authentic relationship?"

"Yes."

He looked up, his midnight eyes looking deeply into my own, intent. "It's because I've had the other kind of relationship, where everything is sugar-coated, just the right words for the right moments. Then those words didn't later match up with her actions. She wasn't who she pretended to be. I just want to know that I can trust your words to be true."

"Liam is a friend. In fact, he's gay. More interested in you than me. And that's the truth."

Adam's hands slipped lightly from my shoulders, down my arms and to my hands, which he held. "Eliza, I'm sorry for how I acted, for how I jumped to conclusions based on my—damn it, I guess you could call it baggage—instead of listening to *you*. I was wrong, and I'm sorry. And that's the truth."

I slid my hand out of his, and wrapped my arm instantly around his neck, pulling him close. There was a pause as our eyes locked, lips centimeters apart, and then I saw the corners of his mouth turn up slightly before he pressed his soft lips to mine.

Adam didn't have long before he had to get back to work, but we decided to head down to the first floor for a quick cup of coffee. He found us a small table in the corner of Starbucks, and I was glad to see few of my colleagues in the café.

"Are you feeling better? Overall, I mean?" Adam asked, holding my hand with one of his, and holding his coffee with the other.

"About us, yes. Life is just crazy, and while knowing we're okay doesn't fix everything else, it does make me feel like I'm regaining some control."

"Everyone's life can get a little crazy. I totally understand."

I tilted my head. Did he understand? "It seems like things are piling up, you know?"

"It always hits all at once. So, what's piling up with you?"

"My roommate was run down, my assistant thinks I killed my boss, and I have to start contacting authors as if life is as normal as can be. I just need to get my mind off the complications for a while."

Adam paused for a moment, before smiling a crooked smile.

I beat him to it. "My office doesn't have a locking door, if that's what you're about to ask me."

"My apartment does."

"I have to work until five at least."

"I have to head up to Oceanside for an interview near my place. I know there is a five-thirty Coaster train that heads from the Santa Fe Station. I could pick you up, and we can find something to distract you."

❧

After Adam left and I went back, blushing, to my office, I picked up the phone with more confidence than I'd had earlier. Ms. Li answered right away, seeing my name on her phone screener. "Eliza Tahan. How is your roommate feeling?"

"Better," I replied.

"How can I help you?"

"I really need to meet with you about this position. When can we talk?"

There was a pause and a muffled salutation. "Sorry about that, Jane just walked in. What were you saying?"

Jane was there. To tattle on me for blaming her, most likely, and maybe to accuse me of a murder. I needed to act quickly, not schedule to meet at a later time. "I want to talk about this position. I really don't feel comfortable with it yet, and was wondering if you'd be able to have another editor fill in temporarily until you hire someone permanently? Jane mentioned that she knows some of the stuff. Maybe she could fill in, I don't know. I'd really prefer to go back to my old position."

"Eliza, I'm sorry. Jane was trying to tell me something at the same time, and I didn't get all that. You're saying you are not planning to apply for the permanent editor position?"

"Sort of. I'm saying I don't want this position at all. I want to go back to my old position, as assistant editor."

"I understand," Ms. Li reassured me absentmindedly. Obviously, Jane was still pulling her attention away from me. "I will cross your name off the list of candidates and we'll do a final call for résumés and then start looking for Ms. Orwell's replacement."

"But for now—"

"Yes," she said absently, "we will let you know when we've hired a new editor. In the meantime, let me know if you need anything else. My door is always open. Have a great day, Eliza." The phone wasn't even hung up before I heard her addressing Jane.

"Now Jane, calm down. Whatever is the matter?"

So that's how it's going to be? I had been thrust into a position I didn't want (well, kind of wanted at first, but never *asked* for) and now I was stuck. To say I was annoyed would be an understatement.

Fine, I thought to myself, *if they won't let me out, then, hell, my next order of business will be grabbing lunch!*

I checked at the clock. Eleven. Close enough to a decent lunch hour. I was off to Horton Plaza and Jamba Juice for a quickie smoothie with "energy boost" that just might set me up for a little something more than a quickie later tonight.

When I headed off to lunch, I saw Jane return to her desk after being MIA all morning. I didn't say a word, but made my way to the elevators, then back to the first floor, and out the glass doors.

Like nearly every day in San Diego, outside it was sunny and warm, with a clear blue sky and a cool ocean breeze reminding me that I lived in a postcard world. Horton Plaza was teeming with tourists, and near the Abercrombie and Fitch store a line was forming for the next trolley tour. I passed people in "I Love San Diego—America's Finest

City" shirts with their cameras out and ready, waiting in line and taking pictures of the U.S. Grant Hotel across the street. My steps matched the beat of the ultra-loud music pouring out of Abercrombie and Fitch's wide-open doors. I grabbed my Strawberry Surf Rider "with energy boost" smoothie and headed up the long staircase to the various upper levels in the open-air mall.

After an hour of touring the shops—the bookstore up near Nordstrom, the Discovery Channel Store, the Victoria's Secret with Adam on my mind— I was on my way down the staircase when I felt a hand rest heavily on my shoulder. I nearly toppled over and down the stairs. But I caught myself on the handrail and whirled around to vent my ire.

There stood California Guy, a stair above and behind me. I had a flutter in my stomach, but for the moment I couldn't recall why I felt so uneasy. It was a bad night when we last met, and I'd almost forgotten about him. "H—Hi, Donnie," I stuttered, still trying to remember why I didn't feel quite right about him.

"Eliza." He glossed over my name as though swallowing it with a shot of good, smooth whiskey. He moved beside me so that we could descend the staircase together. "You seem in pretty good shape. I thought you weren't doing so well."

"Not doing well?"

"Yeah. Sue said you were out for a while. That something had happened."

"Oh, well, I called in sick a few days. It was my roommate, though. I was taking care of him."

"Your roommate?"

"My ex-fiancé. We're friends now, roommates. I'm sorry Sue misunderstood. I hope she wasn't worried."

He gazed around absently, as though there might be something more important going on elsewhere. "I think your assistant told her something like that. I can't remember what she said. They told her when she called to say she wasn't coming in, you know."

I *didn't* know. Jane hadn't told me anything about Sue calling. Of course, it wasn't like we'd had a great catch-up meeting this morning. "How is she?" I asked, hoping to ascertain the situation this way.

"Your assistant?"

"No, Sue."

"Oh, of course." The bright sun played in his sunny hair. "Better, I guess. She's had it pretty bad, as you probably know. But she'll be better soon."

"So, it was the flu or something?"

He looked at me oddly, "No. She isn't *sick*. She was in a little accident. So you didn't know? What did *she* say happened when she called?"

"My assistant only told me that she was out. Is she okay?"

"Oh, yeah. It's no big deal. She's fine. It was just a little accident."

Our feet hit the ground level simultaneously and we stopped. *An accident?* My mind flashed back to the night in the taxi after I had run into Sue and Donnie at Sea World. Flashed back to the fleeting suspicion that California Guy was dangerous. And that he might be abusing Sue. I couldn't think of what to say, hovering somewhere between wanting to know if my concern was justified and wanting to get away from this possibly bad guy.

He must have picked up on my change of mind about him, because he was quick to change the subject.

"You know, her real problem right now is with you." California Guy's blond hair fluttered in the breeze as he waited for me to reply.

"With me?"

"She's upset about her novel. Remember that book she gave you? The one she wanted your opinion on?"

"Of course. I can send her those comments via email this afternoon if she's really that upset about how long it has taken me."

"She already knows you think it's bad."

"Then why did she give it a good review? And pass it along to Ms. Orwell to be chewed up?"

"She wrote it."

"She wrote the review."

"The book."

My stomach churned, brewing a potent mixture of anxiety and guilt. I didn't reply.

"She knows you hate it. Maybe you should tell her something good about it. Not something generic, or something harsh like that *other* editor said about it. Make her feel a little better."

I was speechless.

We said goodbye and I left quickly, assuring him that I'd go easy in my review of the manuscript. About a block from work I let another thought pass over me.

Has Sue really had an accident? Or has Donnie hurt her? If it was an accident, did he mean a car accident? Could Sue have hit Liam? That would make it an accident. I'd no longer be a target! I wouldn't be responsible for Liam's injury.

Unless it meant that she hit Liam on purpose, thinking it was me, angry that I didn't like her book. Was it the same thing with Rain, when she'd written those harsh things about the book?

I felt a chill despite that warm, dry air. It couldn't be. Not Sue.

By the time I boarded the elevator, I'd decided that if the police didn't want me trying to solve mysteries for them, then I'd just do it without them. All I needed was some evidence, not just a vague suspicion. Then I could take the solved crime to Detective Wilson.

And if I can't find any evidence?

That would be even better. It would mean Sue was probably just mad at me, and not murderous.

I made my way to the interns' office, trying to act casual, glad to see that it was empty as it was prime lunch time. I walked along one side of the room towards Sue's section of the long desk. Was there something on her wall that would count as a clue? Just those quotes.

Three of her quotes gave me pause.

"A man's reach should exceed his grasp."—Robert Browning

"Do not go gentle into that good night. Rage, rage against the dying of the light."—Dylan Thomas

"I am the master of my fate; I am the captain of my soul."—W. E. Henley

I continued my search, looked over my shoulder to make sure no one was watching before opening the small drawer next to her chair. Pens, note paper, extra staples. I was turning my attention to the pictures she had in the drawer when I noticed a small, handwritten note stuck to the bottom of the pen sectional. I picked up the pens and read the note.

There was a toll-free telephone number, and then:
#DJS62278 Delta.

This was stapled to another note that read:
LuAnne
Ms. Orwell
Mrs. C
Eliza or Ms. Li

What was this? A hit list? I made copies of these too. Who were LuAnne and Mrs. C? Why was I on there? And Ms. Li? I quickly replaced the pens and took my copies towards the door. Jane was coming in and blocked my exit.

"Jane, hey," I said nervously. What had she seen? Would she tell Sue to be careful of me? Did Jane still think I was the killer, even after I had accused *her*? Would she tell Sue that I was spying on her?

"Hello."

"Say, do you know if Sue sent out those rejection letters yet?" It was the best I could come up with in such short reaction time.

"I have no idea," Jane replied, looking at me sideways and moving out of my way. She was still suspicious of me; her actions were telling. "Why?"

"Oh, I think I gave her a rejection to something I'm reconsidering. I wanted to see if she'd sent it out yet. I'd like to take another look at the manuscript. It was a long shot. Don't worry about it."

"Sue isn't here today. She was in an accident."

"Yeah, I know."

Jane peered at me, as if looking for lies or guilt. "I didn't tell you."

"Yeah, *thanks* for passing along that important message."

"You obviously found out on your own, so who cares if I didn't tell you? How did you find out?"

"Her boyfriend told me."

"Donnie?" she asked, raising an eyebrow. "You hang out with Donnie?"

"I ran into him at Horton Plaza on my lunch break."

"But how do you know him?"

"I met him last week while he was out with Sue."

"And he was at Horton Plaza today?"

"Yeah. He recognized me and told me what happened to Sue."

Jane stepped aside to let me through the door, but continued talking. "And what did *he* say happened?"

"That Sue was in an accident. Sue didn't tell you that when she called in sick? What did she say?"

"Oh, yeah, pretty much that."

"A car accident?"

"Just an accident," she concluded. She then moved past me out the door and to her desk, picking up the phone and dialing before she even sat down.

I couldn't worry about her right now. Who cared if she was still angry at me for supposedly taking her stupid job? She could have it.

I strode out of the intern office, past Jane speaking low on the phone, and into my own office. Once at the computer, I pulled up Delta Airlines' reservation page and typed in "DJS62278." Where was Sue going? And was Donnie involved? Was Jane?

There it was. She was flying into Phoenix, Arizona. Alone on Friday morning. She hadn't even mentioned to me that she'd be leaving so soon. I turned my attention to the photocopied list of names. LuAnne? I checked our internal directory of the people in the company. No LuAnnes. I pulled up *The San Diego Union-Tribune* website and searched the obituaries. No LuAnne in the recent past. Was it code?

"LuAnne," I muttered, varying it slower and faster, with different enunciations. "L'Ann. Lou Ane. Luan. Luam—" I stopped and continued more quietly. "Liam." I glanced back at the photocopy and noted the thin line through the name. *Liam?*

"Ms. Orwell" was obvious. If this was a hit list, Ms. Orwell, with the thin line through her name, was a hit.

Mrs. C? And me? Okay, I had insulted her manuscript, just as Rain had and that was why I was there. But why was Liam, of all people?

Because everyone thinks you still love him, popped into my mind, thinking back to Starbucks when I got back from Greece. Even people from other departments who I barely knew had the dirt on my failed engagement and how I still lived with my old flame. *Did she dare?* I gritted my teeth.

So who was Mrs. C? Someone who had insulted her writing? Someone also connected to me? Someone I cared about?

Cleo!

I hopped out of my chair and closed the office door. Returning to my desk, I decided to call Cleo right away. Her answering machine picked up.

"Oh, come *on*, Cleo," I whined after the beep. "This is really important. You may be in danger. I think I know who the murderer is! The person who killed Rain, and who tried to kill Liam! Please call me as soon as you get this—" I was about to hang up when Cleo picked up.

"Liz?" she was breathless.

I was in no mood for teasing about her romantic life.

"Don't hang up! I'm here!" she gasped.

"Cleo, listen, I need to talk to you. Is your answering machine off?"

"It's in the other room. I'll erase the message as soon as we finish. Are you at work?"

"Yeah, and I think I know who killed my boss and tried to kill Liam."

Cleo was silent for a moment. And then, "They didn't decide it was a murder, did they? I thought you said it was just an accident."

"I think it was a murder. And you may be in danger."

I heard her walking, and then a door shut. "What kind of danger? Is this about work?"

"Yeah," I stammered.

"Did someone call you?"

"No, *my* work, I meant."

Cleo sighed. "Oh geez, you really worried me there, Liz!"

I paused. What was Cleo so paranoid about? "Are you in some kind of trouble with work, Cleo? You're not translating for some shady client, are you?" I queried.

"Of course I am. The government." I heard her leather chair squeal as she slumped into it. "But I shouldn't be in trouble with them. I just worry with some of the government stuff I do. I'm translating taped conversations of some really weird stuff. Some really, really bad people. Sometimes I just get freaked out. It's hard to 'leave your work at work' when you work from home."

"You need to work for corporations instead, Cleo. Really, work shouldn't do this to you."

"Yeah, you're calling me all paranoid about something from *your* work. So look who's talking."

"No kidding."

"So?"

I took a deep breath. "I'm calling about the murderer."

"You don't really think it was a murder, do you?"

"I do think that, actually."

"Is that what the police have settled on?"

"I think so. But they're not telling me anything—"

"So you're just assuming—"

"Cleo, I'm afraid that you're on her hit list."

"The murderer's hit list?" Hearing the words come from Cleo's mouth made them sound sillier than they seemed in my mind.

"Y—yeah. She has a hit list."

"The murderer is a woman, then?"

"If it is who I think it is. It's all in code. Rain and Liam are on it. Rain's name is clear. Liam's is in code. My name is clear on the list, too, and yours is coded as Mrs. C."

"I'm not married."

"What?"

"I'm not married. So I am not Mrs. C. But other than that, if you've got a list with Rain's name and Liam's name and yours . . ."

"Yeah, except Liam's is coded also."

"Mrs. L?"

Cleo chuckled, which annoyed me. This was serious and she was taking it as a joke.

"No Cleo. *LuAnne.* Say it a few times fast and it comes out as Liam."

"Okay, so who is this supposed murderer?"

"If you're not going to take this seriously—"

"What will you do?"

I was without an answer and she drove home her point.

"You'll call Liam? Freak him out and make him feel even more helpless? Will you call Adam and scare him off by making him think you're a crazy woman? Will you call the police who listened so intently when you called them trying to connect Liam's accident and your boss's?"

I was on the verge of tears. "I'm hanging up on you. You're making fun of me."

I heard the leather chair squeal again as Cleo readjusted herself. "Hey, Liz, I'm sorry. I was being silly, but

I didn't realize you were so upset about this. Listen, I'm only taking it lightly because I think you're overreacting. You do this whenever things get out of your control, and with your boss and Liam and the new workload—"

"But—"

"Come on. A hit list? Do you really think someone might leave that in a place you'd find it? It's just a list of names. Look, I'm getting up right now to go to my desk. I'm looking through the papers on this damn cluttered desk and—here, within fifteen seconds I, too, found a list of names. Some are even in 'code.' I promise it is no hit list, though."

"What does it say?"

"It says: Del, J.E.S., Tech, J, Liz. What a hit list *I've* got, eh?"

"She also has a flight reservation number. And why am I on that list, by the way?"

"I don't have a flight," there was a shuffling of papers, "but here is my Hotel Del Coronado reservation code, right on my desk. That's basically the same thing as a flight reservation code. And that's the first on my list, 'Del,' but they are crossed off because I already called them. Hence the reservation code. And that brings me to why I was going to call you. Good news! I am coming down to San Diego for three days next week. I'm staying at the Hotel Del Coronado. I made reservations and then I had to call my boss— J. E. S. are his initials— to make sure the government was going to cover it even though I was not staying at the Marriott downtown, where everyone else will be staying. I always make things difficult, don't I? He said they'd work it out, and so he's crossed off my list, too. I haven't called the tech team yet, but I need to make sure they can secure my new laptop's wireless Internet so that no messages can be intercepted. I was going to ask Jorge— he's 'J' on my list— to come down to Coronado with me after I cleared the hotel with my boss, and I was going to see if you wanted to double date with Jorge and Adam. Am I a murderer, too? Just because I have a list and a reservation code? Please."

Okay, my mystery-solving skills are weak. Fine. But then I remembered the phone number. "She has a mysterious phone number on her desk, too."

"What makes it so mysterious?"

"I don't recognize it."

"Did you call it?"

Cleo was better at everything. *Fine.* "Fine, I'll call the damn number. I'd forgotten about it until now, to be honest."

"If it's the number to Murderers Anonymous or something, then call me back and I'll say you win and call in my government contacts to make the police department actually listen to your detective work. But otherwise, just calm down, sista. *You're safe.*"

"I don't feel safe."

"I think you're mistaking safe with *satisfied*. Of course you're a little paranoid or uncomfortable. You need to move out, work more on your writing, and get a new job. At least you got the love life stuff covered. Or you did until you let Liam get in the way again."

"We talked it over. You were right. Everyone has some kind of baggage. Anyway, I'm seeing Adam tonight. Pizza and a movie to relax."

"Sounds nice."

"Yeah, it does, doesn't it." I relaxed, leaning back heavily against my chair.

"So let's double date when I come down."

"Sure. And thanks, Cleo. I called to save you, and like always, you kinda saved me."

"Except that you weren't in danger."

"So we think."

❦

I didn't call the toll-free number right away, since I no longer was entirely paranoid. Cleo had done an excellent job of reassuring me, and I was pulled between being grateful for her friendship and feeling sorry for myself for not having someone a little closer to make me feel safe on a regular basis. Ironically I was in the midst of feeling lonely when I was boarding a train to see someone just thirty minutes away who made me feel great. Adam might eventually be my safe house.

When I was settled in my seat on the Coaster, I decided that I should just call the number that I had found in Sue's desk now, before I forgot about it again. It was probably nothing, some contest for a getaway for two to Cabo or something. But this way I could get it off my mind once and for all. I pulled out my cell phone, punched in the number, and turned toward the window, watching the ocean speed by.

"Hello," a woman's voice answered.

What kind of 800 number is this? What business answers with a plain old "hello" these days! How unprofessional! "Hello," I replied, not sure what else to say. The sun glared dramatically on the dark ocean.

"May I ask who's calling?"

"My name is Jane."

Oops.

"Jane, may I help you?"

"I found this number."

"Do you need some help?"

"Yes."

"A safe place to stay?"

What?

"Yes. Is that what this is?"

"It is. How much do you know about us?"

"Not much. I just found . . . my friend handed me this number and she said that I should call."

"It sounds like she's a really good friend, Jane. She may have seen something in your life that you are not yet willing to face. Is your friend a former resident?"

"Maybe."

"And do you agree that you are in danger?"

My eyes refocused and I could no longer see the ocean clearly, just my own reflection in the window, openmouthed. "I used to think so, but I don't think so anymore."

"Are you safe right now? Are you in a safe place where you can talk openly?"

"I think so."

"Let me tell you a little about us. This is Bernadette House, a shelter for victims of domestic violence. I can't tell you exactly where we are, for the safety of our residents, but if you need a safe place to go, we are completely donation based, so it is free to come here. We arrange to meet you at the airport of our nearest big city, and we'll drive you to the home from there. Where are you living now?"

"California. San Diego."

"I suggest flying into Phoenix as soon as it's safe. You can call this number twenty-four hours a day and whenever you get here, we'll send someone over to pick you up. Can I get your full name?"

"I'll call you back." I suddenly hung up. I hated having led her on like that, but I justified my rude hang-up by the fact that she should be helping people in real trouble. Still, I could picture the matronly woman on the other end in a dimly lit room, shaking her head over a phone in her hand with a dead tone. She must be thinking that I was not accepting my situation and fearing that I might go home to my abuser tonight.

A shelter for victims of domestic violence. Sue Talley. A victim. A bitter cocktail of anger and helplessness mixed in the pit of my stomach. I couldn't ask Sue if I could help—she would know I was snooping. I couldn't confront Donnie, because he'd think that Sue was telling me about it and Sue would be in even more danger. The main thing was to let Sue get out of town on Friday and make her way to safety, as quickly and quietly as possible.

The Coaster train slowed as we closed in on my stop. I dialed Cleo and was glad that her answering machine picked up since I didn't have a lot of time to chat. The passengers around me began gathering their things.

"Cleo, this is Eliza. Just confirming that you're right about Sue Talley, that intern. She isn't a bad guy. That number was," I dropped my voice very low, "a domestic violence shelter. Sue's idiot boyfriend Donnie is abusing her. I feel really horrible about all this. Thank you for making me think it through a little more. My plan is to be quiet so Donnie doesn't know Sue is leaving, and of course so that Donnie doesn't know that *I* know that she's leaving. I don't want to be a target either. And I'm not going to say anything to her until she says something first. Okay, I'll talk to you more later."

The train stopped and people filed out. I made my way off the train at the last moment, before it left again. Adam was waiting in an orange beam of streetlight, like a refuge.

CHAPTER 14

I sat on the pastel sofa in Adam's apartment, listening to him rummaging about in the kitchen. He was gathering our drinks, plates, whatever. I couldn't see him, but he was sure making a racket. I got up from the couch, taking the opportunity to check out his small studio apartment. We walked right into the living-room-plus-bedroom area when we had first entered. A short hall at the back of the room led to a bathroom on the left, and a small, enclosed kitchen on the right.

He had used his space well in the main room. The rose sofa backed up against the front wall, one of its arms at the edge of the front door so that if it was pushed a little to the side, it might block the door completely. Along the right wall, making an L with the couch was a black futon, currently closed. I pictured it opened up, meeting the couch in length and making for an extra-wide bed.

I pictured him sleeping there.

I pictured his long, tanned limbs exposed.

His long, dark hair falling around those wide shoulders.

I sucked in a quick breath to cool my suddenly hot throat. *Just wait. No need to imagine something you might experience shortly.*

Behind the futon rose several bookcases full of books. The English major in me knew that what was on those shelves would tell me more about Adam than anything else in the apartment, more even than the awkwardly pink couch. I moved closer to the shelves and read a few titles on the spines.

The Essential Rumi.

The Promise of Light by Paul Watkins.

A Coney Island of the Mind by Lawrence Ferlinghetti.

In Dubious Battle by John Steinbeck.

Gods Go Begging by Alfredo Véa.

Meridian by Alice Walker.

Delicious. I removed the Ferlinghetti book of poems and flipped through it, pleasantly surprised that he had underlined passages and written notes in the margins. Most of the books on his shelves earned him high marks. There were a few books that I had never heard of, and one or two that I didn't like, but that was to be expected. Overall, he fared well on the bookshelf test.

Next in importance was the issue of photographs. A guy can bring you flowers and take you out for fancy meals and win you a stuffed teddy bear at a carnival, but if he doesn't have at least one photo of emotional importance in his apartment, he's not worth your time.

I found two mid-sized photo collages opposite the futon. They contained pictures of his family while he was growing up. Four different camping trips. A birthday party for someone other than himself. Two Halloweens.

Then there were a few pictures from college, in a dorm with walls covered in movie posters. In one, he and three other guys were pointing to a doorknob with a sock on it. Hmm. Then there was a picture of a group of people in front of a store full of brightly colored beaded crafts.

I leaned in closer. A snip of blue beyond the store-front hinted at the Mexican coast. Two of the guys were from the dorm room pictures. There was one other guy and three girls. Adam had his arm around the waist of a beautiful blonde woman.

This was taken a long time ago. Don't you dare be jealous.

Adam was suddenly behind me, and I felt his warm breath on my neck. "We're pointing to the sock because our fifth roommate was finally making a move on his girlfriend. We decided to solidify the memory, but were trying to keep quiet because we didn't want to mess things up. We'd just come home and there was the signal sock on the knob. We took the picture for posterity."

He waited for my reply, but I was so wrapped up in feeling his presence close behind me that I said nothing. Adam placed a large hand gently, casually, on my hip, sending an electric shock through me.

When I still didn't reply, he continued, "I guess it seems kind of insensitive now, but it was funny at the time. Guess I need to make some new memories," he concluded and moved toward the couch.

I turned and followed. I didn't care much about the picture in the dorm. Hell, I probably had a similar one somewhere in my box of photos, except that I was the one behind the door with Liam. I was probably trying to make the move, though, and may or may not have been successful. How could I have missed that he was gay? Suddenly, though, that wasn't important anymore.

I was still curious about the girl in Adam's arms. The blonde. *Why did she have to be a skinny blonde?*

"Were you guys in Baja in that other picture? Visiting your family?"

Adam turned to the wall again and looked past me at the collage, as if trying to figure out which picture I was referencing.

"I don't think I have a Baja picture up there. Oh, I see which one you mean. That's Zihuantaneo, past Baja, further down in Mexico. That was the summer after I graduated. I did a little road-trip-around-Mexico thing for a few months, if you can believe it. A couple of friends joined up for a couple weeks."

"So you took the trip alone?"

"Yeah, it was quite the adventure."

"Sounds dangerous."

"Because it's Mexico?" Adam raised an eyebrow.

"No, but, I mean, people *do* get kidnapped all the time." I was getting off track, and tightrope walking on the edge of insulting his heritage. "At least the newspapers show that. But you must speak Spanish, which probably helped you get around."

"*Si.*"

"And these are just friends who joined in for a couple weeks?" I pretended to study the photograph as I asked, "Who are they?"

He came up beside me again to take a closer look at the photo. "That's Matt and Diego, roommates from college. Matt still lives close by. We hang out pretty often, watch movies and drink a little beer and goof off. He's a lot of fun. I can't wait for you to meet him. I already told him about you, and he's looking forward to meeting you."

He's been talking to his buddy about me! I blushed with pleasure.

"Diego is next to his girlfriend-at-the-time, Kylie. Don't hear from Diego much anymore, other than a Christmas card each year. Next to me is Crystal, my ex-girlfriend. Then there's Brody and Barbara. They got married a few years ago. Living up in the Bay Area now, but Barbara was close to Crystal, so when we broke up that friendship kind of dissipated as well. Too bad, Brody was a good guy."

He made his way back to the couch and I ran over the name *Crystal* in my mind. A name to match the girl.

"Sorry," Adam interrupted my thoughts as we sat down, "about the pastelness and eightiesness of this couch. I bought it from Goodwill back in college to save money and I just never replaced it. It's ugly, but comfy. And I like it until I have someone over and then it embarrasses me."

"Please." I waved it off. "Not a problem." I wanted more information about Crystal, not the couch.

It's not as though I'm jealous. I just want to know why you broke up with such a beauty? Is this where your baggage comes in? My own thoughts surprised me.

Adam set the pizza box on a wooden TV tray and opened it, the spicy scent filling the air.

He handed me a slice on a plate and I sank into the couch.

"So," I tried to nudge a little more info, "what happened with Crystal?"

Adam took a bite of his pizza.

"Oh, we just had different values. I'm usually all right with that to some degree. But it came to a head and there were some major lies and things that have stuck with me." Adam stared off for a moment and then shook his head, as though he didn't want to bring those things back to the surface. "Anyway, we dated for something like six months. One of the last months just happened to be when I first went to Mexico. She wanted to go along, but I was a little uncomfortable with the idea, since I knew things would likely be ending soon with us. She came along with my friends anyway to 'surprise' me."

"Uncomfortable."

"No kidding. I broke up with her in the airport the day she left. I didn't want her to wait for me to return and then break up. Ending it with Crystal was a good move." He finished off his pizza. And then, as if to steer the conversation quickly away from Crystal, he asked, "What happened with your last boyfriend?"

"Oh," I replied, trying to be casual about it, "he was gay." I took the last bite of my four-cheese pizza and waited for his response. I pretended it was no big deal, which was getting easier because it was becoming less painful as I pulled away from Liam.

Adam put another slice on each of our plates. He swallowed another bite before answering. "Dang, that must have been awkward, to say the least."

"What? Finding out he was gay, or telling you right now?"

"Both!" Adam set down his pizza on his plate on the TV tray, and he moved closer. "I'm not surprised he was tempted by you. Imagine, even a gay man wanted to date you!"

We laughed together. No one, including myself, had ever taken that slant, and it was a slant I liked. "You make me feel good about myself. About . . . things. About life."

"Life is good." He wrapped one arm around me. "It *should* be good. It ought to be good for you because you're amazing. Smart. Interesting. Fun. Beautiful."

There was a pause and I watched his face, which was turned toward mine, his eyes watching mine.

"I'm glad you came over tonight, Eliza."

"So am I." This was comfortable. This was spicy.

"And you came over even though it was just pizza and nothing fancy."

"I didn't come over for the pizza specifically. That was an added bonus."

"Then you came over for the movie? Should I just go ahead and start it up?" He playfully acted as though he was going to get up.

"Oh, no, you don't!" I grabbed his arm to pull him back to the couch, but he was too strong, and he pulled me up to him, my body pressing against his. "I came over to see you," I whispered, my face close to his, my lips skimming his without intentionally touching them.

"I was hoping that was the reason. I want you to feel good when you're around me because I have a great time with you."

"I feel comfortable."

"Hmm, comfortable? I'm not sure if that's good."

"Spicy comfortable. And that's a good comfortable."

Adam reached down unexpectedly to pick up the pizza box. "Now that you've seen me, I suppose you'll be wanting to leave," he joked, and moved with the box into the kitchen.

I trailed after him, grabbing his forearm as soon as the pizza box hit the counter. "I can hardly say I've *seen* you at all, what with all those clothes covering you up."

A flashing smile, straight white teeth, soft lips. He gave a throaty laugh and I could see the skin on his neck deepen to red.

"These clothes? They always seem to get in the way, don't they?"

He leaned in for a soft kiss as I kept my grasp on his forearm. He quickly followed that up with a long, lingering kiss, his right arm circling my shoulders. His left hand was on my cheek, trailing down from my temple to my neck, increasing sensually with every millimeter. I rested a hand on his hard thigh, and he moved closer to me until we were one shadow on the wall.

His hand brushed over my breast and then pulled away. I felt my body heat build and build. His fingers feathered over my stomach, and his strong palm glided down my hips to my leg. The building pressure was unbearably sweet.

My hands were exploring the hard muscles of his arms and chest, when suddenly his strong hands closed around my waist, and I was up, spinning around until he set me down and pushed me against the counter. I wasn't going to protest.

His hand slid up, his thumbs hooking the bottom of my blouse and pulling it over my head. The tile counter chilled a line on my back, but the rest of my body was on fire as Adam's fingers searched under my skirt, pulling it up, pulling the wisp lace under it down, down and onto the floor.

I couldn't control myself any longer, and I yanked his shirt over his head. His ponytail came loose and his long black hair fell over his shoulders. The look in his midnight eyes was smoldering, daring me to go further. I found his zipper, and once between my nimble fingers it was down, the slacks sliding from his sculpted hips and down over the muscular *tizi* I'd admired from the first time I'd seen him. Adam plucked off my bra in an instant and stepped back to take in the view. Then, in one swift movement, the silky black boxers were off, thrown on top of the panties and bra on the floor.

Adam stood at attention for half a moment before lunging at me with an animal grunt, pushing me again against the counter. His hands traced my hip and thigh, pulling my right leg up, opening me to his greedy embrace.

With one hand tangled in his hair, I pulled his head down, forced my mouth on his, bit his lip hungrily, unconcerned about any pain. This was pleasure. All pleasure.

I heard a throaty growl escape Adam's lips.

"God, Eliza, God!"

One arm circled my waist, one hand circled my thigh, pulling it up until my knee was against his bicep. He leaned onto me, and I could feel the tip of him brushing the outer petals of my most sensitive core, with the tentative control of something about to break free.

I threw my head back, breasts lifting up and connecting with his eager lips. "Yes, Adam. Take what you want!"

That was all the encouragement he needed. He leaned, entered with a force that pulled me off the floor. The heat of him inside of me, combined with the icy tile on my back, sent thrilled shocks over my body. I felt him deep, and needed him deeper.

Adam needed it, too, and unfolded my leg from the crook of his arm and threw it over his shoulder. And there he was, deeper inside me than I knew existed in my body, hitting a point of pleasure over and over with each new, distinct thrust.

And finally, unable to hold off the growing intensity in my body, I released into ecstasy. My high-pitched cry triggered his own low groan. No articulate words, not his name from my tongue, nor mine from his lips. Only raw ecstasy.

When Adam finally drew away, it wasn't in an embarrassed hurry to gather our clothes. Instead, he went nude to a drawer where he pulled out a dove gray washcloth, and then to the sink where he ran it under the faucet until it was dark with cool, clear water.

Without bothering to wring it out, he brought the washcloth to me, dripping on the floor without a care. When he reached the place where I stood, naked and the slightest bit self-conscious, he laid the cold cloth on my forehead, traced it down my cheek and under my chin. "Somehow, Ms. Tahan, you've worked yourself into quite a frenzy."

"I couldn't have done it alone," I chimed in with a coy smile.

Adam moved the cool, welcome cloth down my neck and over each breast. "I couldn't help myself."

I grabbed the washcloth out of his hand and ran it under the water again. And since he didn't care if the floor got a little wet, I held the cloth over his head and rung it out.

This created just the image I was hoping for. Adam's long hair damped in strands, droplets of water beading at the ends and falling onto the tanned chest, running down the curves of the muscles in his arms.

My fingers traced up the path the droplets had taken from his forearm back up to his collarbone and to his cheek. They circled the mauve ribbon of his soft lips, back and forth, until he opened his mouth to kiss my fingertips.

I licked my lips as his arms reached around me and held my naked body close to his.

"You must think I'm a beast," he announced.

His words glided over my mouth between his kisses. "And why would I think that?"

"Because, remember when you told me to take what I wanted?"

Heat rose in my neck and cheeks. Had I said that? Not that I would ever take it back. "I suppose I did say that, didn't I? How does that make *you* a beast?"

Adam moved to the futon and lowered me onto it. "Because I want to take a little more."

By the time we made it to our pizza dinner, we'd worked up an appetite and enjoyed the picnic of cold pizza as we lay tangled up in the sheets on his futon. As it got later, Adam tried to draw out the time that I would be there, asking questions and starting stories that led nowhere. He enjoyed my company, on an intellectual level as well as the obvious physical level, and this made me enjoy him even more.

I snuggled closer to him on the futon. "Adam, it's after midnight and we've both gotta be at work tomorrow."

"How's work going?"

"We talked about it this morning. You know how it's going. You're just trying to keep me here longer."

"Maybe."

I laughed, but I didn't complain. I didn't *really* want to end the night and go home. I was only trying to be responsible.

"Is the new job getting any easier?"

"Some aspects of it. But I've decided that I don't want the job permanently. I even called our HR manager today to try to tell her."

"Wow. I didn't realize that you were that unhappy with the position. Did the HR person agree to withdraw your application?"

"Yeah. I wanted to get out, like, yesterday. I asked if she could have a different editor fill the position immediately and let me go back to my old job."

"What happened?"

"She didn't listen to me. I don't know if she was ignoring me or if she just didn't want to deal with it. For the time being, what happened was *nothing*."

"No, I mean what happened to give you such negative feelings that you wanted out so badly."

"Oh. A lot of things. To be quite honest, I don't think I'm doing a very good job. And I'm still kinda paranoid about the whole thing with Rain's murder and Liam's attempted murder."

"Stay the night, Eliza. No reason for you to go back and sleep alone. I want to be able to protect you."

His words brought tears to my eyes. *He wants to protect me. I've finally found my hero.*

"I only have this one bed, but that hasn't seemed to be a problem yet." Adam flashed me his killer smile.

"I think I need some real sleep, Adam."

"After the last few hours, so do I."

"All my clothes are at home, and I have to go to work early. This is not a rejection, Adam. I just have to go home." When I stood up, Adam grabbed my hand. His eyes didn't leave mine.

"Eliza, I don't want this relationship to be a flash in the pan."

My heart stopped. "Neither do I."

Only then did his eyes drop to my breasts and hips. "You are so beautiful," he muttered.

"Do you mind driving me to the train station? I know you have to get up early tomorrow, too, but if you could—"

"Train station?" he countered. "If you insist on going home, then I'm going drive you home."

When we arrived at my condo, Adam walked me inside despite my protest that he needed to get home and get some sleep. He took a look around the condo and made sure everything was safe. It certainly made me feel very safe.

"I don't mind staying here, you know."

Adam ran one warm hand up my arm, and I seriously considered his offer. The prospect of falling asleep in his arms was tempting. But sleep? Who were we kidding? Making love until the sun came up was more than appealing, but as unromantic as it was, I really just needed a shower and some rest before work.

"I feel much safer now that you've checked things out. I appreciate it, Adam. I'll let you get home and get some real sleep."

"Okay, but call if you need anything, and I'll come back. I'll call you tomorrow," he whispered, kissing me gently. His kiss was every innocent thing that the rest of the night had not been.

After a quick, hot shower, my skin remained warm with thoughts of Adam, and I instantly felt sexy all over again. I could hardly wait to hear from him tomorrow. To be tempting again, as he'd described me. Tempting.

Looking through my drawer for something to sleep in, I decided this night deserved more than the usual frumpy T-shirt and boxers. I outfitted myself in a short, sexy royal purple nightgown and settled between the cool sheets. My tongue explored my mouth for a lingering taste of the recent kiss. Adam hadn't just made love to me, he'd infiltrated every fiber of my body. I wondered if he was close to home yet, if he was experiencing me again, lingering in his car, in his mouth, on his skin.

A half hour later I was still awake, unable to get the events of the evening out of my mind, so I got up, threw on a light robe, and pulled open the curtains. Pale moonlight flooded the room, to which I added a narrow streak of yellow light from the nightstand lamp. I found my notebook from Greece and I removed a blank sheet of paper. I was feeling inspired again, ready to tackle my life-changing resolutions. Filled with determination, I wrote:

Liam:
We need to get to the business of selling the condo.
Liz

I taped the note to his bedroom door where he'd see it in the morning. When I returned to my room, I'd barely switched off the lamp and crawled between the sheets before I fell fast asleep.

CHAPTER 15

On Thursday morning, the first thing I did was rework my comments on Sue's manuscript. We were coming up on the weekend and I needed to get this done before Sue was out of here.

I used the same technique as I did with any promising manuscript, picking out all the good points and really highlighting them. I then mentioned what made it "not quite right" for J Press and ended the review with something a little more hopeful for the future. I tried to be as in-depth as possible, mentioning a couple of obvious things that could use some work.

When I finished, I buried it under a stack of the other manuscripts she had given me (all with comments and rejections), and called the intern office. Murphy, another intern who I rarely saw because he rarely showed up, answered the phone, surprising me. "Oh, hello, Murphy," I said.

"You know my name?"

"Yeah, of course," I replied. *Though you never show up.* "Can I speak with Sue?"

"Sure," he said and I heard some shuffling. It sounded like Sue asked who it was and Murphy said he didn't know. Sue asked if it were a man or woman, and Murphy confirmed it was a woman.

"All right," I heard her say. She picked up the phone and asked softly, "Yes?"

"Sue, it's Eliza."

Sue sighed. Was it in relief? Did she think Donnie was calling her?

"Oh, hey, Eliza. I actually wanted to meet with you. May I come over to your office?"

"Yeah, absolutely. That's why I called. Come on over."

She assured me she would and a minute later she was in my office with several spreadsheets. She shut the door with her elbow and set the spreadsheets on my desk.

"These list all the manuscripts that have been submitted and rejected in the past year," she explained, pushing the spreadsheets closer to me and topping the stack off with a CD-R. "The author's name, title, notes, stuff like that. I printed it out and also saved it electronically since I wasn't sure which you preferred."

I was thoroughly impressed with the sheer number of spreadsheets here. "Wow, Sue, this must have taken forever."

"It *felt* like it sometimes."

"The other interns helped, didn't they?"

"Well . . ."

"You did it without any help?"

"It's just that I'm the only person here on a regular basis. So it kinda fell on me. But I didn't mind."

"I'm sorry about that, Sue. I assumed it would be a project you'd all work on. Not something to get piled onto one person."

"That's how group work goes, isn't it?"

"If I'm remembering correctly from school, yes. I should have thought about that. Please know that we won't be giving full internship credit to *all* the interns. Some of the more, um, unreliable people won't get it. You'll get the credit, though." I flipped casually through the pages, anxious to look through them.

"Yeah, I know, which is why I'm sorry to tell you this. I should have given you more notice, but I wanted as few people as possible to know. Today is going to be my last day."

I tried to look surprised. "I'm sorry to hear that, Sue. Did you get a new job?" I surveyed the yellowing bruises on her face, almost hidden now with the help of time and makeup.

She turned to make sure that the door was closed, then leaned over my desk secretively. "I'm moving out of the state. To a shelter for victims of domestic violence."

"Because of Donnie?"

Sue nodded, folded her hands on the desk and whispered, "I wish I could have told you before. It would have been so nice if you had known. You could have, like, helped me or something. I was confused. He . . . he loves me and he is so supportive and positive most of the time. He just has a temper, as much of a cliché as that sounds. Anyway, I'm not taking it anymore. I knew he'd find me if I went to a friend's house. Or if I went to a shelter in San Diego, he'd find me back at school or work. I want to get really far away from him."

"And so you chose a place out of state?"

"Jane chose it, actually."

"Jane?" I tired to conceal the shock in my voice, but even I knew my attempt was feeble.

"Yeah. She's wonderful, isn't she?"

I didn't answer, but looked at the closed office door and pictured Jane sitting right outside it. *Wonderful Jane? The same wonderful Jane who threatened me with scissors?*

Of course, she had thought I was the murderer. And hadn't I, moments before, glanced at those same scissors as a possible weapon against her? She just got to them first.

"It was Jane that finally confronted me about Donnie. You probably noticed that I had a fat lip at Sea World. Donnie had hit me when I got home from class because I had cancelled our date the next day to come in to work on those rejection letters. I finally agreed to stick with our plan, and then he felt bad about hitting me, so he took me to Sea World for dinner at that barbeque place. Not like it was much of a stretch for him, seeing as we have annual passes. But it got me to forgive what he'd done."

She shook her head and muttered, "So stupid" under her breath. Then she looked up and continued.

"Well, after he hit me, I called work. Jane was still here, I guess it was around four-thirty. I told her I didn't feel well and wouldn't be able to make it into work tomorrow. Jane said I didn't sound sick, and said it was suspicious that I was calling in sick so far in advance. I thought she was being a bitch and giving me a hard time, but she was really just trying to get me to tell the truth. She asked if Donnie was there with me, and when I told her he was in the shower, she said she knew what he'd done. I acted like I didn't know what she was talking about, and then she gave all these examples of stuff she'd noticed. Bruises, this sprained wrist I had, whatever. I started crying and I think that gave it away. I said it would be okay, that we were going out to dinner and that we were still going to go on our date tomorrow, and now he was happy. But just to mark me as 'sick,' if possible. I hope that doesn't reflect badly on me. Or Jane. Other than that, I've never faked sick before. And she was only trying to keep me safe. I promise."

"No, no. Don't worry about it." I pictured her cut lip, how she had smiled crookedly at Sea World, as if to keep her mouth from bleeding again. My stomach hurt, knowing I hadn't said anything. Why hadn't I called the police right then and there, asked them to go to Sue's apartment and arrest Donnie as soon as they got home? My conscience pained me. I hadn't done anything to help. Instead, I had called myself a damn cab.

"After Sea World," Sue continued as if reading my mind, "we got home and the police were there. Jane told me later that she'd called them as soon as she got home that night. Donnie was livid, and I was afraid. I almost told them that Donnie had hit me a few hours before, but then I kept thinking that they might put him in jail and as soon as he posted bail he would come back and kill me. I kept thinking about that. So I said nothing was wrong. When they left, Donnie accused me of ratting him out and demanded to know whom I'd told. I didn't tell him about Jane knowing, even though at the time I didn't know that she was the one to have called the police. He beat me up really bad, yelling at me that I was a liar, and a traitor, and unfaithful, and pretty much every awful thing he could think of. I was almost unconscious and he was still raving. He said he'd kill me if I tried to leave. He'd never threatened me like that before, and at that moment I knew I needed to get away."

Sue was crying now, and I took her hand.

That's all you can do? I accused myself. *Hold her hand? And you've been complaining for weeks about Jane, when she's the one who actually called the police and tried to save Sue?*

"So after Donnie went to bed, leaving me lying on the kitchen floor, I just kept thinking about how I could escape. I called Jane the next day, after Donnie went to work, to ask if she was the one to call the police. I told her how he beat me up and that I wanted her help to get away. She booked a flight for me. She even used her own credit card so Donnie wouldn't know if he checked our statement online. She found the place out-of-state."

Sue pulled out a familiar note. "She put my reservation on a note in my desk here so Donnie wouldn't see it at home. She even listed the people I wanted to tell on the note, too. My sister, my college counselor, and you or Ms. Li. I wasn't sure who should receive resignations. I decided to tell you, though, because I really trust you. Don't tell anyone, please, Eliza. Please. I plan to pretend to go to work on Friday, get on the plane, and never come back. Don't even tell Ms. Li until Monday afternoon. I mean, if that's possible."

"I won't say a thing until Monday. And I'll compose a glowing recommendation letter that you can take with you and use when you're ready to get a new job."

"Thanks, Eliza. You've been just the best boss." She lifted a pen from the cup on my desk and crossed my name off her list.

What a great boss you are, my mind accused sarcastically. But I smiled, picking up the stack of manuscripts for her.

"Here are the manuscripts that you wanted comments on. Maybe you can use them as a training tool for another intern before you leave. I included extensive comments on your . . . the manuscript you were especially interested in. I'm sorry it took so long. You can incorporate however much you'd like into your letter to the, um, author. Even add some of your own comments if you want."

"Sure," she said hesitantly, her anxiety evident, though, by how quickly she grabbed the pages.

I leaned across the desk. "Listen, Sue, do you need a place to stay tonight? You're more than welcome to stay with me."

She waved it off. "No, no, though I appreciate the offer. The woman at the shelter said to sneak off without a trace. I have no excuse to give to Donnie about spending the night at your place. And I don't want him getting suspicious. And if I stay with you, he might assume you helped me escape, and I don't want you to be a target."

A target, I mused, feeling the old worry that I was the real *target* instead of Rain or Liam. I nodded, thumbing the pages of the author list. I was ready to get to the bottom of this and move on once and for all.

Sue nodded towards the spreadsheets and CD. "Do the police think it was an author who killed Ms. Orwell?"

"Maybe. It seems most likely. Could've been a rejected author. You know from checking cover letters that some authors can go off the deep end."

"The world is full of crazy people."

"You said it."

Sue stared past me as her hand moved up her neck to touch her bruised left cheek. Almost to herself she muttered, "You always think the bad guy is the anonymous stranger."

I looked away, feeling as though I were intruding on a personal moment.

Sue then rose from the chair, lifting the manuscripts as she got up. "Thanks for this, Eliza. I really appreciate it. I can't wait to read your comments."

"I appreciate your interest."

She skimmed through the stack and pulled out her manuscript, setting it on top. She saw me watching her and explained, "I'm just most interested in this one. I'll read your comments on this first."

"Sounds good." I looked down at the pages she'd given me. *Will I find the murderer amongst these pages? Will the constant anxiety in the pit of my stomach finally be calmed?*

"Do you have any suspicions about who did it?" I asked Sue.

Our minds had now gone in completely different directions, with me contemplating my new list of suspects and Sue excited to read comments on her novel. Which would explain why Sue assumed I meant "whodunit" from her own manuscript—as though I had read it and rejected it, but was intrigued by the mystery of the submitted first fifty pages. Without meaning to, I had given her hope that her manuscript had potential. Her face burst into a smile. "Well, Eliza, you'll find out when it gets published somewhere else and you can read the rest!" She patted the manuscript, beaming with pride.

"Oh!" I replied, realizing that we were on different pages now. "Okay."

She moved to the door and made her exit, but not before a friendly wink and a cheerful, "Just remember, it's always the person you least expect."

I checked the hard copy of the spreadsheets briefly before putting the CD she'd made into my computer to email the information to the police department. *As though they'll do anything with this information anyway.*

I typed in Detective Wilson's email address and wrote a short note:

Hello Detective:
Per our recent conversation, please find attached the file of all authors who have been rejected in the past year. I have not looked at it yet, but will do so in the next few days. I'll

let you know if I notice anything suspicious. In the mean-time, please feel free to contact me with any questions.

Regards,
Eliza Tahan
J Press

For some reason, holding the spreadsheets listing author names, locations, submission dates, and manuscript details, I was no longer scared. I most likely had the name of a killer in there somewhere, and it was only a matter of time until I figured out who it was. I was in control. I was closing in. And because our murderer hadn't struck again, he must not know that I was getting closer.

But what if he does know?

I shook my head as if to clear the thought. This was not the time to overreact. I was at work. Not only did I not want that tendency to slip into my professional life, I wanted to correct it in my personal life.

Just because you're at work at this moment doesn't mean that you're no longer in danger. Doesn't mean you're safe.

I was on the edge of succumbing to fear again, calling Cleo to have her talk some reason into me, when I got a call saying my car was ready to be towed from the police impound yard.

"What time do you usually close?"

"We close at five every weekday except Monday, when we close at seven."

She added that I should have my insurance pay for the repairs for the time being, that is, if the car could be repaired. If they caught the other driver, his insurance would reimburse the cost. That way I would not have to wait any longer than I already had.

"*When* they catch the other driver," I countered confidently. "Not if."

She was disinterested and already hanging up.

It didn't matter that she didn't reply, because I'd remained calm. I had taken that my car might be totaled very well.

My confidence was back.

"Cleo, my dear," I said, trying to get my things together from my desk while cradling the phone on my shoulder.

"Sounds like you want something," she teased.

Did my sister know me, or what? Luckily, I knew her, too, and was certain she'd have no problem with my request.

"Yeah, yeah. Hey, I'm going to pick up my car on Monday. Sounds like it's in pretty bad shape. Do you think if I had it towed up to Jorge's garage, he'd have time to work on it?"

"Hmmm . . ."

"Oh, I didn't mean for free! I'll pay him whatever he charges everyone else. It's just that I think if *you* trust him with your hot cars, I should trust him with my mine. I just don't want to be taken for a ride, and I don't know enough about cars to know if I am getting ripped off. Jorge is an honest guy, isn't he?"

"Y—Yeah. Let me give you his number."

She rustled through her papers and called out the digits and I jotted them down on a piece of paper. I almost said thanks and ended it there, but I caught myself on her hesitant tone. "So what's going on with you and Jorge?"

She brushed it off. "Oh, nothing really."

I waited, knowing she would follow with what was wrong.

"It's just that he's been really busy. And I sometimes worry that . . . well, that it isn't just his garage that keeps him busy. That maybe there's someone else."

Apply sympathy. "Oh, Cleo! That's awful! How *could* he?"

"I know, I know!"

Follow sympathy with a *small* dose of rationalization. "You know his time could easily be occupied with his job. He's a guy passionate about his trade. That's probably one of the reasons you're attracted to him. You're the same way about your job."

"I know. You're right."

Complete treatment with a helpful offer. "Do you want me to do a little detective work on him? Or do you want to stay with me for a few days?"

"No, that's all right. I'm already keeping an eye on him. Maybe I'm misusing my government-supplied access to information, but I don't think they'll care. Everyone probably does it. And I'll be down next week anyway. We can get together and talk more. But thanks. You're a good sister."

Lace with solidarity. "And you are an amazing woman. If he doesn't see that, he's insane. And *I'll* take my car to someone else. Even if Jorge isn't unfaithful, he still ought to be treating you right, and so he doesn't get any of *my* money."

Cleo sighed. "Thank you, Eliza. And speaking of asshole boyfriends, what happened with the girl at your work who you thought might be abused?"

"She's leaving tomorrow for the shelter. I offered to let her stay with me—"

Cleo gasped. "No, Eliza! You don't want the boyfriend targeting you! We already talked about that!"

"I know. Sue Talley, the intern, said the same thing when I offered it. She said he might assume I helped her escape, and that she doesn't want me to be a target."

"She's right!"

"Yeah. It's nice of her. But hell, I *know* about it, don't I? I'm covering for her, aren't I? I think I'm past being part of her escape. If I'm a target, I'm a target. I can't not do the right thing to help an innocent victim, just because I'm covering my own ass."

"She can take care of herself. Don't get yourself hurt, Eliza."

"I'm not going to worry about it. She'll be on the plane tomorrow morning, and this will be over. I just wish I could have been more help to her."

Cleo remained silent for a moment and then finally replied. "You're a good person, Eliza. And I think you're right—you don't have to worry about David or whatever his name is—"

"Donovan. Donnie."

"Right, whatever. That girl, Sue Talley, is safe, and so are you."

"I can't wait for you to visit next week, Cleo."

"Me either, sista. We are due for some more bonding."

CHAPTER 16

On Friday morning I was quite conscious of Sue's absence. I pictured her in the air on her hour flight to Phoenix to her new and safer life. I felt so heavily *her* safety that I had forgotten that I still had a slight worry about my own.

After a brief meeting with a colleague, a graphic designer responsible for many of the mystery department's covers, regarding an author who didn't like the font she'd chosen for his title, I returned to my office and Jane followed me in, shutting the door behind her.

Instinctively, I scanned her hands for weapons, and instantly felt bad about it. This was the woman who had secured Sue's escape. I forced myself to relax, and said, "Hi, Jane. I actually wanted to talk to you—"

Jane flopped down in the chair, rested her elbows on the desk and let her head fall forward into her hands. Blonde ringlets followed the forward motion of her head.

Is she going to cry or something? Should I say something?

"She told me she'd told you she was leaving." Her words were muffled.

"Yeah, she told me yesterday. I wanted to thank you for what you did for her."

"Have you heard from her yet?"

I looked over at my calendar to be certain it was *the* Friday. "No, it's Friday. She should be on the plane right now. Why?"

Head still in her hands, Jane said, "She's not on the plane."

I froze. "How—how do you know?"

"I checked online. We used my credit card to order the ticket, so I had online access. She never boarded."

"Is she all right?"

"I don't know," Jane said, looking up at me finally. Her voice and eyes plainly showed that she was on the verge of frustrated tears. "I was hoping you knew something!"

"Did . . ." I started and then stopped, as though if I dared to say it, it might make it real.

Jane wasn't as careful. "—Donnie find out? I was wondering the same thing. So I called their place and no one answered. I left a message, thinking maybe someone was screening the call. I said I was calling from work and wondering why she was not in today. I'm so scared for her, Eliza."

I was surprised at her openness, possibly stemming from Sue's trust in me or from the current, desperate situation. "I'm calling the police," I announced, determined to take charge here. Whatever I did not do for Sue in the past I'd make up for right now.

"I don't think they'll go over there again. Last time I called them Sue said everything was okay."

"Don't worry. I know someone. He'll help us." I dialed my own personal contact at the police department.

The phone rang twice before the authoritative voice answered. "Hello. This is Detective Wilson."

"Hi. This is Eliza Tahan, and no, this is not about Ms. Orwell's murder. Actually, I was wondering if you could help me with something else." I explained that a colleague at work who had been consistently abused by her boyfriend was supposed to escape this morning to a shelter, but that she never boarded her plane. I asked if he could see if there was anything reported about her this morning. "If not, maybe you can get someone to go over and check her house. I just want to make sure she's all right."

"What's her name?"

"Sue Talley. Her boyfriend is named Donnie. Or Donovan."

Jane made a face at the mention of his name.

Detective Wilson surprised me by answering, "Is his surname Kelley?"

I gasped, tapping Jane's arm to show her something was up. "I . . . I'm not sure. Just a second." I held the phone aside and asked Jane, "Is Donnie's last name Kelley?" She nodded with as much fear in her eyes as I had in my heart. I confirmed the name with the detective. "Yes, Donovan Kelley. Tall and blond. A surfer-type guy, as though that narrows it down much in this city."

"Your colleague Sue is fine," Detective Wilson confirmed. "She's just shaken up. I can't say the same for her boyfriend, though."

"What's happened?"

"I can't say much right now, but I suggest you check online at *The San Diego Union-Tribune*'s website. They'll have the story with as much detail as I could tell you."

I wedged the phone between my head and my shoulder and immediately began typing in the site. "But Sue's all right? She isn't hurt?"

"No, she isn't hurt. And I don't think she will have to escape anytime soon."

Once the website loaded and I had hung up with Detective Wilson, I turned my computer screen so that both Jane and I could see it. "He said I should look on *The San Diego Union-Tribune*'s site for information."

"But Sue's okay?"

"That's what he said." I scrolled down the page, searching for the familiar name.

"I hope she cut off his—"

But then both our eyes landed on the story. Donovan Kelley, a student at San Diego State, was bicycling to his part-time job early this morning when a driver going through a red light struck him. He died within the hour. There was a headshot of Donnie, probably from his university ID card or driver's license. It was definitely him.

"So he's dead?" Jane asked weakly. "They're sure?"

I re-read the short article, thinking I might have missed something. "It looks that way."

"It didn't say that Sue was okay."

"Yeah, but Detective Wilson said she was. The article doesn't even mention her. If she was hurt, it would've mentioned her."

Jane slumped back in the uncomfortable chair. "Well . . ."

"Yeah."

We were both unsure of how to feel. Creeping up on me was the same ambivalence that I'd felt when Rain was killed. A mixture of relief and guilt. Except with less guilt.

Jane made no motion to leave. Just sat in the chair and stared absently at her hands. Finally she announced with a sigh, "If anyone deserved it, it would be Donnie."

I nodded, finally feeling only relief.

"Eliza, thanks for calling your friend."

"Thank you for setting everything up for Sue. I'm sorry I thought you killed Rain." I laughed at the words, which sounded so cheesy coming out of my mouth.

"I'm sorry I thought *you* killed Rain."

The last few weeks of hostility drained away, and we were back to the way we'd been before Rain's death.

"Thanks for telling me that Sue hadn't gotten on the plane."

"Do you think she'll come back to the company?"

"I don't know. She can do whatever she wants now."

"She's free."

"And she's safe."

Liam was feeling better, and had decided to spend the weekend with James at his apartment. They were polite enough to invite me over on Friday night, saying that they'd just be renting a movie and ordering out from Lotus Thai down the street. I thanked them both, but I declined. I certainly appreciated the offer even if there was no way I'd take them up on it. Besides, I wanted to get through the spreadsheets of rejected authors from San Diego to see if I could come up with a murder suspect.

After a night of that, my eyes were crossing and I couldn't even contemplate another day of it. I called Adam and he was up for a daytime hike, though he had work he had to finish that night. I took him up on the offer, even though I hadn't been hiking in years.

The Boulder Loop trail at Daley Ranch, where he took me, turned out to be the perfect date hike. It was long enough and steep enough that I was able to prove that I could be sporty, and beautiful enough that I could actually enjoy it despite a lack of trees. We wandered off the trail in parts to mosey among the large tan rock formations, laughing together at suggestively shaped boulders. We climbed together on the more accessible formations, and made out in the shadow-cooled dust of an enormous boulder that kept us entirely out of view of the trail.

Adam dropped me off at home around dinnertime and topped off the day with a sweaty, dusty embrace before leaving. I breathed in the scent of him. Rugged. Manly. I soaked it up, hoping I could keep it with me. Rugged Adam. *My* man.

On Monday, the tow truck met me at the impound yard. The driver, a tall, sturdy woman in her late forties or early fifties, was there just in time to see me break down just a little. After settling the paperwork, I'd found the misshapen heap that used to be my perfect-for-me car. It was so mangled on the driver's side that I could hardly imagine how Liam survived.

As I ran my hand over the crushed metal, the tears began to flow. The tow truck driver approached me and rested a sympathetic hand on my shoulder. "Honey, you are lucky to be alive," she drawled with a slight Southern accent. "It doesn't seem right to mourn over an inanimate object when you're alive after an accident like this."

I looked over my shoulder at her. "Are you an author?"

She looked at me blankly. I took that as a no.

"Anyway, I wasn't in the car. It was my roommate."

She bowed her head. "Oh, your roommate. I'm so sorry." Her hand rested even heavier.

"He's alive. He almost didn't make it. Some people deserve what they get," I thought of Donnie, "but my roommate didn't deserve this. It was a miracle that he even survived. I didn't realize how much of a miracle until now." I waved my hand at the wreck.

"I'll say it's a miracle," the driver agreed, and moved back towards her truck. "Now, where are we taking the car?"

"Let's bring it to my place for now. I guess I didn't realize it was really this bad. In the end, I may just have to have it totaled."

"Definitely should be an option for you, honey. This is in pretty bad shape. Now, let me get it hauled up on the flatbed. Is there anything in there that you want to get out before I put it up? Anything that might fly off on the freeway? How far are we going?" She was setting up the device that would pull my car onto the truck.

"Not far. But, of course, this is California so there's definitely a freeway involved. Let me check in the car."

I managed to get the trunk open and retrieve the manuscripts and paperwork from before my trip to Greece. I placed them in the passenger side of the tow truck, and then got the passenger side door open.

When I leaned inside I saw big, black stains dried into the upholstery and carpeting and splattered across the dashboard. For a moment it didn't register.

"What is all this?"

Then my eyes moved up to the windshield. The parts of glass that hadn't shattered had stains as well, and with the light shining on them, I saw the hint of red. Deep red. Blood red.

"Oh, my God," I muttered as nausea spread over me. I backed out of the car in a flash, and began pacing, breathing deeply, and whispering, "Oh, my God."

The tow truck driver saw me and called over, "Hey! You okay there, honey?"

I nodded, but kept pacing.

"You need me to get something out of the car for you?"

I stopped and considered taking her up on the offer. *But why should she have to face all that blood when Liam is my friend, and this is my car? I can do it.*

So I answered, "I think I can do it," and stared at the passenger door. The driver went back to her work.

"Okay," I whispered to myself. "You can do this. In and out. Real quick. Face it once and it's over."

Four large steps and I was at the car again. I leaned in without touching anything, trying to keep my eyes from the seats and carpet and dashboard. I grabbed the few manuscripts, a jacket, and my umbrella from the back seat. I pulled out, dropped them on the ground unceremoniously, and from outside the car, I gazed at the glove compartment.

A few droplets of blood stained the edge, but the handle was clean. I reached in, opened the glove compartment, and with one movement scooped everything out and into my arms. My insurance information, my vehicle handbook, a handful of CD cases.

Then I shut the door and turned my back on it. "It's over," I told myself, and immediately tried to erase from my memory what I'd seen inside.

"I think that's all," I said to the driver as I made my way to the front of the truck again. "Should I just climb in, or do you need my help?"

"Honey, I've been doing this for twenty-three years. And unless you can do something this automatic crank can't, go ahead and hop in the cab."

I passed the minutes in the cab looking through the CDs. *Crossroads. Bringing It All Back Home. The Living Sea* soundtrack.

The Living Sea? That wasn't my CD, and finding it unsettled me.

My mind flashed back to Liam, upset and crying for us to stop the DVD we'd rented of *The Living Sea*.

Cleo had suggested that the other driver might have been playing the CD when he hit Liam.

I was furious at Liam! How could he have made us believe that it was someone else playing this music when he crashed? How could he have given us that false lead? And why did he pretend not to know this music? He was obviously listening to it when he was in the accident or it would not have freaked him out. So why the hell had he assured us that he hadn't heard the music before the accident?

I dialed his cell phone, not caring if he was resting or getting his groove on with his new love. He was going to have to explain this.

"Liam?" I asked when he picked up the phone without a salutation.

"Why are you calling me?"

"How are you feeling?" I asked.

"All right, I guess. Why are you calling? Can I call you back later?"

"I'm picking up my car right now and found a CD of yours in it."

"Cool, just bring it home with you. I'll see you tonight."

"Don't you want to know which CD it is?"

"It doesn't matter. Just bring it home."

"I think you'll want to know."

Liam sighed, "Just a sec." I heard him speak softly, away from the phone, but I couldn't make out what he was saying. When he returned to the phone he sighed again before speaking. "Okay, Eliza, which CD is it?"

"*The Living Sea*!" I declared.

"I don't even know what that is. Must be yours."

"It isn't mine. And you were the last person in my car."

"I told you, I don't know that album."

"It's a soundtrack."

"Listen, Lizzy, I really can't talk right now. I didn't bring any CDs into your car, and unless you borrowed one of mine, then I can't imagine why any of my CDs would even *be* in your car."

I backed down at his logic. "Okay. I guess you *might* be right."

"It isn't a question of who's right. I don't own that CD, and that's plain fact. Okay?"

"Yeah, okay."

"Is that all?"

"Yeah. Sorry for bothering you."

"Okay, Lizzy. I'll be home later tonight. See you then."

We hung up and the tow truck driver hopped in the cab and started the engine. "Okay, honey, ready to get this thing home?"

"I sure am," I assured her, still thinking about the CD.

"Were you on the phone with your mechanic?"

"No, no, just a friend. My roommate, actually. He's the one who was borrowing my car when it was crashed. I thought this CD was his, but it isn't." I held up the CD case, then set it back on my lap.

"Well, if it isn't his, and it isn't yours—"

"Exactly," I interrupted. "Whose is it?"

"I was *going* to say that no one can say no to me popping it in the CD player for the ride to your place." She laughed and I opened the CD case. She grabbed the CD inside and fed it to her CD player.

It began playing as we pulled out of the impound yard and initiated a nice and uncomplicated conversation. The driver was married with no kids but a handful of pets, dogs, cats, and a ferret that she made me swear never to tell the California State Government she had. I told her the broad outline of my situation, living with an ex, dating someone new.

"How does your new man feel about you living with your ex?"

"I think he's all right with it." I thought back to Adam's reaction when he found out I was living with Liam. Had I even told him that Liam and I had been a couple? If not, how *would* he feel if he knew?

The driver, keeping her eyes on the road, continued, "At least you told him. If he's continued to see you, then it must not bother him too much. If you hadn't told him already, I was just going to say that you'll have a confrontation sooner or later about why you're living with an ex-lover. And why you hadn't told him. So, it's good he knows."

I nodded, anxious to talk to Liam about selling the condo. I had been afraid of the hassle of selling it and finding a new place to live when he first brought it up. But now with Adam in my life, the fear had been replaced with a sense of urgency. We had to get this done before Adam found out how deep my relationship with my roommate had once been. Before he took me for some kind of liar. Again. And besides that, I was really ready now to get on with my life.

The driver seemed to know that she had sparked a train of thought and fell silent. I rested my elbow on the edge of the door and looked out the windshield. To the left heading north on Interstate 5, there was a beautiful ocean view with the setting sun turning the sky shades of orange, red, and purple. I glanced away to the passenger-side mirror to check the traffic behind us. We were in the slow lane and I could see people in the passenger seats of the cars behind us pointing at the wreck on the back of the tow truck before passing.

Just then I saw a familiar face in the car behind us, but one that I couldn't quite place. I turned around to look out the rear window, but my crushed car blocked my view. I returned to the mirror. Long blonde hair surrounding pale skin. Who was this?

Not someone from work, at least not anyone I knew personally. Not a college classmate either, that I could remember.

Where have I seen this girl? I kept studying her in the mirror, all the while trying to push down the sick feeling in my stomach.

Why is she following us, and where do I know her from?

"What is it?" the driver asked.

"There's someone in the car behind us that looks familiar. But I can't seem to place her."

"An old friend maybe?"

"No, I don't think so."

"Yeah, you seem too worried for it to be a friend."

"Sorry, I'm just . . ."

"Worried. Right. But why are you worried?"

This wasn't helping. What was I supposed to say? That she might be a murderer who'd found me before I found her? That maybe I'd been followed before? The driver would think I was crazy. Paranoid. And maybe I was, but I wasn't going to let on to a complete stranger.

"It's just annoying me that I can't remember where I've seen her before."

"Let me slow up a bit. They're sure to pass us, and you'll get a better look." She did, and I saw the car move slowly to the left and out of my mirror view. I leaned forward past the driver and she leaned back against the seat to give me a better view out her driver's side window.

The picture on Adam's wall!

This girl, at least from my memory, matched up perfectly. The beautiful blonde wrapped up in Adam's arms in Zihuantaneo.

Crystal.

How could she still look *so* perfect? How many years ago had that picture been taken? Crystal didn't seem to have aged *at all*. Had the picture been taken much more recently than Adam had led me to believe?

The car was passing us slowly, and I now turned my attention to the car itself. I gasped. A burgundy-maroon Mustang. I leaned over even more, but from the height of the tow truck, I could only see the passenger seat.

Drawing in a deep breath, I leaned back to wait for the car to pass us completely so that I could look at the bumper stickers.

Don't love Steinbeck! Please!

They passed us. I saw the sticker: *I –heart- Steinbeck.*

In the driver's seat I could make out the figure of a man, the setting sun throwing him into silhouette.

Either some random stranger and Crystal had stolen Adam's car, or that was Adam out with her.

I shook with disappointment and with fury. How *dare* he? Either they've gotten back together, or he never stopped seeing her.

I'm the other woman.

The driver looked at me and then back at the road. "Not someone you were hoping to see?"

I didn't reply, but bit my lip hard, and she let it go. We didn't speak on the rest of the way to the condo. My mind was filled with curses for Adam and his waif-like little blonde.

After I paid the driver and she left, I pulled out my cell phone and dialed Cleo's house. I sat there in the driveway next to my crushed car, tears in my eyes. When her answering machine picked up, I remembered that she was on her way to San Diego today. I hung up without leaving a message and dialed her cell. If she was still driving, she wouldn't answer. Ever since the accident with Dad she'd been a careful driver who did not approve of distractions while on the road, and that included talking on a cell phone. I was not surprised when her voicemail picked up.

"Cleo, it's me. I'm really, really upset right now. Can you call me back when you get a chance? And I'm not overreacting. So don't say that when you call or I'll be really mad. Okay, call me. I'll be up late."

I paused, wondering how much to tell her. I didn't want her to think I was hurt, so I decided to go ahead and tell her the upsetting news via voicemail. "Okay, here it is. I saw Adam with his supposedly ex-girlfriend *Crystal. Crystal!* And yes, her looks match her perfect little name. I've seen a picture of her in his house and he said it was from a long time ago, and that she was an ex. *Right!* I think he's been cheating on me with her. Or cheating on her with me, which would be even worse. I'm not even in the 'real' relationship. I feel like going over there right now and . . . I don't know what! Kicking him right in the groin or something. Damn it, Cleo, I am so upset. How did I get so wrapped up in him so quickly? And to think he flipped out when he thought Liam and I were a couple! He said it was because his ex had lied and now he's the liar! Sorry for this disjointed message. Call me when you get this. Please, just give me a call. I'm so upset."

I hung up and wanted to sit in the driveway and wait for her to call back, not go inside with my tear-streaked face and have Liam ask what the matter was. I didn't want to admit that my new romance was a fake.

But I didn't even know if Liam was home yet. And who knew how long it would be until Cleo could call me back? And I didn't want to explain myself to any neighbors taking their dogs for evening walks. I hardly knew any of these people, but they'd ask if I was okay and I didn't want to explain it to them. They wouldn't want to hear it all anyhow.

So I left the wreck in the driveway and went inside. I didn't want the sight of it to frighten Liam or upset our neighbors so I covered it in sheets and decided that if I did not have a plan for the thing soon, I'd invest in a car cover.

Of course, the best option would be to make a plan after the guy who hit my car was caught and his insurance could pay for the damages. Or a new car. Maybe a hybrid. Maybe a cute little Miata. Maybe a huge Hummer to smash into Adam's Mustang. Mentally giving myself a shake, I extracted the spreadsheets and manuscripts from my bag to read while I had dinner. Liam wasn't home yet, and I wondered if he'd just said he'd be home tonight to get me off the phone. I didn't want to have the talk with him tonight anyway. I was too damn angry.

With the spreadsheets under my arm, a glass of pineapple-orange juice in one hand and a plate of quesadillas in the other, I climbed to my room and planted myself on the floor. If Liam came home and decided to check on me, fine. But if he didn't, that was even better. I needed to use my time wisely.

I'll figure out this mystery and catch this asshole, no matter how long it takes.

My fury at Adam came out in the compulsive search for a murderer.

After many hours, I was exhausted. My plate was greasy and empty, and I'd continually refilled my glass in the bathroom sink, despite my distaste for unfiltered water. I gulped down the remaining tap water and lay back on my bed. My eyes were starting to blur from reading name after name and title after title. I'd come up with nothing suspicious, but then I hardly knew what I was looking for.

I should just quit.

Someone at the police department was probably doing the same thing, getting paid to do it, and looking at it with a trained eye.

I'm not a detective. I'm a mystery editor. I don't know whodunit until I read the last pages of a manuscript.

But the two alternatives to my headache were far worse. I'd either obsess over Adam and Crystal, or I'd have to try to hide my anger and talk with Liam about the condo. I'd heard him come in through the front door and call my name, but I hadn't answered. I told myself that if he knocked on my door, it would be a sign that I should talk to him. But he hadn't, and I'd left it at that.

Through the pain I pressed onward with the mystery. I decided to give myself to the end of the hour. Then I'd toss out the rest of the stack and leave the detective work to the detectives.

I kept reading.

Name: Tabas, Ian.
Title: "A Far Voice"
Reader: Intern Office

Notes: 3+ spelling errors in cover letter, automatically rejected per standard procedure.

Name: Tadlock, Felicia.
Title: "Mystery in Numbers"
Reader: Eliza Tahan
Notes: Poor grammar & syntax, standard rejection letter.

Name: Tag, Lee.
Title: "Morey"
Reader: Eliza Tahan
Notes: Slow plot, can't connect with characters, standard reject.

Name: Tahan, Sharif.
Title: "Illusions of You"
Reader: Intern Office
Notes: 3+ spelling errors in cover letter, automatically sent back per standard procedure.

I blinked, certain that my blurred eyes were playing tricks on me. "Sharif Tahan," I whispered.

"It's a different Sharif Tahan," I justified, but my voice shook even as I said it. "There is no way in the world that Dad sent in a manuscript."

He's been dead over ten years!

"This list must be old, pulled from the wrong date range. What if he wrote something a long time ago and didn't tell us? Yeah, why would he tell his kids? It's a personal thing." I checked the date range again at the end of the page. The manuscript was submitted just two months ago.

There must be some mistake. I trembled violently.

I struggled with my next step. I knew I should call Cleo, but talk of Dad always disturbed her and brought back her initial survivor's guilt. And I'd already left her a message to call back. But I couldn't just sit on this finding until I saw her. Couldn't just bring it up lightly or something. I needed her advice right now, and I called her again.

Her voicemail picked up. My first sentences were my general, "Cleo, are you there? If you're there, pick up," but then I remembered that this was not her answering machine, she couldn't screen message per message. "Sorry," I muttered, and left a short message saying she must call me right away.

Cleo's not available.

Liam's not home.

I no longer trust Adam.

And I'm far from work, so even that can't distract me.

I couldn't hold back any longer. I lost it. Conspiracy theories ran through my mind.

Maybe the guy who was driving the truck that hit and killed Dad is a writer and took Dad's name as a pen name as some kind of tribute. Or he was driven insane and took Dad's personality.

Or did Dad fake his death for some reason? Had he been in danger? Had he been a spy? Could he be with Mom now? She was supposedly in Botswana, but I had never been there so I could not know for sure. Mom could be anywhere. She could be "anywhere" with Dad.

I picked up the phone and called Detective Wilson. It was late, and I expected to leave a message with all the information so that I could feel somewhat unburdened. I was tired of the police department's inaction. When he answered I was too surprised to speak for a moment. Finally I stated, "You're there late."

"I left you a message, Kai, my sweet," he replied somewhat absently, surprising me more. "This case is becoming increasingly urgent. I won't be home for another hour or so at least."

I coughed in embarrassment for Detective Wilson. "Um . . . I'm not your . . . sweet." I tried to keep a playful tone to keep him from being too embarrassed. "I'm just calling to see if you got a chance to look at the list of authors I sent on Thursday."

He stuttered for a moment and then said, "This must be Ms. Tahan. Sorry about that. I thought you were my wife. I'm rarely late coming home and was worried that she didn't get my message. Anyway, yes, we got the list and it has been helpful. Thank you for sending it."

"No problem. Listen, I've been going through it, slowly of course, because it's so long. But I found something that seems really odd and suspicious."

"You don't need to go through it. We're doing that."

"Yeah, I know. But I feel in danger, and so I needed to take some kind of action."

"Understood. What did you want to tell me about?"

"There's a name on there that shouldn't be on there."

"I know who you are talking about," the detective surprised me again. "Your father's name."

I could not reply. I nodded nervously until he asked if I was still on the line and I mustered up a weak answer in the affirmative.

"We noticed that, too, and we are looking into it."

"Why's he on there, Detective?"

I heard a noise in the background, a man's voice saying that the files he ordered had been picked up. "We are looking into it, Ms. Tahan. Something just arrived that I need to take a look at, but we will hopefully figure all this out soon. Then we can make an arrest and you will no longer think that you're danger. Thank you for calling us with this. Please let me know if you need anything further. Until then—"

"Wait." I stopped him before he could hang up. "Please. What do you mean when you say that you're going to make an arrest? *Who* are you going to arrest? My dad's been dead a long time."

"We know that. But you were correct to realize that the fact that his name is in the list is a key point."

"Okay, so who do I need to avoid? Is it an author in the area?"

"I don't think you need to worry about that. I have to go, and besides, I am not at liberty to discuss this further right now. We will be in touch."

Detective Wilson hung up.

I paced my room, wondering what to do. *I should be comforted*, I told myself. *The police are on the case and*

must have some lead. That author list helped them. They have narrowed it down or something. They are going to make an arrest soon.

It really didn't help right now, though, and I questioned whether I should even go back to work until the murderer had been found. Would the author be looking for me there? Or would I be safer out of the house? I knew for sure that I would be using public transportation now, even if my car had been drivable. I didn't care *what* kind of car the murderer was driving these days; he wouldn't be able to knock a bus off the road and walk away from it.

I decided that, indeed, I should go to work tomorrow. Cleo was in town and I was hoping we could get together. We could talk about Adam. We could talk about what I found on the author list. Or maybe by then I will have gotten a call from Detective Wilson and we can just celebrate that the murderer is behind bars. We could go to a bar to celebrate and I could pick up a new lover, and she could, too. Her Jorge was probably cheating, too, now that I thought about it. Why had I stuck up for him?

I couldn't wait until she arrived. Her trip down here was perfect timing. Even with the anger and fear, my painful eyes and head overcame me. I crawled into bed, turned out the light, and fell asleep.

I had received no call from Cleo or Detective Wilson by my lunch break, and I tried Cleo's cell phone again. When there was no answer, I reminded myself that she was down here for meetings, and not at my usual disposal while working from home.

As soon as I hung up, my cell phone rang. Adam's number appeared on the screen, but I didn't answer because I didn't want to speak to him. I did, however, want to hear what he had to say, so I waited five minutes to give him a little time to leave a message and then immediately dialed the voicemail.

"Hey, beautiful. I got your message. I can definitely meet up tomorrow at six. And yeah, that Greek place is good. Do you need a ride, or are you going to take the ferry over? I can definitely give you a ride if you want. I have something to show you. Just let me know. If I don't hear from you before then, I'll just meet you at the Greek place at six. Can't wait to see you!"

What is he talking about? Did I invite him to dinner before I found out about Crystal?

I searched my memory. *No, Cleo's in town, and we hadn't discussed yet when would be a good time for all of us to get together. I wouldn't have just made plans with Adam before working out a good time with Cleo.*

Could it be that the message was for Crystal, and he was already mixing up his Aryan chick with his Arab chick? Could he be so careless?

I decided that was all right. It was perfect. I'd show right up at the "Greek place" and surprise them. He'd mentioned taking the ferry, so the Greek place he was talking about must be Spyro's Gyros right off the ferry landing in Coronado. I'd take the ferry over around five-thirty, and maybe even see Crystal, if she took the ferry. In fact, she probably would take the ferry around the same time, especially since she would not have received the message with Adam's offer to pick her up.

I imagined the look on her face when I walked up to her on the ferry and told her that her boyfriend was a two-timing jerk. Maybe we could walk up to him together, just to see his reaction. I began to feel better about the situation. More in control.

If Cleo ever returned my call, for goodness sake, we could go together. That way, if I didn't meet up with Crystal, Cleo could be there to support me. Make sure I didn't overreact in public. She always grounded me when I went a little crazy, just as she had when I'd overreacted to the situation about Sue.

By the time I ran downstairs to the Grab-and-Go deli and brought my grilled cheese sandwich and diet soda back to the office, my lunch break was pretty much over. I closed my office door and put on the mysterious *The Living Sea* CD, which I still had in my bag. I needed some background music as I ate and plowed through more manuscripts and made more authors hate me.

I knew I shouldn't be listening to the soundtrack that was associated with Liam's accident, but as soon as the music started, I couldn't turn it off. It was just so good. Plus, now that I knew *he* was the one listening to it and not some murderer, I didn't feel as threatened. As the third song began, I looked up from my stacks of manuscripts and my sandwich and said, "Wait a minute!"

I stood up, a light of discovery shining in me.

If Liam was listening to this at the moment of impact, why wasn't it in my car CD player? If anything, it should be crushed inside my crushed car!

I walked around to the front of my desk, my steps keeping time to the music. I paced back and forth in the office until I finally shut off the CD. In the first moment of silence, the realization came upon me.

Someone put this in my car after *the accident. And it wasn't me and it wasn't Liam.*

I picked up the phone to call Cleo again. I stopped myself, though, knowing that she was in meetings all day, and that I had already left several messages. But I was not overreacting on this one. This *was* important.

CHAPTER 17

Cleo didn't call me back on Tuesday. By the end of the workday Wednesday, Cleo still had not called me and I was getting worried. She was my best friend and sister and she never ignored me like this. I spent a lot of time wondering if I had done something to make her mad at me, but I could think of nothing. That made me even more worried. What if something had happened to Cleo now? I decided to find her, even if it meant calling the President of the United States and demanding to know where my sister, one of his government's employees, was. Enough was enough.

First I called Cleo at home, even though that wasn't where she was supposed it be. I left a message on her answering machine just in case.

I called her cell phone and left another message. "This is Eliza. You need to call me back right away. I'm worried about you."

I called the number she'd given me for Jorge, but no one picked up there either. I left a message stating who I was, that I needed to get in touch with Cleo, and that she was not returning my calls. I asked him to call me back as soon as possible.

Then I remembered that she had said she'd be staying at the Hotel Del Coronado and I decided to try her there.

"The famous Hotel Del Coronado," the friendly voice on the line answered. "How can I help you?"

"Yes, hi. I'm trying to get hold of my sister. She's staying there while going to some kind of Homeland Security conference. Can you connect me to her room? Her name is Cleo Tahan."

"Just a moment, I'll check. But I think the people going to that conference—the Homeland Security one—are booked downtown. At the Marriott, I think."

"I know, but my sister was going to get approval to stay at the Del instead."

"Her name is not coming up. Tahan is spelled T-a-h-a-n?"

"Yes. No Tahans at all?"

"I'm afraid not. Her bosses must not have approved the hotel switch. They like to keep everyone in the same hotel. Probably get a group discount or something. I'm sorry I can't be more helpful."

My next step was to call the Marriott. They had no one checked in under Cleo's name, but noted that the rooms were reserved by the organization, and room numbers were assigned when people checked in. They told me it was possible that Cleo was staying there, and that she hadn't checked in yet.

This didn't help my anxiety. If she hadn't checked into her hotel and been at the conference, where had she been?

It was time to get serious.

Within minutes of hanging up with the Marriott, I was searching the Homeland Security website for any name that sounded familiar. Cleo had mentioned her boss's name many times, but I just couldn't remember it. I was hoping I'd see it and recognize it.

Russ Goodwyn, that was it! I redialed the Marriott to inquire after him. The man on the line said Mr. Goodwyn had left forwarding instructions for a short list of people, but if I wasn't on the list he could direct me to the room voicemail.

"My name is Ms. Tahan," I said, knowing I would not be on the short list, but that Cleo might be.

"Tahan. Yes. And your first name?"

"Cleo," I lied.

"Here you are. I apologize for the inconvenience of waiting. I'll connect you to his cell phone, Ms. Tahan."

"Thank you."

After a moment a bass voice answered the line.

"Hello. This is Goodwyn."

"Yes, this is Eliza Tahan—"

"Who gave you my cell phone number?"

"I—I'm Cleo Tahan's sister. Listen, I'm sorry to call you in the middle of your conference but I haven't been able to get hold of Cleo. She said she would be here this week, and that she was staying at the Hotel Del Coronado, but when I called them they said they didn't have her name on record. So I called the Marriott and they don't have her listed either. They put me through to you because of my last name. I guess my sister was on your list of people to connect to your cell phone or something. It's important that I talk to Cleo."

"This is her sister?" he asked simply, after my long monologue.

"Yes, Eliza Tahan. I know she's down here for the conference, and she was probably in meetings yesterday and today, but she hasn't called me back and she always does, so I'm worried about her. Plus she is not at the hotel she was supposed to be at. Do you have her hotel information?"

He cleared his throat and said gruffly, "Miss Tahan has not showed up for any of our meetings, yesterday or today. She never said anything about the Hotel Del Coronado, and as of this morning when I inquired, she hadn't checked into the room we reserved for her at the Marriott. We try to keep an eye on our agents, even the ones who are unlikely to be in harm's way, so we've been trying to track her down. When was the last time you heard from her?"

He seemed frustrated and accusatory, and I found myself lying to cover for her even before I thought it out. "Oh, um, this past weekend, I guess."

"How was she acting?"

"Acting?"

"Was she acting normal? Angry? Distracted?"

"Normal, I guess. Actually, I probably talked the entire time. So I can't really say."

"Did she mention whether she was planning to miss meetings?"

"No. I think her car may be in the shop. The last time she was down here, she had to use a rental car."

"Her government-issued car was in the shop? She never reported that."

I was getting her into hotter water. "I'm . . . I'm not sure which car it was. She has several cars."

He cleared his throat again. "I didn't know that. But if she has several cars, and one was in the shop, then why didn't she use a different one? Having a car in the shop is not a reason for her missing these meetings."

I paused and conceded, "Good point, Mr. Goodwyn."

"She's missed quite a few meetings lately," he continued. "Just a moment, let me find a spot to sit and start up my laptop."

After a moment during which I assumed his laptop was booting up, he began clicking open files and then typing. He didn't say a word the entire time, and I wasn't going to speak first. Finally he asked, "Did you talk to her on the twelfth?"

"Of . . ."

"This month."

The date jarred my memory. "I think I did."

"That was the date of the last meeting she missed."

"Oh! That makes sense, actually. She was with a friend of mine in the hospital. The hospital called her because they couldn't get hold of me. She was on her way down here for the meeting, so she wasn't planning to skip or anything. It was just an emergency."

"Where's 'down here'?"

"San Diego."

There was a silence then a quick mouse click and keyboard typing. "Keep going," he said finally.

"That's all. She was down here for the meeting—not the conference, of course, just the usual one. She must have missed it because of my friend's accident."

Russ Goodwyn cleared his throat. "She wouldn't have been in San Diego for our usual meeting. The meetings are in L.A."

"But you're in San Diego now, right? For a meeting."

"For a conference. It's completely different. Our regular meetings are in L.A. At the West Coast headquarters. Cleo knows that. She's been to dozens. So why was she coming down to San Diego for a meeting that she *knew* was in L.A.?"

I had no answer, though it was obvious that this question needed one. "Well . . . I don't keep track of her at all times. I'm sorry. Why not call her? Or email her or something? Maybe she thought the meeting was in San Diego. Maybe she got mixed up, what with the usual meetings in L.A. and then the conference coming up in San Diego. It could happen. Maybe she was just confused on the meeting location."

"Maybe she was going to a different meeting."

"I don't think so."

"Do you have a number I can reach you at later? To check in and find out if Cleo has gotten in touch with you?"

"I'm going to head over to Coronado for a while this evening—"

"You said you called the Del and Cleo was not there."

"Oh, yeah. This is something else. I'm not even going down to the Del if she's not there."

"Where in Coronado will you be?"

"At the ferry landing meeting someone."

"The ferry landing. Okay. Meeting someone to go shopping over there?"

"No, I'm just meeting someone."

"Where at?"

Is he going to follow me? I hoped I wouldn't have Homeland Security showing up during my plot to find out if Adam was really cheating on me. "Spyro's Gyros. But it's a personal matter. Nothing to do with Cleo."

"I understand. Is there a number where I could reach you?"

I gave him my cell phone number, and the conversation abruptly ended with his command to tell Cleo to call him right away if I heard from her. I hung up with the shivers.

The meetings are in L.A.? I scanned my memory. I was almost certain that she'd said she was down here for a meeting when she got a call from the hospital and went to see Liam. *But what if I'm mistaken? What was she down here for?*

I worked halfheartedly until five, then began getting ready to meet Adam. I was not as into my scheme to trap him as I had been yesterday, and now I was more than a little worried about what was going on with my sister. I decided to call Liam, not for advice, but for plain old information.

"Hey, Lizzy, is everything okay?" he asked. "You never call me anymore."

"Everything's fine," I lied. "I have a quick question for you, though."

"Of course, and we need to have that talk, like you said in your note. We keep missing each other. And hey, what's up with your car? How long are you going to leave it in the driveway? It gives me the creeps every time I pass it."

"I know. I'm sorry. It kinda freaks me out, too."

"So, soon then?"

"Soon, I promise. I'm waiting for the insurance stuff. And we'll talk soon about the note, too. About the condo. For now though, I need you to look in your wallet and pull out your emergency card."

"Um, okay. Just a sec," he answered. "Okay, I've got it."

"Can you read me the names listed on the 'in an emergency' part?"

"Sure. It's your name, and it has your work number and cell number. I put it on there when we were still engaged. And I guess it makes sense to keep it that way since we're still living together. I'll change it when we sell the condo."

"Anyone else?"

"What?"

"Who else is on there?"

He laughed a moment. "No one, Lizzy. You know those cards that come with new wallets have, like, *no* space."

"You don't have Cleo's name on there?"

"Cleo? Why would I have her name on there? There wasn't even enough room to list my *parents*. And if there were room, don't you think I'd list them or my work or my friends before *your* sister?"

"But the hospital called her when they couldn't get in touch with me."

"I thought you called her. She came later."

"No, she was there all night with you before I even showed up. You were unconscious."

"Oh, seriously? I didn't realize that."

"I'm sure you had other things on your mind."

"Like coming out of a coma. But I should thank her for coming over. That's pretty nice of her, especially since she doesn't even like me."

"No, she likes you."

"Please, Lizzy. There's no need. It isn't like it's a big secret, and I don't really blame her. She's your sister. She's protective of you."

"Yeah. Thanks for the info."

"Hey, is everything okay?"

"Sure," I replied before hanging up, but it was a lie.

Why was Cleo called to the hospital? Why was she in San Diego? A sick feeling boiled in my stomach.

I checked my watch, and realized that if I were going to catch Adam and Crystal, I had to leave now. Of course, the issue with Adam was rapidly diminishing in importance, but it wasn't like I could get hold of Cleo. I had a plan for the evening and if I were going to keep control over my life, I needed to follow through on my plan. It wasn't as though I had anything else I could be doing, and to sit around waiting for the phone to ring would drive me crazy.

I walked to the ferry stop and looked around for Crystal, but she was nowhere in sight. I handed over a couple of bucks and boarded the ferry.

Crossing the bay, watching the lights of downtown begin to twinkle, I hugged myself as a chill ran through me. My stomach turned, and it was not caused by the waves.

Could Cleo have crashed into Liam?

I felt guilty even thinking about it. My best friend, my sister, my confidant. If she could have tried to hurt Liam—if *she* could have done something so evil—there was no hope for the world. She was one of the good guys. She spent every day translating for a government agency that had her helping to protect all Americans. She always came to my rescue, whether I needed an idea for an outfit, an ear to vent into, or someone to talk some sense into me. She was sensible. She would never try to hurt me. I'd give my life to protect her, and she'd do the same for me. I was not on her hit list—that was for certain. She might be the one in danger now, since she'd seemingly disappeared. I tried to shake the idea of her guilt, not sure if the idea of Cleo as criminal or victim was worse.

I'm overreacting, like Cleo always says I do. I tried to shake the feeling, shake the thoughts. Turning away from downtown and toward Coronado, I watched the island get closer. The ferry landing was already bustling with tourists and locals. I tried to take in the oncoming island but could not gather any thoughts other than those that insisted on my attention. Deep inside, I didn't *feel* like I was overreacting. I felt like I was closing in.

But could Liam have been her planned hit? Could she have come to San Diego for the sole purpose of hurting him? Hurting him for hurting me?

She had gone to the hospital without being called, without any notification that Liam was there. And she'd lied about being on his emergency card. She hadn't had a meeting in San Diego after all, and was in fact supposed to be in Los Angeles.

Even if she planned to come after Liam, she could've just been trying to scare him.

That didn't make me feel any better about the situation. If she was the one who hit him, whether she meant to scare him or not, she'd almost killed him. Had she *meant* to hurt him? To kill him? To get him out of my way, so I could have the condo to myself and my life to myself?

This would mean that all this time I had been worried for my own safety, I was not a target after all. The accidents were unrelated. One angry author whose target was only Rain and one overly protective sister whose target was Liam. Unless . . .

I tried to think back. Had I ever mentioned S. Rain to Cleo? I must have. I'd complained all the time to Liam, and as he grew away from me, I must have turned to Cleo, venting the same way I did with pretty much every subject.

But Rain had been killed by an author. She had been found with a rejection letter.

But I'd complained to Cleo about my horrible boss who made my life miserable. And my horrible boss was killed when her car was purposely rammed.

I'd complained to Cleo about the roommate who broke my heart and made me feel like I could not move on. My roommate was almost killed when he was purposely rammed, albeit in my car.

I trembled. My teeth chattered and it was not because of the cold. The wind whipped my hair as we pulled up to the ferry landing.

Getting off, I almost lost my footing because of my nerves. I was no longer angry or panicked about Adam and Crystal. I was too afraid of the new vision of my sister I'd conjured up.

Who else had I complained about? Jane? Sue? Were they still alive, or was Cleo on some kind of killing spree as I went forward with my superficial and spiteful spying on Adam?

"Adam!" I gasped, remembering my last voicemails to Cleo. I looked around for him, not sure of what I was expecting. He wasn't driving right now, and Cleo would never know that he was on this date with Crystal. He was safe for the moment, but I needed to find him. Even if he were with Crystal, I would pull him away and talk to him, warn him. We could call the police together. After all, Adam and I weren't committed. I was still living with my ex-fiancé, for heaven's sake. All that mattered was that Adam was safe.

Then I saw him in the distance, sitting at a tiny table outside the Greek café. He was looking around, and it seemed that Crystal had not shown up yet. It was just as well. We needed to team up and get to the police post haste before Cleo got my message and before she found the newest subject of my venting, poor Adam. He might not be innocent, but his crime didn't merit the death penalty either.

I was getting close to him when he spotted me. I was surprised that he didn't seem panicked, but smiled and began to stand. He'd been expecting *me*, not Crystal. But who had set up this date if she hadn't and I hadn't?

I heard sirens in the distance, multiple sirens, edging closer. Then suddenly, out of the corner of my eye, I saw a red Corvette speeding far too fast for the tight parking lot in front of the ferry landing. The license plates were off the car, and the front bumper was smashed in. The sirens in the distance were quite close suddenly. A green kerchief and dark sunglasses covered the driver's head and face, but I recognized the cheek structure and the long thick hair that I'd envied for most of my life.

Cleo was on the island. And she was on her way.

To Adam.

Still watching me, he didn't even see Cleo coming. And Cleo, focused on Adam, didn't see me coming.

I rushed toward him, toward his surprised face. He was smiling, laughing. A woman in the parking lot screamed as she jumped away from the Corvette that didn't stop for her. Adam turned to look over his shoulder and saw the Corvette as it was speeding directly at him. His mouth dropped, the smile wiped away.

I broke into a full sprint toward him without thinking twice.

My body mass came in handy for once as I made contact with his strong chest, knocking him as far away as I could. Wheels squealed close or in the distance; it sounded like both at once. Red flashed in front of my eyes. Sirens whined and I hit the ground, feeling a horrendous pain shoot through my neck and down my entire body. I skidded across the cement, but even as my skin was tearing, the sting simply blended into the shocking pain throughout the rest of my body. My breath caught and my lungs seemed to collapse deep inside my core.

My body came to a halt with the sickening thud of my skull hitting the pavement.

There were shouts, screams, and sirens all around me. The smell of wet air and oil sank into my nostrils as I lay on the ground, the pain so great that my vision came and went.

Then there was silence. Blackness before my eyes. I realized I might have only seconds of consciousness left, but at the same time I felt certain this was not the end. I was not facing nothingness.

The pain cut across my shoulders, and I let myself escape into darkness.

CHAPTER 18

When I opened my eyes, I knew I wasn't in hell. Everything was too clean and light. I couldn't possibly be in heaven either, because I was in a hell of a lot of pain. My eyes wouldn't focus, and I realized I didn't have my contacts in around the same time that someone handed me my glasses.

"I didn't know you wore glasses."

The deep, warm voice flowed over me like a river of honey. Unless I was mistaken, it was Adam Mestas. I put on my glasses and focused on his handsome face. He wore a light bandage along the length of his arm.

He was smiling. He was safe.

Crystal was not at his side. He was at mine.

"I usually wear contacts," I muttered, and it seemed new and difficult to speak.

"I like your glasses," he replied. "They're cute." He kissed me on the forehead between my eyebrows.

"I felt that. That must mean I am alive." My words were weak, as though I wasn't sure that my assumption was accurate.

"Yeah, thank God," Adam said. I heard Liam's nervous chuckle behind him, but I didn't peek around to find him. Adam rested a hand on my hand.

I coughed, gaining better control over my voice. "I was hit by a car."

"You weren't hit."

"I tried to push you out of the way and then the car hit me."

"You knocked me out of the way, and in the process went skidding across the pavement," Adam said, petting my hand. When I looked at him, I could see his midnight eyes misting. "You saved my life, Eliza."

"But everything hurts. I saw the car—"

"When you knocked me out of the way, you fell on your shoulder and broke your collarbone and your wrist. And your side is totally scraped up, too. Mine is, too, but I didn't break anything. The driver saw you at the last minute and skidded. She just missed us and plowed into some trees and tables. But no one was hit."

"But I was unconscious. That doesn't come from broken bones."

"You hit your head on the concrete. An ambulance brought you here, and I admit I was scared. But they did an EEG and you still had lots of brain waves and they said that this meant you weren't, what did they say, comatose. They were almost certain you would wake up soon. In a day or so, they expected. No more than two. And that you'd be fine."

"Has it been two days?"

"Not even a day. You're an overachiever." Adam smiled. I heard Liam laugh behind him again and I wondered how much they'd spoken during the hours that I'd been out.

"Is this ICU?" I asked, remembering the term from Liam's recent visit.

"Yeah, but I think now that you're awake, they're probably going to move you to a regular room and then let you go home."

I looked at the cast on my arm briefly and felt with my other hand for the brace at my shoulders. "Did they set these while I was unconscious?"

"Yeah. And it was probably a blessing in disguise that you were unconscious for that broken collarbone. The doctors said it's the most painful bone to break."

"Well, it sure hurts now. Did they give me drugs?"

Adam looked around, as though there might be a bottle of Vicodin sitting out just in case, and I smiled at his thoughtfulness. "I don't know. Maybe you just tell them when you need drugs and they bring 'em. I'll go get a nurse."

"No, not yet. I just want to relax for a minute. Thanks for being here, Adam."

"I wasn't going home until I knew you were okay."

It hurt, but I leaned forward so that I could see Liam, who was sitting in the chair against the wall. "And thank you, too, Liam, for being here."

"No problem, Lizzy," he muttered, but I suspected he might be getting a little bored with the whole hospital situation. I didn't blame him. Didn't I feel the exact same way after sitting with him for a few hours when our roles were reversed?

I looked around the room and asked, "Did anyone call Cleo?"

The moment I said her name, however, I saw a flash of her face behind the wheel of her Corvette, plowing towards Adam. Then the surprised, gaping mouth when she saw me appear next to her target. "Cleo!" I gasped.

"Um, she's all right," Liam said. "Don't worry about her for now."

Adam turned to him. "Come on. She deserves to know the truth." He turned back to me to me. "Cleo was the one driving the car that tried to hit me, Eliza. I'm sorry. They think she is responsible for hitting Liam and your boss, too. Maybe even other people, but of course they can't say much yet. She's in police custody right now, being held without bail."

Liam cut in, "Her lawyer said he wants her to plead not guilty at the arraignment, but that she hasn't agreed. I'm not really sure what's up with that. The lawyer wants to say it was an accident or something."

"She hasn't agreed to plead not guilty? Why not?"

"Probably because she *is* guilty," Liam muttered, but Adam broke in.

"We're not sure. Her lawyer just came in briefly to drop off those flowers on the table and see how you were doing. He said Cleo wanted to know how you were."

"I—I need to talk to her. When's her trial going to be?"

"She'll have a preliminary hearing in a week or two, just to make sure they have enough evidence to hold her in jail for now."

Jail. It blew me away. Cleo. My best friend. My little sister. The star. In jail.

"Did her lawyer say why she did this?" Then I remembered why she might have done it and didn't want to discuss it further.

"He didn't say. We were wondering that, too, though, Liam and I. We thought you might know something."

"Maybe she was trying to look out for me. She knew when Rain upset me, when most anything made me anxious. Liam, after you and I began, um, drifting apart, Cleo became my new confidant."

Liam spoke up, not impressed. "Thanks for talking smack about me behind my back." There was the drama. There was the sarcasm. He was, after all, still in a cast, possibly because of this confidant of mine.

Adam responded to Liam before I could even think of a comeback. "Hey, man. Give her a break. It isn't her fault that you're hurt—it's Cleo's. And from what you've told me about your relationship with Eliza, you don't seem like the kind of person she'd want to confide in anyway."

Liam backed down under Adam's quiet but firm voice. Or maybe it was his flashing eyes and the way he pushed a long ribbon of black hair away from his face. Adam was on my side. He was my champion.

Liam backed down. "Sorry, Lizzy. I guess you had more than enough to vent about."

Adam turned back to me, and I noticed Liam slipping out of the room. I wasn't sure if he was leaving in embarrassment or just to give Adam and me some privacy. A few months ago, I would have been sad to see how far we'd drifted apart. At this point, though, I barely gave him a second thought and just waited on what Adam was about to say.

"I have a question, Eliza. I hope you don't think I am prying. If it's too much to discuss right now, I can wait. Just say the word."

I imagined the question. *Why didn't you tell me Liam was your ex? Why did you lie? You realize, don't you, that we're history as soon as you get better?*

"Did I do something to upset you?"

"What?" I asked. This was not the accusation I expected.

"Your sister obviously thought so. But I thought we were doing good. Weren't we? I mean, was I misreading this whole relationship?"

I thought of just dismissing the issue; he was here with *me*, wasn't he? But I realized that I cared for him enough to give him the honesty that he so highly regarded. He had a right to defend his actions.

"I found out about Crystal."

Adam stared blankly at me. "Who?"

So much for honesty! "Crystal! Your supposed ex-girlfriend! I saw her in your car on the freeway. And don't even say it wasn't your car. It had the bumper sticker and everything." My voice trailed off. I was losing steam. My shoulder was hurting. Everything was hurting. And by the look on Adam's face, my assumption left something to be desired.

He shook his head, smiled, and took my hand. "That was *not* my car and *not* Crystal. I sold my car, Eliza. I'm still friends with Crystal's family, by way of my parents, anyway. Our families have lived next door to each other since elementary school. My mom told me that Crystal's *younger sister* was going to move to college soon after she finished this last semester. Mom said that Crystal's parents were looking to buy her sister an older car she could use while she was away. I had already been thinking about selling my car. I thought I'd mentioned it. That I was ready for a new car. I'm sure we talked about it. Remember, we talked about the Steinbeck Museum?"

I nodded.

"So finally her parents came out to San Diego to visit Crystal, who lives here with her *husband and kids.*" He lifted an eyebrow in my direction. "I met up with her parents when they were out here. The car was a surprise and their parents sent the girls shopping while they met up with me."

"She looked just like Crystal in the picture."

"She probably looks *a lot* like Crystal did at that age. They have that whole waifish blonde thing going on. I haven't seen her in a few years. But I wonder why Crystal's sister was driving. I know they were going to present it to her before they headed back home to Arizona, but I thought her folks said that she needed to learn how to drive a stick shift first. It's been less than a week, and I'm kinda surprised they were letting her drive it."

"She wasn't driving," I muttered. Admitted. "She was in the passenger seat. I couldn't see the driver from where I was sitting. I was in a tow truck. I just assumed it was you because it was your car."

"There ya go."

"I'm sorry for assuming. I just saw a girl who looked like the girl in the picture, and she was in your car and my relationship with Liam was based on so many lies that I just reverted to the defensive."

"Don't you remember in my voicemail I said I had something to show you and that I could pick you up for our date? It was my new car that I wanted to show you."

I blushed and was happy to be interrupted by a nurse, a freckled brunette, coming in to check my vitals. I waited for Adam to check her out. He never did, not even a side-glance. She said I was doing well, and he nodded to her politely as she left. Maybe I really was Adam's type. Maybe Adam was really my man.

"I thought that call was for . . . geez . . . this sounds so silly now, after all you said . . ."

"How could that call be for anyone else? It was to *your* phone."

"You didn't mention my name, and it was right after I'd seen who I thought was Crystal in what I thought was your car. I thought you might have been calling Crystal back, but accidentally dialed my number."

Adam pulled a chair up next to my bed. "I am not the cheating type, and even I know not to invite another girl to go along on a date I've been invited on. I've seen the sitcoms!"

I laughed and ached. "But I didn't invite you on that date."

"Sure you did," he explained, flipping open his cell phone. "I saved your message so I could make sure to remember the right time and all." He dialed his voicemail and handed me the phone.

I listened. I knew it would have sounded like me to anyone else. She said she was Eliza, and asked to meet Adam in Coronado at the Greek café at the ferry landing. I closed the phone. "You should save that for the police. That's Cleo. She was setting you up."

He took back his cell phone, his face turning pale. "She set me up to be there so she could hit me? So she could kill me?"

I sighed. How could Cleo have gotten so out of control? What happened to her fear of crashing? And her love of her cars? Not to mention her tendency to do the right thing in every situation.

"If you hadn't been there, Eliza . . ."

"Good thing you called me."

"Good thing you came. Even after thinking I was supposed to be on a date with another woman. For heaven's sake, Eliza, why did you even come?"

I was about to dash this new relationship to a bloody

death upon the rocks of honesty. "I wanted to catch you with Crystal. I'm sorry."

Adam regained his composure just as I noticed the nurse and doctor standing outside the door. They moved in and the nurse took my vital signs again. The doctor looked at my chart. She told me what bones had been set, what to expect, what pain medications she would pre-scribe and that they planned on releasing me the next day if I continued to do well. She said I probably felt much worse than I actually was.

When they left, Adam followed them for a moment, and I heard him asking if he could take me home, or if they needed a next of kin or something. "I plan on taking care of her, and her family is not available. So is that okay? I don't want her to have to stay here just because no one's here to take her home." They explained that I was an adult and could check myself out. And that cer-tainly he could take me home if I approved.

When he walked back into the room, he said, "I think I need to stop watching sitcoms and hospital dramas." He laughed and sat back down. "Do you mind if I take you home, or do you want me to call your room-mate?"

"I'd love it if you could take me home."

"Good, then it's a done deal."

I lowered my eyes. "I thought I'd died or something."

"It probably feels that way with your broken bones and all. Eliza, you must tell me why you pushed me out of the way when you thought I was cheating on you. Please. You should've just let me get hit. Or just shouted to warn me. But you risked your life. When you thought I was there to meet another woman."

I shrugged, "I was really mad, but—"

"But when you saw me in danger, your instinct and some emotion in you caused you to jump out in front of a speeding Corvette to get me out of the way."

"But I didn't want to *die* for you."

"But you might have, and you took that chance. Why?"

"I don't know. I guess, when it came down to it, I was giving you the benefit of the doubt. I still cared for you."

"I told you before that my relationship with Crystal was based on lies, and how honesty was so important to me." Adam sighed and looked down. "I don't like to talk about it, Eliza. It's just really hurtful and hard to talk about."

I touched his arm. He didn't have to tell me. I didn't care anymore. I just didn't want to see him hurting so badly. "Don't worry about it, then."

"No, I want you to know what she did that tore me away, so you can believe once and for all that I am indeed torn away. She aborted our baby, Eliza. Without telling me she was even pregnant until after it was over. Now, I know it was legally her choice and that I had no say in it. But it was my baby, too, and now I have to live with the fact that I have a dead child I couldn't save. It was over between us after that, to say the least."

I didn't begin to know how to respond. I thought about his dramatic response to my white lie about Liam. I thought about how open he'd been with how he felt about me. I thought about when he'd said he wanted a completely honest relationship. No wonder. "I don't know what to say."

"Don't say anything, Eliza. Nothing you can say will take away what happened. Everyone has something they have to live with. Your dad's death. My baby that won't ever be born. And now your sister with this side of her you never knew existed. I don't want our pasts to get in the way of our future. It affects us, but shouldn't freeze us."

I only nodded, trying to push through the news.

"You need to rest, Eliza. I'll leave you alone for now. I am going to phone work and let them know I'm all right."

"Okay. Hey, what day is it?"

"Thursday afternoon. Do you want me to call your work?"

"Yeah, that would be great. They probably think I've been playing hooky."

"No, they know what happened. I called your HR person. Liam had the number."

"I appreciate that. Thanks."

Adam planted a little kiss on the tip of my nose before exiting, and I began to relax. I decided to ask the nurse for some painkillers. I'd been enough of a hero. I didn't need to suffer through the pain any longer. And besides, I had to contend with the pain of realizing what my sister had done. I wished my nurse could administer morphine for my soul.

The painkillers were stronger than I'd expected. This was no OTC aspirin I'd been given. It didn't take long until the room blurred and pixilated. Thoughts of death, of Liam, of Adam, and of Cleo marched across my mind.

I began to sob, sending piercing pain throughout my body. I couldn't stop. And I didn't want to.

I deserved a good cry.

CHAPTER 19

The rain was pouring from the sky and inside my heart when I left the hospital. Adam held an umbrella over me while he wheeled me to his car, but that didn't stop the rain from brushing against my face, hiding the tears I could not keep inside. Maybe it was the painkillers that distorted the world at this moment, or maybe it was the shattered life I was returning to, but the droplets falling from the sky were a visual symbol of what I was feeling. Sad, so sad.

I'd spoken to Liam on the phone this morning, and he'd said he would not be at the condo when I returned. He'd tried to forgive my part in his "accident," but he couldn't get it out of his mind. He wasn't mad at me *per se,* but he felt we were eternally broken now. I told him that we'd been "eternally broken" for a long time, but I had stuck by him in the exact way that he was *not* sticking by me now.

Liam would stay at James's apartment until the condo was sold. He made it clear that I could keep the condo if I wanted to buy him out.

"I want to start anew," I'd explained this morning, holding the phone to my ear with my good arm while I sat up in the hospital bed. "Let's sell it as soon as possible, pay off the loan, and split the profits."

"Do you realize we'll profit almost one hundred thousand dollars, Lizzy? In just a couple years. You can't get that kind of return with any other investment."

"Thinking about putting a down payment on a bachelor pad?"

"I'm not really a bachelor anymore. I liked James before the accident, and now I've seen how he really stuck by me, you know. That kind of person is, well, not the kind of person you just let go of."

I thought of Adam, who'd spent hours and hours in the hospital with me, talking, playing cards, anything to take my mind off the situation. "So, you and James are thinking about getting a place together?"

"I'm going to move into his apartment for now. But we're hoping to buy something soon. Together. Probably in the Hillcrest area, since it's kinda close to both our jobs and the area's very hip."

"Can you call that realtor we spoke to when we were thinking of selling before?"

"Yeah, I'll call today. Do you need a ride home?"

Liam's offer was refreshing, as I was not expecting it. I was glad he'd put aside his uncomfortable feelings regarding the accident to come to my aid if I needed him to. "No, Liam, but I appreciate the offer. Adam's coming in a few hours."

"He's a nice guy, Lizzy. We were talking in the room when you were unconscious. He likes you a lot. He said you were sharp and fun and gorgeous."

"Gorgeous?"

"His words, I swear. You guys going to move in together?"

"I think I'm going to live alone," I said, deciding it as the words came out of my mouth. Saying it aloud made me feel stronger. More decisive. And more sure of my choice. "Not even a roommate. And I don't think I'm going to live with a boyfriend again. Not that it hasn't been fun, Liam. But I'm not going to live with a man I'm not married to ever again. It kinda clouds things. Keeps you from seeing things that you might see otherwise, because you assume more of a commitment than you actually have. I shouldn't be saying 'you' there, though. It kept *me* from seeing things *I'd* see otherwise. Anyway, I am looking forward to having a place of my own."

Now that I was home, with Adam tucking a blanket over my legs and setting up a movie in the DVD player, I thought back on my assertion that I'd live alone. Had it been the painkillers that had given me such confidence in myself? Or was it just who I was becoming?

"Are you all right?" Adam asked.

"I am, Adam. Thank you. For picking me up, for getting me all comfy here, for being here for me. For being you."

"You're sweet, Eliza. I'm glad to help. Can I get you something to eat that isn't hospital food? Maybe a bowl of ice cream or some popcorn or . . . hey, I can make a mean grilled cheese sandwich."

"I don't think we have any of that stuff here. But thanks anyway."

Adam pulled on his jacket and grabbed his umbrella. "Everything's set up for the movie, and the remote is right next to you. Will you be okay if I run to the store for a minute? Get you some supplies?"

This was a man who wanted to take care of a woman. Of me. "That sounds great. I'd love a grilled cheese sandwich."

Adam smiled and I melted. "I'll be back soon. Here's the phone, call me if you think of anything you need while I am at the grocery store. Or if you need me here, I'll come back right away."

As Adam closed the door behind himself, I thought I might have another cry. But while the rain continued outside with mind-numbing percussion, I realized that I didn't need to cry anymore. I wanted to *think* about my future instead of *worry* about it. I didn't have a sister to confide in or to ask advice from anymore, but I had a new confidence in myself as a courageous individual. If I could jump in front of a car to save someone's life, I could face a new life. And now I had to deal with the drastic change in one of the people I loved most.

I don't know the first thing about the legal system. How am I supposed to free Cleo? Then again, if Cleo really did all she's been accused of doing, then am I supposed to be fighting for her release at all? Would a conviction mean that she'd get therapy she never received when Dad died?

Why hadn't she said anything? Why did she pretend everything was fine?

Cleo wouldn't have an answer for me, at least not until I spoke to her in person. And I wasn't ready for that.

I might never be ready emotionally, but I'd already decided I'd go to see her as soon as I was physically able.

And the rest of my life? It had all seemed so complicated before. Now, compared with the ordeal with Cleo, this would be the easy part.

I'd definitely quit my job and maybe even recommend Jane for it. I might take a part-time job at a bookstore. Or freelance as a reader for J Press. I'd rent an inexpensive apartment, which I could do if I was freelancing since I didn't need to be near downtown. I would have my nest egg from the condo to supplement my income if needed.

And I'll write. I'd finish my book. Maybe I'd get published. Maybe not. But I would do what I said I would do. I'd write.

Maybe I'd visit Mom in Botswana. I'd never even considered it before. I'd just assumed that she would come to me.

And Adam. He was as interested in me as I was in him. And he'd opened up to me with his most hurtful memory because he trusted me and because he wanted me to feel confident in trusting him.

By the time Adam returned, hands loaded down with grocery bags, I had just started the movie. I wasn't even past the opening credits.

"I see you are really enjoying the DVD," he joked, kissing me lightly on the lips before setting down the bags.

"I was thinking about a lot of stuff," I explained, getting up gingerly to follow him into the kitchen, trying not to move my shoulder much.

He began unloading the bags of groceries, and I saw that he'd picked up much more than cheese and bread. Milk, PopTarts, apples, crackers, an olive medley, and three different kinds of cheese, among other treats.

"What's all this?"

"Thought I'd stock you up so you don't need to carry heavy bags until your collarbone heals. So, what have you been thinking about?" He continued to move food into the fridge and the cupboard.

"Liam and I are going to sell this condo, so I was thinking about what I'd do with my share of the profits, and where I'll live. I think I'm going to quit my job."

"You don't like your job? I thought HR had said you could go back to your old position when they hired someone new."

"To be honest, I'm a little burnt out on mystery. Too much of it in real life these days."

"As long as you don't get burnt out on romance . . ." Adam flashed me a smile, and popped a kiss on my lips as he set the milk in the fridge. "So, writing then?"

"Yeah. I've always wanted to finish a novel I began in college."

"Haven't had the time?"

"That's what I've been telling myself. The truth is that I just haven't had the grit."

"You've had a lot going on lately."

"True. But I could've sat down and written something. I just didn't. And now I'm going to."

He paused and leaned against the counter. "Good. I'm glad you're ready to tackle that dream. And I'd be happy to edit it, or whatever you need."

"Thanks, Adam. I may take you up on that."

He put his arms around me, careful not to squeeze anything broken. "My woman, the writer. I like the sound of that." He kissed my forehead and paused for a moment.

It sounds wonderful, I thought as I held my breath.

"Eliza, as you make your plans, if you feel the same way about me as I feel about you, I hope you'll keep our relationship."

"Keep our relationship what?"

"Just keep our relationship. Sell your condo. Quit your job. But keep us."

I nuzzled close to him. "I wouldn't have it any other way."

CHAPTER 20

As soon as I could get around without much pain or medication, I asked Adam to drive me to the jail to see Cleo. I still loved her and I needed to hear what she had to say.

If I had not seen Cleo's face in the driver's side of the windshield as she was headed toward Adam, and if I had not seen the determination and decision set in her jaw, I would have been my sister's strongest defender.

I sat in the room waiting for Cleo to be brought in, not quite sure what to say.

Hey, Sis, how are things going?
Look what you did to me.
Why?

The guards walked in with a woman who could not possibly be my sister. She was escorted to the chair on her side of the glass opposite me. The jail outfit hung like pajamas on her frame and made her look smaller than usual. Her face's raggedness and uneven tones showed how tired she was, and her unkempt, loose hair partially covered her features. She sat down behind the glass and pushed back her hair, tucking it behind her ears, and I realized how much she resembled herself as a teenager, after the accident. Shunned by her friends and uncomfortable around her mourning family, she had withdrawn, slept and ate little. She looked like that tired and troubled child.

When she didn't move, I made the first attempt at communication and lifted the phone to my left ear. I tapped gently on the glass and pointed to the phone in my hand. I saw her chest rise and fall in a sigh before she picked up the phone on her side.

"Hey, Cleo," was the brilliant opener I had came up with. Right.

"There's no touching allowed. That's why we have to use these little phones. As if someone is going to slip me a weapon or drugs or something. I'm not a damn dead-beat," she muttered.

I could barely hear her. "But at least we get to talk. Are they treating you all right in here?"

"Yeah," Cleo replied finally, still not looking up. "It's not that bad. Most of the women are nice to me."

I longed for my sister to look up, to make eye contact. It was difficult to read her when I couldn't see into her eyes, and the body language I was reading otherwise was not painting a pretty picture of her condition. Cleo was not herself, was disappearing inside her own mind, so that she was only half-conversing with me. We were both uncomfortable. I was about to excuse myself for both our sakes, when all of a sudden Cleo's face shot up and her olive eyes met mine. She was clear-eyed and alert. She'd snapped back into life.

"I was so scared I'd hit you, Liz. The police told me I didn't, that you fell. But when they took me away, they were putting you into an ambulance and I thought you'd be in a coma maybe forever or you'd wake up and be a vegetable and that I'd never be able to see you again. I am *so* sorry that you got hurt. *So sorry.* I should have stopped quicker. Driven slower. Or come earlier. *Something.* I just didn't know you were going to be there. And the police were following me. They'd figured it out. I think the police were in touch with my boss or someone. Maybe somebody at work was scanning my computer to see who I'd been tracking or something. I don't know how, but they knew. They'd connected me with the others. I just feel so bad that you got hurt. That is the *last* thing I wanted."

I couldn't believe my ears. *That* was what she was sorry for? That I happened to be there and that I personally got hurt? "You were going to kill Adam. *That's* what you should be sorry about! You didn't even hit *me*!"

Cleo squinted, confused. She lowered the phone for a moment and looked to the side as though she were trying to comprehend what I had just said. Then she pulled the phone back to her ear. "Adam was cheating on you. You said so yourself in that message. You left a couple of upset messages and you said Adam was cheating." She nodded, as though that was a reasonable explanation.

"I never said you should hurt him!"

"I know. I was trying to help. You can't just say someone is hurting you and expect me to be okay with it. I'm your sister."

"I was *venting* . . . like I always do!"

"You vent, but you never take action. He deserved a payback and I knew you couldn't—or wouldn't—give that to him. So I did. He *deserved* it, Liz."

"He wasn't cheating. I was mistaken."

"But you told me he was cheating on you."

"Jorge was cheating on you and you didn't go after him!"

"It wasn't like that with Jorge. He kept my secrets."

"I thought I was your confidant."

"Not about this kinda stuff. He knows people who have helped me out."

"With what? What exactly could Jorge's friends do that was so important?"

"They could fix up my cars. Take some apart. Move them down to Mexico. Make them disappear when they needed to disappear. He's a different kind of confidant."

"God, Cleo, this sounds so shady! This isn't you."

"Listen, Liz, the point is that *no one* hurts my sister."

"*Lots* of people hurt me! Lots of people hurt everyone! It's just a part of life!"

"Who else has hurt you?"

"Lots of people! You *know* that. And lots of people hurt lots of other people, too. You can't get around that!"

"But who hurt *you*? Give me a name."

I paused before answering. "You have."

She blinked and began to put the phone back in its cradle.

I looked around and wondered if the phone conversation was being recorded. I tapped on the glass and pointed to the phone again. She picked it up and I continued the conversation. "The other hysterical voicemail I left you, it wasn't about Adam. It was more important and I wasn't sure how to bring it up, but I am not hesitant about it now. I thought an author had killed Rain, and had hit Liam, so I was looking through a list of authors who had been rejected to see if any might be Rain's murderer when I came across a manuscript submitted by . . . Dad."

Cleo shuddered. To keep her safe from another bout of depression, I rarely spoke about Dad. Now though, I figured things couldn't get much worse. She surprised me by replying calmly, "Yeah, I know."

"It was submitted recently . . ."

"*I* submitted it."

I was my turn to be speechless. I set the phone on my lap and looked at the counter. Cleo assumed my question correctly: *Why?*

She tapped on the glass and mouthed something I couldn't hear. I lifted the phone to my ear.

"Because I knew I'd be rejected and I needed that letter."

"To put on Rain's car?" I looked to the cameras.

"I wanted it to look like an author. You know, so you wouldn't be a suspect. Same reason I waited until you were on vacation."

Not a suspect? I'd wavered between feeling like a suspect and a potential victim because of her terrible planning. "Cleo, you've been doing so well for all these years. You'd seemed to get over the accident. You did so well in school, in college, at work. You're this sophisticated woman with a great job. What happened?"

"Was I ever really fine? Just because we never talked about it doesn't mean I was peachy-keen, Liz."

"I still deal with all the sadness, too, but we've both been functioning all right. So what happened?"

"I got a letter. Actually a card. From the guy who killed Dad. The guy who hit our car. He went on about how he's been carrying around all this guilt and felt that writing an apology would be 'healing' or something."

"You're kidding."

"Nope. He wanted 'closure.'"

"Closure for *himself.* Reopening a wound for you."

"Exactly. It opened an old wound that I'd hoped had been scarred over forever. That guy was so selfish, acting as though curing his guilt was worth wounding the victim again. It just got me thinking about you and Mom. I wanted to be *sure* that I could protect my remaining family."

"But we're okay, me and Mom."

"But you guys weren't! And Mom is half a world away."

"That's her life, Cleo. It isn't your responsibility."

She ignored my rebuttal, and continued on her original train of thought.

"I used my connections in the government to have Mom transferred to a safer place in Botswana, just doing some office work for the organization and not out at the school or the center. And I wanted to keep an eye on you. You weren't standing up for yourself, so someone had to."

"I was fine. Maybe a little bored with life, but never in danger."

"Bored with life? Your life was at a standstill and you were burying yourself in work so you didn't have to deal

313

with your issues with your boss and Liam. Not only that, you purposely put yourself in harm's way!"

"Please! When did I put myself in harm's way?"

"By helping that intern. Her boyfriend could have found out how you had helped and gone after you. I read about that kind of thing happening all the time. You should have let the girl deal with her own issues. But no, you couldn't leave it alone. So I had to clean *that* up, too."

"Donnie?" *Who is this woman caged in glass, and where is my sister?*

"To protect *you*," she answered.

I shook my head, getting frustrated with Cleo. "Of course, when you were trying to hit Liam, he was in *my* car. You could have hurt me in your twisted plan to protect me." My shoulder ached.

"I made sure his car would be in the shop. Or, should I say, I had *friends* make sure. Knowing him, I knew he'd beg you to use your car. And knowing you, I knew you'd let him, because you let him walk all over you."

Cleo's eyes were fast becoming dazed again. I nearly expected her to rattle off her crimes one by one, right here and now.

"I'm sorry about your car, but because it was yours, you weren't blamed, right? Plus, I didn't have a vehicle available that could do enough damage if he were in his sturdy little SUV."

I stood up and motioned to the guard. "I think she's getting tired or something. She shouldn't be talking right now." I spoke into the phone while still standing. "Cleo, you need some rest."

"You're leaving?"

"You look tired, and you're saying . . . you're just saying stuff you probably should discuss with your lawyer or something. I'll see you soon."

I stayed on the phone as the guards moved toward her. She mumbled to me, "Did you get your car back?"

"I thought I'd told you that I had."

"Can you look for my CD before you have it towed away? I think I'd like it back now."

"Which CD?" I asked, though I knew the answer.

"You'll know it when you see it. I put it in the car when it was in the impound yard after the accident. I wanted to put it in the CD player, but there was blood all over the dash and I couldn't touch it. It should be in the CD case. I just wanted you to think that Liam—"

She struggled with the guards for a moment and the phone fell to the tabletop. She was led out the door.

I sat in the chair a moment. I wanted to put my head in my hands and bawl my eyes out. But I realized that I shouldn't. Not right now. I didn't need to break down. And I realized that I could control myself. Oh, I'd cry later. There was nothing wrong with showing my sadness and hurt. But Adam was waiting in the parking lot, and I was in control of myself. So I got up slowly, with dry eyes, and made my way to the door.

In his new metallic blue hybrid, not yet pasted with bumper stickers, Adam asked if there was anything I needed. Anywhere I wanted to go. Anything that would make me feel better.

"I'm not in a huge amount of pain anymore, Adam. I'm just bummed."

"My offer still stands. Is there anything that would make you feel better? Anywhere you want me to take you? Anywhere at all?"

I thought for a moment. "Could you take me to the Amtrak station?"

"Leaving town, are you?"

"I want to go up to Orange County."

"I can drive you up there."

"That's sweet of you, but I need to go up there alone."

"Then to the train station it is. Call me when you get back and I'll pick you up." I was thankful he didn't push the question about where I was going. It was hard to lose my freedom by losing my car, but at least I didn't have a nosy taxi driver.

❧

I spent the train ride trying to remember the exact location of where I was heading. Directions from the train station. Whether I could walk from the station or if I'd need to hire a taxi.

I ended up hiring a taxi, mainly because it had been a while and I wasn't sure I could find my way and didn't want to be wandering around trying to find it while I was still in a moderate amount of pain. The taxi driver knew exactly how to get to the cemetery, and the ride there was short.

I hadn't been to Dad's grave in years, but had no trouble finding it. I was surprised to see fresh flowers in the inground vase next to the headstone—roses—but as I came closer I could see that they were silk, in varying degrees of fading. I pictured Dad's friends here, bringing him flowers that couldn't die, wondering why they never saw his wife or daughters visiting anymore.

I used to come here every day after school, but after graduation my visitation dropped to once a week, then once every other week. Once I began college, I'd visit infrequently, wanting to spend my time at home with my mom and sister instead of sneaking away to see Dad's grave. It always felt like sneaking, because I was afraid Cleo would find out and sink back into the depression that she was slowly emerging from.

Now, as I lowered myself to the grass next to the flat headstone in the ground, I felt guilty for how I'd treated Dad's memory. Dad, who was always laughing and joking and enjoying life. I'd hidden my hurt, but also my entire memory of him, just so that Cleo wouldn't feel uncomfortable.

From the start, I should have brought up good stories about him with Cleo. It would have hurt for a while, but she would have been comforted with the good memories at least. Instead, Dad's memory only invoked guilt and pain for her.

"I'm sorry, Dad," I said, touching the smooth dove-gray marble that lay flush against the recently mowed grass. My fingers traced his name, Sharif Tahan, over and over. "I was still a kid . . . I didn't know the best way to help Cleo deal with her guilt. I didn't know the best way to deal with my own grief."

I crossed my legs under me, positioning myself for the least amount of pain. I touched the silk roses in the vase. "Who brought these for you? Smart idea—the silk ones last longer. Was it someone from church? Work? You touched so many lives that it could have been anyone."

I began pulling out the most faded rose. The silk petals were graying now from too much time under the sun, but as it emerged from the vase, I saw that the plastic stem remained a rich green. I pulled it out the rest of the way and was surprised to find a small, winkled piece of paper wrapped around the stem. Not tissue paper, but notebook paper. I unwrapped the paper gingerly, careful not to rip it, and set the rose aside.

Unfolding the page, I smoothed it flat. I saw the writing, but had to look carefully to read it, as the ink had run.

My eyes skimmed the page, left to right. Left to right. Left to right. Over and over was written, "I'm sorry."

In Cleo's handwriting.

She *had* come to Dad's grave. She'd left him a silk flower and a note. And she'd filled the entire note with her apology.

I set the note aside and chose another silk rose at random and unwrapped the paper around it.

I'm sorry.

I grabbed another rose and another and another.

I'm sorry. I'm sorry. I'm sorry. I'm sorry. I'm sorry.

I continued until the vase was empty of flowers and my eyes were full of tears. *She's been coming to see you, Dad? For how long? Since the guy who hit you sent her that note? Since . . . forever?*

Tears rolled down my cheeks as I sat clutching notes full of apologies in each hand, surrounded by silk flowers and more apologies. "She's sorry, Dad. Look at these notes! Couldn't you have just made a quick appearance to tell her she's not to blame? Tell her you're okay and to live her life? Tell her not to hurt anyone? Couldn't you have done something?"

I gathered up the notes and stuffed them to the bottom of the vase. "Why did you let her drive without her glasses? Why didn't you notice the truck before it hit you and tell her to stop? Why didn't you pull through and recover after the accident? Don't you see how this has destroyed your daughter? Your *daughters*?"

I stuck the roses back into the vase, and they sat higher than before, perched on the wadded-up papers at the bottom. "Can you see from where you are what Cleo's done? What she did? With all she's been through?"

There was no answer from above, and no ghost-version of my father appeared next to me. I wasn't expecting either to happen. I knew there weren't any answers.

I placed my palm against his headstone, touching the engraved words. Sharif Tahan. Devoted husband and father.

I suddenly thought of my mom. Her husband had been taken from her in their prime, leaving her with two teenage daughters demanding answers about how this could happen to their family. She'd had to deal with our grief on top of her own.

When our family's world fell apart, I became a weak version of my previous self, a person more likely to complain and panic than actually take care of herself. My sister withdrew into herself, and shortly after she gained control over her life, she began a violent crusade to keep her remaining family safe.

When my mom's world fell apart, she mourned. Grieved. Yet did the job of mother and father to finish raising Cleo and me. And when she was done with that, she moved on, to mothering the world. She was being a role model as to how to honor Dad, but we hadn't seen it.

She could have taken my path. She could have taken Cleo's path. But she didn't.

And Cleo and I didn't take her path.

I got up, trying to minimize the pain. I brushed the grass off my pants and asked, "What do I do now, Dad? Cleo's in a lot of trouble, and I can't do anything about her legal issues. So how do I help her get better? Go on with working out my own problems while she works on hers? Support her as best I can by doing whatever she needs me to do while she's serving her time? Making sure they're helping her, instead of just punishing her? Be there to support her when she gets out? *If* she gets out?"

Yes.

This confident answer was not from beyond the grave. It was from inside me. And I now knew my part in helping my sister was the same as my part in honoring my dad.

My part was to continue living life.

EPILOGUE

Adam wrapped his arms around me, hugging me tightly now that I'd had several months to completely heal. "Still don't know when you'll be back?" he asked.

Around us, people shook hands with associates, hugged relatives, rushed with their luggage into San Diego International Airport. Others fumbled outside into the sun after flights, scanning the loading zone for rides. Next to me on the ground sat a piece of rolling luggage, cerulean blue, and the backpack I'd brought to Greece.

"The return ticket is open-ended. I won't be too long, though. If anything, I'll be rushing back just to see you, Adam."

"I know I should say not to rush, especially since this is the first time you'll be visiting your mom in Botswana. But I'm going to miss you." He leaned in for a delicious kiss. When he pulled back, I looked deep into his midnight eyes.

"I'll miss you, too. And I'm sure I want to be with you."

"And I'm sure I'll be waiting for you when you get back. Ready to be part of this new life you're starting."

When I pulled out of Adam's arms, gathered my things, and turned toward the glass doors of the airport,

I watched his reflection. As much as I was looking forward to my adventure, I knew that it would not be long until I began to long for Adam Mestas again.

I inhaled deeply, a breath full of crisp ocean air.

This adventure to Botswana to see Mom isn't meant to change me, I thought as the automatic door slid open for me, the reflection of the handsome Adam Mestas. *The real adventure will be when I come home . . . to his arms.*

I turned once, smiled in response to his wave, and without hesitation walked through the open door.

ABOUT THE AUTHOR

Trisha Haddad is a writer in her twenties living in San Diego. She began a career in the publishing industry directly out of college, first at a literary agency and currently in academic publishing. Her passions include writing, reading, travel and spending time with her husband and best friend, Derek. Her life as a writer has been inspired from childhood by her grandmother, Helen Haddad, a mystery writer. *Best of Luck Elsewhere* is Trisha's first published work of fiction.

2009 Reprint Mass Market Titles

January

I'm Gonna Make You Love Me
Gwyneth Bolton
ISBN-13: 978-1-58571-294-6
$6.99

Shades of Desire
Monica White
ISBN-13: 978-1-58571-292-2
$6.99

February

A Love of Her Own
Cheris Hodges
ISBN-13: 978-1-58571-293-9
$6.99

Color of Trouble
Dyanne Davis
ISBN-13: 978-1-58571-294-6
$6.99

March

Twist of Fate
Beverly Clark
ISBN-13: 978-1-58571-295-3
$6.99

Chances
Pamela Leigh Starr
ISBN-13: 978-1-58571-296-0
$6.99

April

Sinful Intentions
Crystal Rhodes
ISBN-13: 978-1-585712-297-7
$6.99

Rock Star
Roslyn Hardy Holcomb
ISBN-13: 978-1-58571-298-4
$6.99

May

Paths of Fire
T.T. Henderson
ISBN-13: 978-1-58571-343-1
$6.99

Caught Up in the Rapture
Lisa Riley
ISBN-13: 978-1-58571-344-8
$6.99

June

Reckless Surrender
Rochelle Alers
ISBN-13: 978-1-58571-345-5
$6.99

No Ordinary Love
Angela Weaver
ISBN-13: 978-1-58571-346-2
$6.99

2009 Reprint Mass Market Titles (continued)

July

Intentional Mistakes
Michele Sudler
ISBN-13: 978-1-58571-347-9
$6.99

It's In His Kiss
Reon Carter
ISBN-13: 978-1-58571-348-6
$6.99

August

Unfinished Love Affair
Barbara Keaton
ISBN-13: 978-1-58571-349-3
$6.99

A Perfect Place to Pray
I.L Goodwin
ISBN-13: 978-1-58571-299-1
$6.99

September

Love in High Gear
Charlotte Roy
ISBN-13: 978-1-58571-355-4
$6.99

Ebony Eyes
Kei Swanson
ISBN-13: 978-1-58571-356-1
$6.99

October

Midnight Clear, Part I
Leslie Esdale/Carmen Green
ISBN-13: 978-1-58571-357-8
$6.99

Midnight Clear, Part II
Gwynne Forster/Monica
   Jackson
ISBN-13: 978-1-58571-358-5
$6.99

November

Midnight Peril
Vicki Andrews
ISBN-13: 978-1-58571-359-2
$6.99

One Day At A Time
Bella McFarland
ISBN-13: 978-1-58571-360-8
$6.99

December

Just An Affair
Eugenia O'Neal
ISBN-13: 978-1-58571-361-5
$6.99

Shades of Brown
Denise Becker
ISBN-13: 978-1-58571-362-2
$6.99

2009 New Mass Market Titles

January

Singing A Song...
Crystal Rhodes
ISBN-13: 978-1-58571-283-0
$6.99

Look Both Ways
Joan Early
ISBN-13: 978-1-58571-284-7
$6.99

February

Six O'Clock
Katrina Spencer
ISBN-13: 978-1-58571-285-4
$6.99

Red Sky
Renee Alexis
ISBN-13: 978-1-58571-286-1
$6.99

March

Anything But Love
Celya Bowers
ISBN-13: 978-1-58571-287-8
$6.99

Tempting Faith
Crystal Hubbard
ISBN-13: 978-1-58571-288-5
$6.99

April

If I Were Your Woman
La Connie Taylor-Jones
ISBN-13: 978-1-58571-289-2
$6.99

Best Of Luck Elsewhere
Trisha Haddad
ISBN-13: 978-1-58571-290-8
$6.99

May

All I'll Ever Need
Mildred Riley
ISBN-13: 978-1-58571-335-6
$6.99

A Place Like Home
Alicia Wiggins
ISBN-13: 978-1-58571-336-3
$6.99

June

Best Foot Forward
Michele Sudler
ISBN-13: 978-1-58571-337-0
$6.99

It's In the Rhythm
Sammie Ward
ISBN-13: 978-1-58571-338-7
$6.99

2009 New Mass Market Titles (continued)
July

Checks and Balances
Elaine Sims
ISBN-13: 978-1-58571-339-4
$6.99

Save Me
Africa Fine
ISBN-13: 978-1-58571-340-0
$6.99

August

When Lightening Strikes
Michele Cameron
ISBN-13: 978-1-58571-369-1
$6.99

Blindsided
Tammy Williams
ISBN-13: 978-1-58571-342-4
$6.99

September

2 Good
Celya Bowers
ISBN-13: 978-1-58571-350-9
$6.99

Waiting for Mr. Darcy
Chamein Canton
ISBN-13: 978-1-58571-351-6
$6.99

October

Fireflies
Joan Early
ISBN-13: 978-1-58571-352-3
$6.99

Frost On My Window
Angela Weaver
ISBN-13: 978-1-58571-353-0
$6.99

November

Waiting in the Shadows
Michele Sudler
ISBN-13: 978-1-58571-364-6
$6.99

Fixin' Tyrone
Keith Walker
ISBN-13: 978-1-58571-365-3
$6.99

December

Dream Keeper
Gail McFarland
ISBN-13: 978-1-58571-366-0
$6.99

Another Memory
Pamela Ridley
ISBN-13: 978-1-58571-367-7
$6.99

Other Genesis Press, Inc. Titles

A Dangerous Deception	J.M. Jeffries	$8.95
A Dangerous Love	J.M. Jeffries	$8.95
A Dangerous Obsession	J.M. Jeffries	$8.95
A Drummer's Beat to Mend	Kei Swanson	$9.95
A Happy Life	Charlotte Harris	$9.95
A Heart's Awakening	Veronica Parker	$9.95
A Lark on the Wing	Phyliss Hamilton	$9.95
A Love of Her Own	Cheris F. Hodges	$9.95
A Love to Cherish	Beverly Clark	$8.95
A Risk of Rain	Dar Tomlinson	$8.95
A Taste of Temptation	Reneé Alexis	$9.95
A Twist of Fate	Beverly Clark	$8.95
A Voice Behind Thunder	Carrie Elizabeth Greene	$6.99
A Will to Love	Angie Daniels	$9.95
Acquisitions	Kimberley White	$8.95
Across	Carol Payne	$12.95
After the Vows	Leslie Esdaile	$10.95
(Summer Anthology)	T.T. Henderson	
	Jacqueline Thomas	
Again My Love	Kayla Perrin	$10.95
Against the Wind	Gwynne Forster	$8.95
All I Ask	Barbara Keaton	$8.95
Always You	Crystal Hubbard	$6.99
Ambrosia	T.T. Henderson	$8.95
An Unfinished Love Affair	Barbara Keaton	$8.95
And Then Came You	Dorothy Elizabeth Love	$8.95
Angel's Paradise	Janice Angelique	$9.95
At Last	Lisa G. Riley	$8.95
Best of Friends	Natalie Dunbar	$8.95
Beyond the Rapture	Beverly Clark	$9.95
Blame It On Paradise	Crystal Hubbard	$6.99
Blaze	Barbara Keaton	$9.95
Bliss, Inc.	Chamein Canton	$6.99
Blood Lust	J. M. Jeffries	$9.95
Blood Seduction	J.M. Jeffries	$9.95

Other Genesis Press, Inc. Titles (continued)

Bodyguard	Andrea Jackson	$9.95
Boss of Me	Diana Nyad	$8.95
Bound by Love	Beverly Clark	$8.95
Breeze	Robin Hampton Allen	$10.95
Broken	Dar Tomlinson	$24.95
By Design	Barbara Keaton	$8.95
Cajun Heat	Charlene Berry	$8.95
Careless Whispers	Rochelle Alers	$8.95
Cats & Other Tales	Marilyn Wagner	$8.95
Caught in a Trap	Andre Michelle	$8.95
Caught Up In the Rapture	Lisa G. Riley	$9.95
Cautious Heart	Cheris F Hodges	$8.95
Chances	Pamela Leigh Starr	$8.95
Cherish the Flame	Beverly Clark	$8.95
Choices	Tammy Williams	$6.99
Class Reunion	Irma Jenkins/	$12.95
	John Brown	
Code Name: Diva	J.M. Jeffries	$9.95
Conquering Dr. Wexler's Heart	Kimberley White	$9.95
Corporate Seduction	A.C. Arthur	$9.95
Crossing Paths, Tempting Memories	Dorothy Elizabeth Love	$9.95
Crush	Crystal Hubbard	$9.95
Cypress Whisperings	Phyllis Hamilton	$8.95
Dark Embrace	Crystal Wilson Harris	$8.95
Dark Storm Rising	Chinelu Moore	$10.95
Daughter of the Wind	Joan Xian	$8.95
Dawn's Harbor	Kymberly Hunt	$6.99
Deadly Sacrifice	Jack Kean	$22.95
Designer Passion	Dar Tomlinson	$8.95
	Diana Richeaux	
Do Over	Celya Bowers	$9.95
Dream Runner	Gail McFarland	$6.99
Dreamtective	Liz Swados	$5.95

Other Genesis Press, Inc. Titles (continued)

Ebony Angel	Deatri King-Bey	$9.95
Ebony Butterfly II	Delilah Dawson	$14.95
Echoes of Yesterday	Beverly Clark	$9.95
Eden's Garden	Elizabeth Rose	$8.95
Eve's Prescription	Edwina Martin Arnold	$8.95
Everlastin' Love	Gay G. Gunn	$8.95
Everlasting Moments	Dorothy Elizabeth Love	$8.95
Everything and More	Sinclair Lebeau	$8.95
Everything but Love	Natalie Dunbar	$8.95
Falling	Natalie Dunbar	$9.95
Fate	Pamela Leigh Starr	$8.95
Finding Isabella	A.J. Garrotto	$8.95
Forbidden Quest	Dar Tomlinson	$10.95
Forever Love	Wanda Y. Thomas	$8.95
From the Ashes	Kathleen Suzanne	$8.95
	Jeanne Sumerix	
Gentle Yearning	Rochelle Alers	$10.95
Glory of Love	Sinclair LeBeau	$10.95
Go Gentle into that Good Night	Malcom Boyd	$12.95
Goldengroove	Mary Beth Craft	$16.95
Groove, Bang, and Jive	Steve Cannon	$8.99
Hand in Glove	Andrea Jackson	$9.95
Hard to Love	Kimberley White	$9.95
Hart & Soul	Angie Daniels	$8.95
Heart of the Phoenix	A.C. Arthur	$9.95
Heartbeat	Stephanie Bedwell-Grime	$8.95
Hearts Remember	M. Loui Quezada	$8.95
Hidden Memories	Robin Allen	$10.95
Higher Ground	Leah Latimer	$19.95
Hitler, the War, and the Pope	Ronald Rychiak	$26.95
How to Write a Romance	Kathryn Falk	$18.95
I Married a Reclining Chair	Lisa M. Fuhs	$8.95
I'll Be Your Shelter	Giselle Carmichael	$8.95
I'll Paint a Sun	A.J. Garrotto	$9.95

Other Genesis Press, Inc. Titles (continued)

Icie	Pamela Leigh Starr	$8.95
Illusions	Pamela Leigh Starr	$8.95
Indigo After Dark Vol. I	Nia Dixon/Angelique	$10.95
Indigo After Dark Vol. II	Dolores Bundy/ Cole Riley	$10.95
Indigo After Dark Vol. III	Montana Blue/ Coco Morena	$10.95
Indigo After Dark Vol. IV	Cassandra Colt/	$14.95
Indigo After Dark Vol. V	Delilah Dawson	$14.95
Indiscretions	Donna Hill	$8.95
Intentional Mistakes	Michele Sudler	$9.95
Interlude	Donna Hill	$8.95
Intimate Intentions	Angie Daniels	$8.95
It's Not Over Yet	J.J. Michael	$9.95
Jolie's Surrender	Edwina Martin-Arnold	$8.95
Kiss or Keep	Debra Phillips	$8.95
Lace	Giselle Carmichael	$9.95
Lady Preacher	K.T. Richey	$6.99
Last Train to Memphis	Elsa Cook	$12.95
Lasting Valor	Ken Olsen	$24.95
Let Us Prey	Hunter Lundy	$25.95
Lies Too Long	Pamela Ridley	$13.95
Life Is Never As It Seems	J.J. Michael	$12.95
Lighter Shade of Brown	Vicki Andrews	$8.95
Looking for Lily	Africa Fine	$6.99
Love Always	Mildred E. Riley	$10.95
Love Doesn't Come Easy	Charlyne Dickerson	$8.95
Love Unveiled	Gloria Greene	$10.95
Love's Deception	Charlene Berry	$10.95
Love's Destiny	M. Loui Quezada	$8.95
Love's Secrets	Yolanda McVey	$6.99
Mae's Promise	Melody Walcott	$8.95
Magnolia Sunset	Giselle Carmichael	$8.95
Many Shades of Gray	Dyanne Davis	$6.99
Matters of Life and Death	Lesego Malepe, Ph.D.	$15.95

Other Genesis Press, Inc. Titles (continued)

Meant to Be	Jeanne Sumerix	$8.95
Midnight Clear (Anthology)	Leslie Esdaile	$10.95
	Gwynne Forster	
	Carmen Green	
	Monica Jackson	
Midnight Magic	Gwynne Forster	$8.95
Midnight Peril	Vicki Andrews	$10.95
Misconceptions	Pamela Leigh Starr	$9.95
Moments of Clarity	Michele Cameron	$6.99
Montgomery's Children	Richard Perry	$14.95
Mr Fix-It	Crystal Hubbard	$6.99
My Buffalo Soldier	Barbara B. K. Reeves	$8.95
Naked Soul	Gwynne Forster	$8.95
Never Say Never	Michele Cameron	$6.99
Next to Last Chance	Louisa Dixon	$24.95
No Apologies	Seressia Glass	$8.95
No Commitment Required	Seressia Glass	$8.95
No Regrets	Mildred E. Riley	$8.95
Not His Type	Chamein Canton	$6.99
Nowhere to Run	Gay G. Gunn	$10.95
O Bed! O Breakfast!	Rob Kuehnle	$14.95
Object of His Desire	A. C. Arthur	$8.95
Office Policy	A. C. Arthur	$9.95
Once in a Blue Moon	Dorianne Cole	$9.95
One Day at a Time	Bella McFarland	$8.95
One in A Million	Barbara Keaton	$6.99
One of These Days	Michele Sudler	$9.95
Outside Chance	Louisa Dixon	$24.95
Passion	T.T. Henderson	$10.95
Passion's Blood	Cherif Fortin	$22.95
Passion's Furies	AlTonya Washington	$6.99
Passion's Journey	Wanda Y. Thomas	$8.95
Past Promises	Jahmel West	$8.95
Path of Fire	T.T. Henderson	$8.95
Path of Thorns	Annetta P. Lee	$9.95

Other Genesis Press, Inc. Titles (continued)

Peace Be Still	Colette Haywood	$12.95
Picture Perfect	Reon Carter	$8.95
Playing for Keeps	Stephanie Salinas	$8.95
Pride & Joi	Gay G. Gunn	$8.95
Promises Made	Bernice Layton	$6.99
Promises to Keep	Alicia Wiggins	$8.95
Quiet Storm	Donna Hill	$10.95
Reckless Surrender	Rochelle Alers	$6.95
Red Polka Dot in a World of Plaid	Varian Johnson	$12.95
Reluctant Captive	Joyce Jackson	$8.95
Rendezvous with Fate	Jeanne Sumerix	$8.95
Revelations	Cheris F. Hodges	$8.95
Rivers of the Soul	Leslie Esdaile	$8.95
Rocky Mountain Romance	Kathleen Suzanne	$8.95
Rooms of the Heart	Donna Hill	$8.95
Rough on Rats and Tough on Cats	Chris Parker	$12.95
Secret Library Vol. 1	Nina Sheridan	$18.95
Secret Library Vol. 2	Cassandra Colt	$8.95
Secret Thunder	Annetta P. Lee	$9.95
Shades of Brown	Denise Becker	$8.95
Shades of Desire	Monica White	$8.95
Shadows in the Moonlight	Jeanne Sumerix	$8.95
Sin	Crystal Rhodes	$8.95
Small Whispers	Annetta P. Lee	$6.99
So Amazing	Sinclair LeBeau	$8.95
Somebody's Someone	Sinclair LeBeau	$8.95
Someone to Love	Alicia Wiggins	$8.95
Song in the Park	Martin Brant	$15.95
Soul Eyes	Wayne L. Wilson	$12.95
Soul to Soul	Donna Hill	$8.95
Southern Comfort	J.M. Jeffries	$8.95
Southern Fried Standards	S.R. Maddox	$6.99
Still the Storm	Sharon Robinson	$8.95

Other Genesis Press, Inc. Titles (continued)

Still Waters Run Deep	Leslie Esdaile	$8.95
Stolen Kisses	Dominiqua Douglas	$9.95
Stolen Memories	Michele Sudler	$6.99
Stories to Excite You	Anna Forrest/Divine	$14.95
Storm	Pamela Leigh Starr	$6.99
Subtle Secrets	Wanda Y. Thomas	$8.95
Suddenly You	Crystal Hubbard	$9.95
Sweet Repercussions	Kimberley White	$9.95
Sweet Sensations	Gwyneth Bolton	$9.95
Sweet Tomorrows	Kimberly White	$8.95
Taken by You	Dorothy Elizabeth Love	$9.95
Tattooed Tears	T. T. Henderson	$8.95
The Color Line	Lizzette Grayson Carter	$9.95
The Color of Trouble	Dyanne Davis	$8.95
The Disappearance of Allison Jones	Kayla Perrin	$5.95
The Fires Within	Beverly Clark	$9.95
The Foursome	Celya Bowers	$6.99
The Honey Dipper's Legacy	Pannell-Allen	$14.95
The Joker's Love Tune	Sidney Rickman	$15.95
The Little Pretender	Barbara Cartland	$10.95
The Love We Had	Natalie Dunbar	$8.95
The Man Who Could Fly	Bob & Milana Beamon	$18.95
The Missing Link	Charlyne Dickerson	$8.95
The Mission	Pamela Leigh Starr	$6.99
The More Things Change	Chamein Canton	$6.99
The Perfect Frame	Beverly Clark	$9.95
The Price of Love	Sinclair LeBeau	$8.95
The Smoking Life	Ilene Barth	$29.95
The Words of the Pitcher	Kei Swanson	$8.95
Things Forbidden	Maryam Diaab	$6.99
This Life Isn't Perfect Holla	Sandra Foy	$6.99
Three Doors Down	Michele Sudler	$6.99
Three Wishes	Seressia Glass	$8.95
Ties That Bind	Kathleen Suzanne	$8.95

Other Genesis Press, Inc. Titles (continued)

Tiger Woods	Libby Hughes	$5.95
Time is of the Essence	Angie Daniels	$9.95
Timeless Devotion	Bella McFarland	$9.95
Tomorrow's Promise	Leslie Esdaile	$8.95
Truly Inseparable	Wanda Y. Thomas	$8.95
Two Sides to Every Story	Dyanne Davis	$9.95
Unbreak My Heart	Dar Tomlinson	$8.95
Uncommon Prayer	Kenneth Swanson	$9.95
Unconditional Love	Alicia Wiggins	$8.95
Unconditional	A.C. Arthur	$9.95
Undying Love	Renee Alexis	$6.99
Until Death Do Us Part	Susan Paul	$8.95
Vows of Passion	Bella McFarland	$9.95
Wedding Gown	Dyanne Davis	$8.95
What's Under Benjamin's Bed	Sandra Schaffer	$8.95
When A Man Loves A Woman	La Connie Taylor-Jones	$6.99
When Dreams Float	Dorothy Elizabeth Love	$8.95
When I'm With You	LaConnie Taylor-Jones	$6.99
Where I Want To Be	Maryam Diaab	$6.99
Whispers in the Night	Dorothy Elizabeth Love	$8.95
Whispers in the Sand	LaFlorya Gauthier	$10.95
Who's That Lady?	Andrea Jackson	$9.95
Wild Ravens	Altonya Washington	$9.95
Yesterday Is Gone	Beverly Clark	$10.95
Yesterday's Dreams, Tomorrow's Promises	Reon Laudat	$8.95
Your Precious Love	Sinclair LeBeau	$8.95

Order Form

Mail to: Genesis Press, Inc.
P.O. Box 101
Columbus, MS 39703

Name _____
Address _____
City/State _____ Zip _____
Telephone _____

Ship to (if different from above)
Name _____
Address _____
City/State _____ Zip _____
Telephone _____

Credit Card Information
Credit Card # _____ ☐ Visa ☐ Mastercard
Expiration Date (mm/yy) _____ ☐ AmEx ☐ Discover

Qty.	Author	Title	Price	Total

Use this order
form, or call
1-888-INDIGO-1

Total for books _____
Shipping and handling:
$5 first two books,
$1 each additional book _____
Total S & H _____
Total amount enclosed _____
Mississippi residents add 7% sales tax